Simply Learning, Simply Best!

Simply Learning, Simply Best!

倍斯特出版事業有限公司
Best Publishing Ltd.

一次就考到

雅思口說 6.5⁺

倍斯特編輯部◎著

MP3

運用影子跟讀法 同步強化「說」、「聽」
聽力專注力提升和口說能力狂飆

4大學習法

1 收錄百則道地用語，修正中式表達且實質性提升口語整體分數
> ► 道地用語的使用即刻提高口說分數段「0.5-2.0」分，達到理想申請成績。

2 熟悉必考語庫話題，出考場走路都有風
> ► 由必考語庫練習，考試前就佔盡先機，在考場從容不迫完成所有回答。

3 規劃一問三答，精彩的回答讓考官印象深刻
> ► 有更豐富和多樣的答案選擇，從中修正並組織成最適合自己的表達。

4 強化話題卡題應答，不再畏懼兩分鐘回答
> ► 多元的答題思路搭配語庫練習，能無形中進入「話匣子」模式，兩分鐘話題卡題還要考官提醒時間到了。

在《刻意練習》一書中提到"...still much of your improvement will depend on practice you do on your own."。而其實在學習過程中確實是如此，一切最終還是回歸到自己本身的學習上面。自己本身的練習很大程度地影響自己的進步程度。但要如何使自己進步最多呢？或在最短時間內獲得最大的進展呢？很多時候我們都是單向接收訊息，老師授課、買官方題目來寫等等，但是卻不是最能使我們在短時間內達到理想成績的方式。因為當中牽涉到許多因素，例如教科書的表達和道地英語的落差、缺乏最有效率的學習等等。我們不像在遊戲中那樣的靈活，不用思考就能構思出要如何與團隊合作、運用自己角色的長處等來打副本等，使用短路徑就能達到成效且將角色能力最大程度的優化。所以要使自己獲取最大程度的進步你需要...

❶ 熟悉道地用語且用各種生活主題做刻意練習

■ 雅思口說的三個部分雖然迥異，但是所測驗的話題都是大家所熟習的生活情境。大多數時候，被問到某些話題時，並非我們英語程度未達到某個分數段，但是不熟悉的話題就影響的我們的應對能力，進而被判定在某個分數段。書籍中4個part包含許多在雅思考試中許多考生答不好的話題，像是音樂、湖泊等，其實你需

要的是掌握這4個part的所有話題和所有回答中出現的道地用語，將每單元回答的道地用語變成自己的表達語庫，更自然的表達英語，並且用這些話題做刻意練習。掌握道地用語跟能自然地用於各生活情境中就是高分關鍵。

❷ 利用影子跟讀法，同步練習「說」、「聽」，迅速達到理想成績

■ 學習過程中，其實你更需要的是了解「聽」、「說」、「讀」和「寫」四個技能的關係，因為這四個技能是相互影響的，只有能充分掌握這些關係的人，才能在最短時間內獲取最理想的成績。例如，「聽」跟「讀」的關係好了，聽力能力差的人某部分也反映出閱讀能力差，因為你會需要不斷根據關鍵詞在文章段落中去找訊息，但聽力不只在考試中不能重覆再聽一次，在現實生活中不斷去詢問客戶或講者表達內容也反映出你本身聽力不夠好。

■ 書籍中規劃了影子跟讀的部分，跟著音檔同步唸出英文訊息，修正本身唸某些字彙的發音、仿效語調等，並進一步強化聽力跟聽力專注力。此外，這個步驟也能修正某些考生的錯誤學習方式，將口說答案當成範文在閱讀，而忽略的這是口說考試，所以看完口說書後，在口試上分數仍停滯在某個分數段。所以務必透過本書4個part確實做紮實的跟讀練習，最終的學習效果會讓你感到吃驚！！！

倍斯特編輯部 敬上

使用說明 INSTRUCTIONS

Unit 16 迪士尼樂園、奧蘭多的環球影城冒險島樂園和洛杉磯環球影城的鬼屋

MP3 016

迪士尼樂園 ❶
Disneyland!! It is just the best amusement ever. I've been to almost all the Disneyland in the world, and I can't say I like any particular one.

迪士尼樂園！它就是最棒的遊樂園啊！我幾乎去遍全世界所有的迪士尼樂園，但是我說不出來我最喜歡哪一個。它們都有自己獨特的地方。

迪士尼樂園 ❷
They are all unique in their own ways. Who doesn't like Disney Land really? Cinderella's castle, the carousel, and all the magic in the park. It feels like a dream come true when I'm in Disney Land.

不過說真的怎麼可能會有人不喜歡迪士尼樂園？仙杜瑞拉的城堡、旋轉木馬還有園內所有的魔法。在迪士尼樂園裡就好像是夢想成真一樣！

Schlitterbahn 的水上樂園 ❶
My favorite amusement park is actually a water park called Schlitterbahn. It hands down the best amusement park in the world. The countless water slides are all very long and fun.

我最喜歡的遊樂園其實是一間叫做Schlitterbahn 的水上樂園。它真的是我認為世界上最棒的遊樂園。數不清的滑水道都很長又很好玩。

Schlitterbahn 的水上樂園 ❷
You can carry the tubes around the park to do all kinds of slides or just float around the floating river. There are always long lines, but no one seems to care too much once they get on the ride.

你在園內也都可以拿著游泳圈去各式各樣的滑水道，或是只是在漂漂河上漂。雖然都要排隊很久，但是大家都是坐到之後就不會在意了。

奧蘭多的環球影城冒險島樂園 ❶
The Universal's Islands of adventures in Orlando! It's both intriguing and exciting. Once you graduate from DisneyLand, you would enjoy this place so much.

在奧蘭多的環球影城冒險島樂園！它又好玩又刺激。你在迪士尼樂園畢業之後，你就會很喜歡這個地方。

1 道地高分句
2 一問三答
3 結腦卡回答
4 即席應答

078　079

快速累積「道地用語」語彙庫

· 針對雅思 part 1-3 常考話題規劃 28 個單元，融入許多道地用語在短句描述中，便於閱讀且能在短時間內累積更多口語句型。

提升說服力和表達力

· 每單元涵蓋許多實際旅遊景點和實際體驗等，能拓展表達能力跟知識面，能更有說服力的講出自己到過的博物館跟國家公園等地方。

由一問三答，表達更多元、豐富
· 針對雅思 part 1 話題精選 36 個主題，並規劃一問三答，**答案的選擇更多元、豐富。**

修正中式表達
· 三個回答等同與三個外籍友人練習口說，修正自己較不道地的中式用語，不用補習也能達到理想成績。

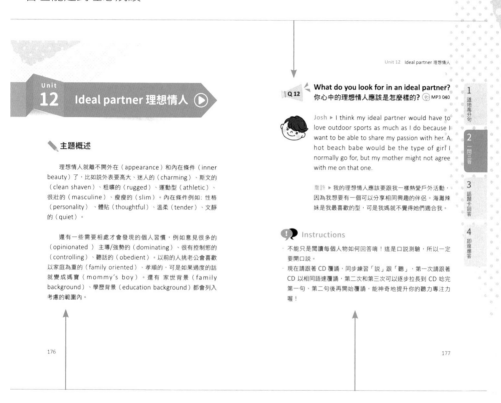

· 透過主題概述，最短時間內進入狀況，掌握更多形容詞和名詞用字，強化細節描述、降低詞窮情況和重複性使用某些字太多次的情況。

利用「影子跟讀法」，同步強化口說跟聽力用最短路徑達到與其他學習者相同的學習成效
· 開口說，且同個學習時間點中，運用「兩樣」技能，強化「專注力」跟「口說表達力」。
· 練完口說要寫聽力題時，也能感受到聽力無形中進步了，除了能省掉更多學習時間外，也能減少聽力時因專注力不夠而失分的情況。

透過拓展話題，不用再為了想回答的主題苦思或想破透頭，面對同樣的話題，能選擇更多自己本身想表達的話題來表達，例如「重要的決定」這個話題也可以選其他八個話題中的其中一個話題，來當作回答的話題，也可以避免在考試時與其他人回答相同【撞車】。

Unit 04　重要的決定：唸哪個科系

話題拓展

◎ 決定一：升學或就業 Work or study
◎ 決定二：出國留學 Study aboard
◎ 決定三：買房子 Buying a house
◎ 決定四：投資理財 Investment
◎ 決定五：分手 The break up
◎ 決定六：結婚 Marriage
◎ 決定七：辭職 Resignation
◎ 決定八：北上找工作 Heading north

Please describe an important decision in your life.
請描述一個你人生中重要的決定

290

念哪個科系 Choosing major　MP3 068

I had a hard time making the decision about the major I'm going to take, knowing it would have a major impact on my career life in the future.

選科系的時候我實在很難下決定，因為我知道這會影響我未來工作的方向。

I always like dancing and I always dream to be a professional dancer one day I have been taking dance classes since I was little, and I was pretty talented, too. But when I start to look at the reality, I am not confident that I can make a living as a dancer. I know I am a good dancer and with more training, I will be an outstanding one !

我一直都很喜歡跳舞，也想像有一天可以當個專業舞者，我從小就學舞，而且也蠻有天份的。可是當我想到實際面的時候，我實在沒把握當舞者可以填飽肚子。我知道我跳得很好，如果透過適當的訓練我會變得更傑出。

291

1 邁進高分句

2 一問三答

3 話題卡回答

4 即席應答

雅思口說 part 2 話題卡題

· 許多人懼怕的題型，常常信誓旦旦要答某個話題但最後講兩三句後不知道該回什麼，或是兩分鐘回答時間中不知道要答什麼。

· 如果上述有這些情況請務必熟悉整本書的口語表達和背誦這個 part 規劃的回答。累積一定表達句型後，會突然覺得兩分鐘回答其實沒有那麼難。

· 另外要說明的是，其實表達沒什麼文法錯誤且話題卡題有講完兩分鐘，分數就能達到 6.5 分或 6.5+，**其實比準備其他單項簡單很多，這是許多考生在備考後期才有的恍然大悟，原來口說這麼好拿分的念頭，但時間已經流逝 XDD。**

006

Unit 13 Shopping 購物

Q 01 Do you prefer to shop online or visit the stores?
你喜歡上網購物還是到實體店面去？ MP3 103

I actually like them both, but it depends how much time and how urgent I need the item. If I had a lot of time and just trying to pick out something I want for a long time, I will browse online and compare the price and specification. I know it will take a few days at least for it to be delivered, but I can wait because I am in no hurry.

我其實兩個都喜歡，可是要看我有多少時間或是我急不急著要那個東西。如果我有很多時間可以只是想慢慢挑一個我喜歡的東西，那我會上網逛逛比較一下價格跟規格。我知道送來要等好幾天，可是無所謂我不急。

However, if I need to pick out something at the last minute, say I just realised it is a friend's birthday, and I

need a present for him today, I will definitely go to thestores. I know I might pay more inthe store, but it doesn't leave me with a choice really.

可是如果今天是臨時需要一個東西，就好像剛發現朋友生日，需要一個禮物，那我就會去店面裡買。我知道可能會貴一點但是我也沒辦法。

 Instructions

· 不能只是閱讀每個人物如何回答喔！這是口說測驗，所以一定要開口說。
· 現在請跟著 CD 覆誦，同步練習「說」跟「聽」，第一次請跟著 CD 以相同語速覆誦，第二次和第三次可以逐步拉長到 CD 唸完第一句、第二句後再開始覆誦，能神奇地提升你的聽力專注力喔！

388

389

· 每個話題又細分成兩個小問題，其實在 part 1 和 part 3 都會考到，書中是將其規劃成雅思口說第三部分常考的，來到考試最後一階段了，面對考官連續針對一個問題的提問，還是要耐心地答完。
· 這個部分的回答都是經過思考、接續性回答一主題。
· 適用於無法連貫性回答一主題的考生、回答一主題過於簡短等狀況的考生。
· 考生可以將答案遮起來，看自己遇到相同問題是否也能夠回答到範例答案的句子數，通常可以回答到的考生，在回答雅思第三部分就沒什麼太大問題。

目次 CONTENTS

Part 1 道地高分句

Part 2 一問三答

地點類

人物類

Part 3 話題卡回答

Part 4 即席應答

生活主題＋道地表達＝獲取高分

雅思口試不論是哪個部分，其實都跟我們生活中的大小事息息相關，但很奇怪的是考生在回答問題時卻常會感到無話可說或在事後遺憾自己本可以表達得更好，這其實只是因為缺乏有系統的把生活中的許多事以英文表達出看法，這個part 收錄的 28 個生活中熟悉的主題，且每個回答都非常道地，透過這個 part 的練習，除了能掌握許多道地用語外，更能使自己在口試 3 個 part 中有顯著的突破，在考試時不慌不亂的回應完所有問題。

Part

1

道地高分句

尼加拉瀑布、非洲的維多利亞瀑布和夏威夷大島的彩虹瀑布

🎧 MP3 001

尼加拉
瀑布 ❶

■ Niagara Falls is my favorite waterfalls.The falls are big, beautiful and very loud. And you get to travel to New York and Canada since it's right in the middle of the two places.

■ 尼加拉瀑布是我最喜歡的瀑布。那裡的瀑布又大，又美，而且超大聲的。而且你還可以順便去紐約或是加拿大旅行，因為它剛好在兩個地方的中間。

尼加拉
瀑布 ❷

■ At night time the falls are even lighted up with colorful lights. I'm definitely going there for my honeymoon. It's just very romantic in general.

■ 在晚上的時候他們還會有不一樣顏色的燈亮起。我一定要去那裡度蜜月。整體來說那就是一個很浪漫的地方啊。

1 道地高分句

2 一問三答

3 話題卡回答

4 即席應答

非洲的維多利亞瀑布 ❶

- My favorite one is Victoria Falls in Africa. It's one of the Seven Natural Wonders of the world, and it's so easy to see why once you're there.
- 我最喜歡的是在非洲的維多利亞瀑布。那是世界七大奇景之一，而且一旦你到了那裡之後你就會很輕易地知道為什麼它是七大奇景之一。

非洲的維多利亞瀑布 ❷

- The hardest part is to get there I guess. It is one of the largest and most inspiring in the world. The waterfall is about 108 meters long. I am still in awe of it.
- 我想最難的地方就是要先到非洲吧。那是世界上最大也是最激勵人心的瀑布之一。整個瀑布大概有一百八十公尺長。我到現在還是覺得很驚人。

夏威夷大島的彩虹瀑布 ❶

- I really like the Rainbow Falls at Big Island, Hawaii. Just like its name suggests, the rainbow can be seen every sunny morning at around 10 am.
- 我真的很喜歡在夏威夷大島的彩虹瀑布。就像它的名字一樣，每個晴天的早上十點左右都可以看到彩虹。

夏威夷大島的彩虹瀑布 ❷

- The waterfall flows over a natural lava cave, which was believed to be one of the Hawaiian goddess's homes. How romantic is that?
- 瀑布是從天然的火山岩洞穴傾流而下，那個洞穴也聽說是夏威夷一個女神的家。真的超浪漫的！

瀑布與攝影 ❶

- I usually try to find the best angle to take a picture with the waterfall. That's all it's about for me really. I finally make it that far to the waterfall.
- 我通常都會試著找跟瀑布照相最好的角度。對我來說那是最重要的。我好不容易才到了瀑布。

瀑布與攝影 ❷

- All I really want is to have a decent picture with the waterfall. It's a good incentive to hike to the waterfall for me.
- 我真正最想要的只是一張跟瀑布的漂亮合照。對我來說那是健行到瀑布很好的動力。

抱膝跳水 ❶

- There are so many things you can do at the waterfall. My friends and I like to jump off the rock and swim. When the water is clean, it is the most refreshing feeling you can get.
- 在瀑布有很多事情可以做啊。我的朋友跟我都很喜歡從石頭上跳下去游泳。當水很乾淨的時候，那是最令人覺得清新的感覺。

抱膝跳水 ❷

- We usually do a cannon ball or just dive under the waterfall. Of Course, we only jump off when it is safe at that place.
- 我們通常都會抱膝跳水製造很大的水花或是潛到瀑布底下。當然那是在安全的狀況之下我們才會跳水啦。

大自然的聲音

- Sometimes I like to meditate on the rock while listening to the waterfall. It's like one of those nature sounds CDs only it's real there.
- 有的時候我也喜歡聽著瀑布的聲音然後坐在岩石上面打坐。那就好像是在聽那些大自然的聲音 CD 一樣。

MP3 002

紐西蘭湖邊
❶

■ My cousin's family has a property by the lake in New Zealand. We visit them from time to time, but I just don't know what to do rather than sitting by the lake and get tanned.

■ 我表姐他們家在紐西蘭的湖邊有棟房子。我們有時候會拜訪他們，可是我真的不知道除了坐在湖邊曬太陽之外還可以做什麼。

紐西蘭湖邊
❷

■ At first, I was impressed with the beautiful scenery, but then I thought to myself: "I would spend my money on somewhere else." I feel like I automatically get old when I'm by the lake.

■ 一開始的時候我對那裡的美景很驚艷，可是後來我跟自己說：「我會把錢花在別的地方」。每次我在湖邊的時候我就覺得我好像自動老了好幾歲。

1 道地高分句

2 一問三答

3 話題卡回答

4 即席應答

湖邊兒時回憶

■ Campfire, fishing, and refreshing morning swims. I think it would be so awesome to just stay a few days or weeks by the lake.

■ 營火、釣魚，還有清涼的晨泳。我覺得如果可以在湖邊待上個幾天或是幾個禮拜一定會超棒的。

湖給人的印象

■ The lakes always give me an impression of calmness. I try to think about lakes when I'm really angry sometimes.

■ 湖總是給我一個很平靜的印象。有時候我很生氣的時候我就會試著想著湖。

湖與生活

■ When I'm very stressed about work, I'll try to think about lakes, and it always brings me peace.

■ 我如果工作壓力很大的時候我就會想像著湖泊，然後我就會平靜一些。

露易絲湖 ❶

■ Lake Louise! I saw it on the magazine randomly, and I was very impressed with the hotel there.

■ 露易絲湖！我有一次不小心在雜誌上看到就對那裡的飯店印象深刻。

露易絲湖 ❷

■ I heard it costs a fortune to stay there for a night, but I guess it's worth the money. I tried to call the travel agency about one of their tour packages there, but it's all booked out.

■ 聽說在那住一晚超級貴,但我想應該是值得的。我有試著打給旅行社問他們那裡其中一個行程,可是全部都訂光了。

蘇格蘭的尼斯湖 ❶

■ I've always wanted to go to the Loch Ness in Scotland. All those myths and legends you heard growing up.

■ 我一直都很想要去在蘇格蘭的尼斯湖。從小聽說了那麼多關於它的神話和傳說。

蘇格蘭的尼斯湖 ❷

■ When I first knew about Nessie, unlike everybody else, I was not surprised at all. I've always believed that there are some kinds of monsters in the lakes.

■ 當我第一次聽到 Nessie 的時候,我沒有像其他人那麼驚訝。我一直都覺得在湖裡一定住著某種怪物。

帛琉的水母湖
❶

■ I heard about the Jellyfish Lake in Palau, and it really got me curious. It's pretty much a lake full of jellyfish. Sounds scary, but miraculously all the jellyfish aren't poisonous at all.

■ 我聽說過在帛琉的水母湖然後就一直對它很好奇。它其實就是一個充滿了水母的湖。聽起來很恐怖，可神奇的是在那裡所有的水母都沒有毒。

帛琉的水母湖
❷

■ The jellyfish were originally from the ocean but the land rose, so the jellyfish were trapped in the lake. Overtime, they lost their predators, so there was no reason for them to be poisonous anymore.

■ 本來那些水母來自海洋，直到有天陸地上升，所以那些水母就被困在湖泊裡。隨著時間過去，水母們失去了牠們的天敵，而也就沒有需要毒素的必要。

MP3 003

墨西哥的巨型
水晶洞穴 ❶

■ Have you heard about the Cave of Crystals in Mexico? I randomly read about it in a magazine, while I was getting a haircut, and I have been really interested about going to see it.

■ 你有聽過墨西哥的巨型水晶洞穴嗎？你不覺得聽起來就很吸引人嗎？我有一次在剪頭髮的時候不小心在雜誌上看到的，然後我就一直想去看。

墨西哥的巨型
水晶洞穴 ❷

■ I really want to see this giant crystal, but I heard it's disturbingly hot in that cave. Well...no wonder the crystal is still there....

■ 我是真的很想去看這個巨型水晶，但是我聽說在洞穴裡是超級熱的。哎…難怪那些水晶都還在那…。

義大利卡布里
島的洞穴 ❶

■ There is an interesting cave on the island of Capri in Italy. It's interesting because there's an eerie blue light in the cave.

■ 在義大利卡布里島有一個很有趣的洞穴。它很有趣是因為它洞穴裡有一道很詭異的藍光。

義大利卡布里
島的洞穴 ❷

■ I went to that cave in the afternoon, which was a really good time to visit because that was the time when the sunlight was filtered through seawater and created a blue reflection.

■ 我去的時候是在下午，聽說那是一個很好的時機，因為那時候陽光會透過海水照進洞穴，然後就會產生反射的藍光。

紐西蘭的阿拉
努伊洞穴 ❶

■ When I was doing the Working Holiday in New Zealand, I went to Aranui cave that is known for its glowworms.

■ 我在紐西蘭度假打工的時候有去一個以螢火蟲聞名的阿拉努伊洞穴。

洞穴與螢火蟲 ❶

- Glowworms are very much like fireflies, but they are different from each other. It's a must see in that area.
- 在洞穴裡的這種螢火蟲跟一般的螢火蟲不太一樣。在那個區域是必看的。

洞穴與螢火蟲 ❷

- When I went in the cave on a boat ride, there were thousands of glowworms glowing. That was the most beautiful scene I've ever seen.
- 我坐船去那個洞穴看的時候，那裡有上千隻螢火蟲在發光。那是我目前為止看過最美的景象。

洞穴體驗 ❶

- It was just so wet and muddy in the caves. I ruined a white T-shirt and my brand name shoes the last time I was in a cave.
- 我有一次去洞穴裡的時候就毀了我一件白色 T 恤和一雙名牌的鞋子。

1
道地高分句

2
一問三答

3
話題卡回答

4
即席應答

洞穴體驗 ❷

- I've heard a lot of stories when people got stuck in the caves. So, I think for me, I would want to bring extra food and water. Ropes and warm clothes to prepare for the worst.
- 我有聽過很多人被困在洞穴裡的故事。所以我想對我來說，我會要帶多點的食物和水，繩子還有保暖的衣服來作最壞的打算。

洞穴與準備用品 ❶

- Of course you need to bring a helmet, flashlight, and extra lights actually just in case.
- 當然你會需要安全帽、手電筒，還有額外的燈以防萬一。

洞穴與準備用品 ❷

- A raincoat would come in handy when you go exploring the caves. You have to watch out for some cave creatures, so you might want to bring company.
- 有雨衣的話，在你去探索洞穴的時候也是很方便的。還要小心一些洞穴裡的生物，所以帶個夥伴也是一個好主意。

MP3 004

中國的九寨溝
國家公園 ❶

- I've been to several National parks in the world, but I would tell you that Jiu Zhai Gou Vally National Park in China is just magical.
- 我有去過全世界很多座國家公園，但是我覺得最夢幻的是中國的九寨溝國家公園。

中國的九寨溝
國家公園 ❷

- The five-colored lakes, the clear sky and the evergreen forests are just amazing on their own. Heaven on earth would be the best description for it.
- 五色沼、晴朗的天空和常青的森林分開看就已經很美了。對它最好的描述就是人間天堂。

1 道地高分句

2 一問三答

3 話題卡回答

4 即席應答

哥斯大黎加的 Arenal 國家公園 ❶

- I've been to Arenal National Park in Costa Rica. I heard many movies were shot in that National park.
- 我有去過哥斯大黎加的 Arenal 國家公園。我聽說很多電影在那裡拍攝過

哥斯大黎加的 Arenal 國家公園 ❷

- It's just so lush and there is an active volcano within the national park! Because of the volcano, there are plenty of hot springs as well.
- 那裡真的很翠綠，而且還有一個活火山在國家公園裡。因為有火山，那裡也有很多的溫泉。

優勝美地國家公園 ❶

- Yes, I've been to Yosemite National Park. The view there is just breathtaking. I went in spring and that was when all the wildflowers were in bloom.
- 有啊，我有去過優勝美地國家公園。那裡的景色真的美不勝收。我是春天的時候去的，在那個時候所有的野花都盛開。

優勝美地國家
公園 ❷

- Besides, the crystalline lakes and the pine forests just make perfect postcard-worthy views all around you!
- 除此之外，清澈的湖水和松樹森林讓你周遭的景色都好像明信片一樣。

國家公園
與騎馬

- I expect to join a guided tour in the National Parks. Horseback riding tours, or some private tours would be ideal.
- 我預期可以參加國家公園裡的導覽。騎馬行程，或是一些私人行程都很理想。

國家公園與
野生動物

- I expect to see a lot of wildlife in the National Parks for sure. Some National Parks even give out maps of where to see those animals. Bear, bighorn sheep, bison, elk, and river otters all wander in the parks.
- 我一定是預期在國家公園裡看到很多野生動物。有一些國家公園甚至會給你一個地圖去看動物。熊、大角羊、美洲野牛、麋鹿和水獺都在公園裡到處遊蕩。

國家公園與熊

- I was once really close to a bear. It was frightening, but also amazing to see a bear in such a short distance. I was in awe to see such a beautiful creature in the National Parks.
- 我有一次很接近一隻熊。其實蠻恐怖的，但是同時也是很神奇可以這麼近看著熊。我那時候看到這麼美的生物真的很震撼。

國家公園與 實際感受

- I've always imagined the stars are all over the place in the National Parks, the forests and all that jazz.
- 我總是想像在國家公園裡到處都是星星、森林諸如此類的。

國家公園與 阿凡達

- Avatar is what I have in mind when it comes to the National Parks.
- 想到國家公園我就會想到阿凡達。

安全性、西藏雅魯藏波峽谷、吸引力和真實性

MP3 005

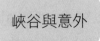
峽谷與意外

■ Do you know how many accidents happened at the canyons? People fall in there all the time. Alright, I might be a little dramatic, but you get the point.

■ 你知道在峽谷有多少意外發生過嗎？大家一天到晚都掉到峽谷裡。好啦，我是有點誇張，可是你知道我的意思。

峽谷的安全性
❶

■ And who knows, what if it rains, there might be falling rocks! I certainly do not want to wear helmets when I'm traveling. I travel with style. Period.

■ 而且誰知道啊，如果下雨的話，還可能會有落石耶！我真的不想要戴安全帽旅行。我要很時尚的旅行。就是這樣。

峽谷給人的
感覺 ❶

■ I went to the Grand Canyon a few years ago, and it didn't disappoint me in any way! It's just as grand as I imagined.

■ 我幾年前有去過大峽谷，而且他也完全沒有令我失望！那就跟我想像的一樣那麼大！

峽谷給人的
感覺 ❷

■ I feel so teeny when I was there. It's definitely a place that humbles you. The Native Americans consider this place a holy place, and I can see that.

■ 我在那裡的時候覺得我好小喔。那個地方真的會讓你覺得很謙卑。那裡同時也是印第安人覺得是很神聖的地方，我看得出來。

西藏雅魯藏波
峽谷 ❶

■ I was traveling in Tibet, and had a chance to visit the Yurlung Tsangpo Canyon. They claim that it was the highest river in the world.

■ 我有去西藏玩然後去了雅魯藏波峽谷。他們號稱那裡是世界上最高的河流。

1 道地高分句

2 一問三答

3 話題卡回答

4 即席應答

西藏雅魯藏波峽谷 ❷

■ that's why the name of the canyon meant "The Everest of Rivers". It is a place that's really close to heaven I think. Very pure and clean.

■ 那也是它名字的意思。意思是說那是河流裡的聖母峰。而且我也覺得那裡是最接近天堂的地方。非常的純淨跟乾淨。

峽谷的安全性 ❷

■ Honestly I have no clue. I guess people would say something about the wonder of the nature blah-blah-blah, but what about safety?

■ 老實說我真的不懂耶。我想大家可能會說因為那是大自然的奇景啊這類無聊的話，但是安全怎麼辦？

峽谷的安全性 ❸

■ What happens to treasuring your own precious life? Many people go missing in the canyons, and I can imagine where they went.

■ 要怎麼保護我們寶貴的生命呢？很多人在峽谷裡失蹤，我可以想像他們是去了哪裡。

峽谷的吸引力 ❶

■ I like it because it's just a great reminder to stay humble, and it's only natural to be drawn to something so grand.

■ 我喜歡是因為那是可以提醒我保持謙卑的地方，而且我覺得是很自然而然被這麼巨大的地方吸引。

峽谷的吸引力 ❷

■ Not to mention that none of it is man-made. We only live in small parts on this planet, and I can't wait and I know for sure that more wonders will be discovered in the future.

■ 更別提它完全不是人造的。我們只住在這個星球上很小的一部分，我等不及要看，而且我確定有更多的奇景在這個世界上等著被探索。

峽谷的真實性

■ then you started watching Discovery or National Geographic channel. It's one of the most amazing things, and it must be true because the textbooks and Discovery and National Geographic don't lie.

■ 然後你就開始看探索或是國家地理頻道。那是世界上最驚人的事物之一，而且也一定是真的，因為課本、探索，還有國家地理頻道不會騙人。

美容覺、值得性和搭乘馬車看日出

MP3 006

日出和美容覺 ❶

■ Sunrise is beautiful but not beautiful enough for me to sacrifice my beauty sleep. Waking up in midnight just so that I can catch the sunrise for a little bit.

■ 日出是很漂亮，可是沒有漂亮到讓我想要犧牲我的美容覺。要大半夜起床所以我才可以看到日出一下下。

日出和美容覺 ❷

■ Excuse me, all that waking up at midnight, hiking and all the fuss that ends up with nothing? What's wrong with stargazing, moonrise or those activities that take less effort?

■ 不好意思你說什麼？所以半夜起床，然後爬山到山頂還有所有做的麻煩事到頭來什麼都看不到？觀星、看月亮升起，還有那些不用那麼辛苦的行程有什麼不好的？

1 道地高分句

2 一問三答

3 話題卡回答

4 即席應答

日出的值得性 ❶

■ You wake up early when it is still dark, you bundle yourself up and hike to the highest point so that you can peek at the best view of something that secretly happens every day.

■ 你早上在天還是黑黑的時候起來，把你自己包滿了保暖的衣服，然後爬到最高的點，你就可以窺視到這個其實每天都偷偷在發生的美景。

日出的值得性 ❷

■ The colors of the cloud and the moment when sun shows up at the horizon just makes me feel that all that work is worthwhile.

■ 雲的顏色，還有當太陽出現在地平線的那一刻，就讓我覺得這一切都是值得的。

日出的神聖感 ❶

■ There is something magical and holy about it. Many people go all the way to the mountain just to bid their good morning to the sun.

■ 我覺得他有一種很神奇跟神聖的感覺。很多人爬上去就只是為了要跟太陽說早安。

日出的值得性 ③

■ However, in exchange, you have to wake up so early that you might as well just stay up late. I drank so much coffee that I was shaking.

■ 但是，要看到這美景，你就得要很早起床。早到你乾脆熬夜不要睡好了。我那時候喝超多咖啡喝到我都發抖了。

搭乘小火車看日出

■ When I was there, I had to lower myself to everyone's level to get in the tiny train to get up to the mountain.

■ 想當初我去看時可是勉強搭乘小火車上去？

搭乘馬車看日出

■ I'd always imagined that we'd get in a luxurious chariot at 3 or 4 in the morning and just wave around the sparklers.

■ 我一直覺得該乘坐豪華馬車零晨三四點左右，乘著馬車邊拿著仙女棒朝著天空劃呀劃的。

攜帶美食

■ So dreamy, and then some servers would have delicious food ready on the side when you were enjoying the sunrise. I guess it didn't live up to my expectations at all!

■ 蠻夢幻的。然後隨從們還準備好美食，在看曙光時享用。我想他們一點也沒有我預期的那麼好。

1 道地高分句

2 一問三答

3 話題卡回答

4 即席應答

茂伊島的哈來阿卡拉看日出

■ I went to Haleakala in the Island of Maui. My friends and I got up at 3 so that the traffic to the mountain wasn't too bad.

■ 我去茂伊島的哈來阿卡拉。我的朋友跟我三點就起床了所以比較不會塞車。

周遭景色的變化

■ When the sun was about to rise, the colors of the cloud changed so quickly that I had no choice but to keep taking a lot of pictures. When the sun rose, everyone was in awe of the scene in front of us.

■ 當太陽快要升起的時候，雲的顏色一直很快的變化所以我只好一直拍。當太陽真的升起的時候，大家都對眼前的景色感到震驚。

看日出迎接新年

■ My friends and I decided that we wanted to catch one of the first sunrises in the world to welcome the upcoming New Year, so we went to Fiji and it was very nice. We completed our first of the year by scuba diving afterwards as well!

■ 我的朋友和我想要看到世界上最早出來的日出來歡迎新的一年，所以我們就去斐濟，然後也真的蠻棒的。我們看完日落之後就去深潛來讓這新年的第一天更完美。

攜帶驅蟲液、防曬乳和羽絨枕頭和水壺和碘

MP3 007

攜帶驅蟲液

■ Bug repellent is definitely one of the most important things I'll bring. I only use the ones with natural ingredients since I have sensitive skin.

■ 驅蟲液一定是我會帶的東西之一。我只用天然成分的驅蟲液因為我是敏感肌膚。

野外的昆蟲

■ I'm born to attract all kinds of bugs. They eat me alive in the wild. A scar is probably the one souvenir I don't want from the trip.

■ 我生下來就是會吸引各種的昆蟲。在野外他們會把我生吞掉。旅行的時候我唯一不想帶回來的紀念品就是疤痕。

1 道地高分句

2 一問三答

3 話題卡回答

4 即席應答

防曬乳和羽絨枕頭

- Also, sunscreen is a must when I'm outdoors. Who wants to travel with sunburn? Not this girl! Oh, and my feather pillow to ensure a good night's sleep.

- 還有，如果我在戶外的話，防曬乳也是一定要的。誰想要邊旅行邊曬傷？不會是我！噢還有我的羽絨枕頭，確保我晚上睡得很好。

水壺和碘

- A water bottle and iodine are always good to have when you need to track down the water source.

- 如果你需要找水源的話，有水壺和碘在身邊的話是很好的。

釣竿

- I bring my fishing pole with me whenever I'm going to be close to the water. It's good to kill time, and you might catch a nutritional dinner.

- 如果我知道我會在水邊露營的話，我也都會帶我的釣竿。那很好殺時間而且說不定你有可能會抓到你的營養晚餐。

太陽能電池的提燈

■ I have this lantern with a solar battery. It's called Luci. It's pretty fantastic. It's light, and lasts for a long time. The bottom line is that the price is so reasonable as well.

■ 我有一個太陽能電池的提燈。它叫 Luci。它超棒的。很輕又可以持續很久的時間。最重要的是它的價錢也很合理。

烏魯魯露營

■ To be honest, I haven't really camped that many times yet, but I'll say that the time when I was at Uluru was pretty good.

■ 老實說，我還沒有露營很多次，但我可以說我在烏魯魯的時候還蠻不錯的。

烏魯魯前喝香檳和吃 buffet

■ I went with a luxurious package where we had champagne and buffet right in front of Uluru. I cannot imagine anyone who doesn't do this when they finish the day hike there.

■ 我選了奢華旅行行程。我們在烏魯魯前喝香檳和吃 buffet。我無法想像任何人在健行完之後不選擇這個行程。

1 道地高分句

2 一問三答

3 話題卡回答

4 即席應答

划塑膠皮艇、釣魚，和泛舟

■ I had a blast when I was at Jasper National Park last year. There are countless beautiful lakes where you can gokayaking, fishing, white water rafting, etc. You name it.

■ 我去年在賈斯柏國家公園裡玩得很開心。那裡有數不清的湖泊，在那裡你可以划塑膠皮艇、釣魚，和泛舟等等。你說的出來的都有。

玩音樂和分享彼此的故事

■ I met some really cool world travelers at the campsite that evening. We spent our evening playing music and sharing stories under the stars.

■ 我那天晚上在營地也遇到很多很酷的正在環遊世界的人。我們那天晚上就在星空下玩音樂和分享彼此的故事中度過。

優聖美地國家公園露營

■ I scored big when I was in Yosemite National Park. Camping is relatively affordable for the accommodation already. However, the fee to camp at Yosemite ranged from 6 to 26 dollars per night.

■ 我在優聖美地國家公園裡拿到超好的優惠。露營本來就在住宿裡算比較負擔得起的了。但是在優美聖地裡露營的費用從六塊美金到二十六塊美金一個晚上不等。

MP3 008

全身肌肉痠痛

■ I don't see the point of walking for miles and miles up and down mountains. You get all sweaty and out of breath. The worst thing is that the next day all your muscles ache.

■ 我不懂為什麼要長途跋涉的爬上山，再爬下來。你會流汗，然後喘不過氣。最糟的是隔天你全身的肌肉都會痠痛。

落湯雞和
被蜜蜂螫

■ Of course it'll rain, and you'll get soaking wet. If it's sunny, you'll get sunburn. To make things really bad, you might fall over and twist your ankle or get stung by a bee.

■ 當然你健行的時候會下雨，然後你就會變落湯雞。如果是晴天的話，你就會被曬傷再更糟的是，你可能會跌倒然後扭到你的腳踝還是被蜜蜂螫到。

不一樣的地形和風景

■ I don't mind hills, but I prefer a varied terrain or scenery to keep it fun. I also enjoy hikes that end with a waterfall.

■ 我是不介意爬一些坡度，但是我比較喜歡有不一樣的地形和風景讓健行的時候比較好玩。我也很喜歡有一些步道的終點是瀑布。

流很多汗

■ After you got all sweaty hiking, it'd be so nice to jump in the water to get reenergized.

■ 在你健行完流很多汗的時候，可以跳進水裡充電一定很棒！

享受周遭的風景

■ I like to stop frequently to enjoy the scenery, the view, and the flora and the fauna.

■ 我很喜歡一直停下來享受周遭的風景、景色、還有花草跟動物。

**可拍照的
漂亮步道**

- so it's best when the hike has a great view for me to stop and take pictures; preferably a shaded hike, just so that it's more comfortable walking long distances.
- 所以如果是一個可以一直讓我停下來拍照的漂亮步道最好。更好的是還有遮蔭的步道，所以長途走下來也比較舒服。

互相問謎語

- I don't really do long hikes, but when I'm doing repetitive workouts with my friends at the gym, we like to ask each other riddles.
- 我不作長途健行，不過如果我是跟我朋友在健身房裡做一些反覆的運動的話，我們喜歡互相問謎語。

辨識路上的植物或是菌類

- My friends and I love to identify the plants and fungus along the way or share some crazy stories from our trips. A lot of the topics are really random, too.
- 我朋友和我喜歡辨識路上的植物或是菌類，我們也喜歡互相分享一些旅行的瘋狂事蹟或是聊一些超無厘頭的話題。

1 道地高分句

2 一問三答

3 話題卡回答

4 即席應答

大吃幾個披薩

- For example, where are some of the weirdest tattoos you have ever seen? On the way back though, we like to talk about how many pizzas we are going to slay when we get back.
- 像是你看過最奇怪的刺青是什麼？在回程的時候，我們喜歡聊回去之後要大吃幾個披薩。

交換意見

- My friends and I are always contemplating our next purchase and swapping notes, pros and cons. It's really good because I feel like we are utilizing time well.
- 我和我朋友最常一起討論我們下一個要買的東西，我們會交換意見然後做一些優劣分析。我覺得很好因為我們有好好地利用時間在對的事情上。

八卦彼此的感情狀態

- and we really got some good advice from each other. However, we also like to gossip about each other's relationships or our mutual friends'. Girls will always be girls.
- 而且我們也有得到很好的建議。不過啦，我們也喜歡八卦彼此的感情狀態，或是共同朋友的。啊呀，女生就是這樣嘛！

把線丟到水裡、像是在放風箏和魚上鉤的興奮感

MP3 009

不喜歡魚的味道

■ Not at all. I just don't like the smell of fish. Growing up, I never liked going to the fish market with my mother.

■ 完全沒興趣。我就是不喜歡魚的味道。從小我就很不喜歡跟我媽媽去魚市。

不喜歡釣魚

■ I can't imagine catching them myself, let alone unhooking them and all that work. Ew, and the bait. Oh my, I don't think it'll ever be my thing.

■ 我無法想像自己抓魚,更別提把魚從鉤上拿下來還有所有那類的事。噁心,還有魚餌。我的天啊,我覺得我應該永遠都不會喜歡釣魚。

1
道地高分句

2
一問三答

3
話題卡回答

4
即席應答

**魚上鉤的
興奮感**

■ It's so exciting when you have a fish on. I kept thinking whoever came up with fishing was such a genius. He must have been so thrilled when he found out it actually worked!

■ 魚上鉤的時候真的是超刺激的。我都一直在想當初第一個發明釣魚這件事的人真是一個天才。他那時候發現真的釣得到魚一定超興奮的！

綁魚線的結

■ It's actually a lot more complicated than what it looks like. How to tie the knots, hook on the bait, fight the fish, even how to reel the fish in.

■ 其實釣魚比看起來還要複雜很多。你要知道怎麼綁魚線的結，怎麼樣把魚餌勾在鉤上，怎麼鬥魚，怎麼把魚拉進來。

**想要試試看
釣魚**

■ I like to eat the fish to say the least, but I have never been taught how to fish or I never had enough opportunities to fish. I'm interested in trying though.

■ 至少我喜歡吃魚啦，但是從來沒有人教我釣魚或是我也沒什麼機會釣過魚。我蠻想要試試看的。

享受在戶外的時候

■ It just seems so relaxing and I guess for me it's not about catching, it's about being out there and enjoying being outdoors. I'm so tired of being trapped in the office.

■ 好像蠻令人放鬆而且我想對我來說釣魚並不是真的要釣到魚，而是因為可以享受在戶外的時候。我真是受夠被關在辦公室了。

把線丟到水裡

■ I tried fishing with my cousins at the lake in New Zealand. None of us was really good at fishing, so we were just throwing the lines in the water, and hoping for the best.

■ 我有在紐西蘭跟我的表姐妹試過。我們其實都不太會釣魚，所以我們也只是把線丟到水裡，然後做最好的打算。

像是在放風箏

■ I was secretly hoping nothing would bite mine. It was really more like flying a kite except that the lines were in the water. More like a social thing for us I would say.

■ 其實我偷偷希望沒有東西會咬我的餌。那天其實真的比較像是在放風箏，只是我們是把線丟到水裡。 對我們來說，釣魚是比較像是在社交的活動。

- I've tried a lot of different kinds of fishing. Deep-seafishing, fresh water fishing, kayak fishing, Jet ski fishing,spear fishing...etc.
- 我有試過很多不同種的釣魚。深海釣魚、淡水釣魚、皮艇釣魚、水上摩托車釣魚和魚叉獵魚等等。

深海釣魚、淡水釣魚、皮艇釣魚、水上摩托車釣魚和魚叉獵魚

- I have to say that I like kayak fishing the best because kayaking is a good exercise and it's just you and your fishing poles out there. Really nice.
- 不過我必須要說我最喜歡皮艇釣魚因為它是很好的運動，而且你只需要你和你的釣竿。真的很棒。

最喜歡皮艇釣魚

- I fished offshore one time at the beach with some friends. I mean, I wasn't really fishing. They set everything up for me to fish, and when we caught a fish, I reeled it in. It was really fun.
- 我有跟朋友在海邊的近岸釣魚過一次。其實我是說我朋友他們把一切都弄好，我沒有真的釣魚啦，只是我們釣到魚的時候，他們讓我拉起來。真的很好玩。

海邊的近岸釣魚

MP3 010

特克斯和凱科
斯群島的一個
私人島嶼

■ The best one is definitely the one that I went to as an exclusive private island in the Turks and Caicos with my parents. We stayed at the Parrot Cay Retreat.

■ 最棒的一定是跟我爸媽去位在特克斯和凱科斯群島的一個私人島嶼。我們住在 Parrot Cay 渡假飯店。

去室外的花園
按摩池

■ They also have a yoga studio, which is 1,300 square feet if you wish to practice indoors. We also went to their outdoor jacuzzi garden after the SPA. Hands down it was foremost relaxing yoga experience I've ever had.

■ 如果你想要在室內上瑜珈課的話,他們也有一千三百平方英尺大的瑜伽教室。我們做完 SPA 之後也會去他們室外的花園按摩池。這一定是我去過最令人放鬆的瑜伽體驗。

■ I think the time when I went to the Wanderlust Festival in Melbourne was a pretty memorable one. It was a huge event and there were so many people doing yoga and meditation with you.

■ 我想我在墨爾本的時候參加的 Wanderlust 節還蠻令人印象深刻的。那是一個超大的活動，而且也有很多人在那跟你一起做瑜珈和靜坐。

墨爾本的時候參加的 Wanderlust 節

■ Everyone that joined the event was all really cool and with really positive vibes. It was definitely something different. I really had a great time.

■ 參加的人都很酷，而且也有很多正面的能量。真的是蠻不一樣的經驗。我真的玩得很開心。

很多正面的能量

■ The first thing that popped up in my mind was the time when I was traveling in Hawaii. I saw some groups of people doing yoga in the park.

■ 我第一個想到的就是在夏威夷的時候，我看到有一群人在公園做瑜伽。

公園做瑜伽

自由付費

■ I approached them and understood that the practice was open to anyone and was donation-based. I thought that was such a cool thing, so I joined them the next day and from what I understood, 5 dollars was more than appropriate.

■ 我跟他們接觸之後知道那是大家都可以參加的，而且下課之後是看你要捐贈多少錢的。我覺得很酷，所以我隔天就加入他們。據我所知，給五塊美金就蠻好的。

名牌的緊身運動褲

■ But I can tell you a story from a friend of mine. So she said she was wearing these really cool and brands-named workout leggings.

■ 不過我可以跟你說我一個朋友的故事。她說有一次她穿了一件很酷又是名牌的緊身運動褲。

穿同一條緊身褲

■ However, it was not until a girl that was late for the class came to the spot in front of her did she realize that the girl was wearing the same pair of leggings as her.

■ 但是，一直到有另外一個女生上課遲到，接著那個女生選了在她前面的位置，她發現那女生跟她穿的是同一條緊身褲。

胃不適

■ Haha the most embarrassing moment was definitely when I went to the yoga class right after dinner. A lot of yoga poses included twisting your body, and my stomach didn't like that too much.

■ 哈哈，最尷尬的一定是我吃完晚餐就立刻去上瑜珈課的那次。那天很多姿勢都是要扭轉身體，我的胃不太喜歡那樣。

Savasana
或者是
corpse 姿勢

■ I normally go the yoga class after work. That said, I'm usually pretty tired to begin with already. After a series of yoga flow, it always comes to the last pose, Savasana, or corpse pose.

■ 我通常工作後會去上瑜珈課。也就是說，我通常已經相當疲憊了，才要開始。在一系列的瑜珈律動後，總是到了最後的姿勢 Savasana 或者是 corpse 姿勢。

尷尬時刻

■ I always fall asleep during the last pose. The most embarrassing moment was when I woke up one time, the other class was getting ready to start their session.

■ 到最後姿勢期間我總是睡著了。最令人感到尷尬的時刻是，當我有次醒來時，其它的課程正準備開始他們下個課程。

MP3 011

女子世界盃足球賽

- I was invited to the 2015 FIFA Women's World Cup in Canada because a friend I grew up with was playing for USA.
- 我有一個從小長大的朋友他代表美國隊參賽，所以我受邀去加拿大看 2015 年的女子世界盃足球賽。

VIP 座位

- I got VIP seats to watch the game and joined them for the after party to celebrate the victory. It was quite an experience to witness my friend add World Cup Champion to her already amazing career.
- 我有 VIP 座位，而且後來還加入她們慶祝勝利的派對。親眼看到我朋友把世足冠軍列入她本來就很好的職業生涯真的是很棒的經驗。

NBA 季後賽

■ I went on a road trip in California. It was during the time of the NBA playoffs, we couldn't pass the game in Los Angeles when the Lakers are playing against the Miami Heat.

■ 我到加州公路旅行，那個時候正好是 NBA 季後賽的時候，所以我們不想錯過在加州的湖人隊跟邁阿密熱火隊的賽事。

現場的 NBA 季後賽

■ It was quite an exciting game to watch. You can't beat live NBA playoffs. It was totally worth the drive.

■ 那場比賽真的很刺激，而且你真的無法超越現場的 NBA 季後賽。完全值得我們開那麼遠的車去看。

義大利當交換學生的時候

■ I watched a college volleyball game in Italy when I was doing a student exchange program.

■ 我在義大利當交換學生的時候去看了一場大學排球賽。

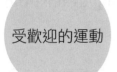

受歡迎的運動

■ I didn't know what to expect, but they were actually really skilled. Apparently, it has become a very popular sport in Italy. It was really fun watching the game for sure.

■ 我不知道該預期什麼，但是他們真的很厲害耶。很顯然的在義大利，排球已經漸漸成為一個蠻受歡迎的運動。至少是很好看的比賽。

紐約市空中
瑜珈

■ I tried Aerial Yoga in New York City when I was on a business trip last time. It definitely turned my world upside down.

■ 我上次去紐約市出差的時候有試過空中瑜珈。那真的是把我的世界弄得翻天覆地的。

吊床來練習瑜
珈和皮拉提斯

■ It's basically a combination of Yoga and Pilates with the use of a hammock. I felt really good after the workout.

■ 那其實就是用吊床來練習瑜珈和皮拉提斯的綜合版。我在運動後真的覺得很棒。

1 道地高分句

2 一問三答

3 話題卡回答

4 即席應答

莫斯科有嘗試尾流衝浪

■ I tried wake surfing in Moscow. It's really cool because you are basically surfing the wake created by the boat in front of you.

■ 我在莫斯科有嘗試尾流衝浪。那很酷因為你就是在衝你前面的船幫你製造出來的浪。

湖上衝浪

■ Who knows that you can surf in a lake as well?I mean it's nothing crazy, but it's awesome to get on your board and have some fun.

■ 誰知道你也可以在湖上衝浪？我是說，那沒有衝很瘋狂的浪還是什麼的，可是可以拿你的板子出來就玩得很開心真的很棒。

巴西的卡波耶拉

■ I tried Capoeira when I was in Brazil. It was really spontaneous because I was walking down the street from my hostel when I ran into a group of people circled together doing this thing called Capoeira.

■ 我去巴西的時候有試過卡波耶拉。那真的很隨性因為我只是從我的青年旅社走出來，然後就遇到一群人圍成一個圈圈在做這個叫做卡波耶拉的運動。

MP3 012

浮潛

■ I don't like water sports...If I really have to pick one, I would probably go with snorkeling. It's pretty cool to peek at what's under the ocean without getting too involved.

■ 我不喜歡水上活動…不過如果真的硬要選，我應該會選浮潛吧！可以看看海裡面有什麼是還蠻酷的，而且也沒有跟他們太近。

飯店的浮潛
行程

■ There are a lot of hotels that have snorkeling packages you can join or some hotels even have a pool where you can swim with fish.

■ 很多飯店都會有浮潛的行程可以加入。有的飯店還會有游泳池是你可以在裡面浮潛，跟魚一起游泳的。

衝浪

- My favorite water sport is definitely surfing. Nothing else can make you feel so free. And I'm more focused at the moment when I'm surfing.
- 我最喜歡的水上活動一定是衝浪。沒有任何事可以讓你覺得那麼自由自在。

衝浪與人生的道理

- You have to observe your surroundings constantly and live in that moment because once you daydream, the wave is gone already. I learned a lot about life from surfing.
- 而且我在衝浪的時候會更專注在當下。你要一直觀察你周遭的環境，然後活在當下因為你只要一發呆，浪就過了。我從衝浪學了很多關於人生的道理。

潛水解憂

- My favorite water sport is diving. I love going diving when I'm troubled in life. Every single noise just instantly goes away once I'm in the water.
- 我最喜歡的水上活動是潛水。每次我人生遇到難題的時候我就會去潛水。一下水，每個雜音都立刻消失。

1 道地高分句

2 一問三答

3 話題卡回答

4 即席應答

放鬆又很平靜的感覺

- I can only hear my breath and the bubbles I created from the oxygen tank. It's a really relaxing and peaceful feeling down there.
- 我只聽得到我呼吸的聲音和從氧氣筒呼吸時製造的泡泡聲。在水裡真的是很放鬆又很平靜的感覺。

澳洲的大堡礁浮潛

- I don't think it's a secret, but the Great Barrier Reef in Australia is always something people talk about when it comes to snorkeling or other water sports.
- 我覺得這個應該不是秘密了，不過每次提到浮潛還是其他水上活動，大家就會提到澳洲的大堡礁。

照顧大堡礁的工作

- Remember the campaign for the best job in the world back in 2009? The job was to take care of the Great Barrier Reef. I don't want to admit it, but I applied for the job as well...
- 還記得 2009 年那個全世界最棒的工作的宣傳嗎？那個工作就是可以照顧大堡礁。我不想承認，可是我那時候也有應徵那個工作啦…。

1 道地高分句
2 一問三答
3 話題卡回答
4 即席應答

菲律賓的
Cloud 9

- Cloud 9 is a really good surfspot in the Philippines. They have some world-class waves there. It's not as crowded as many famous surf spots, and there are a lot of bed and breakfasts there where you can stay for a cheap price with healthy meals there.
- Cloud 9 是在菲律賓很有名的衝浪點。那裡不像很多其他有名的浪點一樣擁擠，在那裡你付很少錢就可以住在那裡的民宿，而且那裡還有提供健康的餐點。

夏威夷群島的
烏龜清洗站

- There are a lot of turtle cleaning stations in the Hawaiian Islands. The turtle cleaning stations are just a huge flatrock where turtles just come and sit on the rock and the little fish will come out and clean their shells.
- 在夏威夷群島裡有很多的烏龜清洗站。烏龜清洗站其實就是一塊平坦的大石頭，烏龜們會來坐在那石頭上，然後很多小魚就會來清洗龜殼上的髒東西。

爵士樂、雷鬼樂、獨立搖滾和紐奧良的典藏廳

MP3 013

爵士樂

■ My favorite type of music is Jazz. It's the perfect music for the morning, the afternoon and the evening. I just can't get enough of it.

■ 我最喜歡的音樂就是爵士樂。早上、下午和晚上聽都很棒。我就是聽不膩爵士啦。

爵士樂具感染力

■ There are so many emotions in Jazz and I always feel like when people are talking about music being contagious, I think they are referring to Jazz.

■ 爵士樂裡有很多的情緒。當大家在説音樂很有感染力的時候,我都想説他們一定是在説爵士樂。

雷鬼樂

■ I'm gonna go with Reggae. I've been traveling in a lot of islands, and they start to grow on me one day, and before I know it, I'm humming the reggae tunes all day.

■ 我應該是會選雷鬼樂。我已經在很多的島嶼旅行過了。突然有一天我漸漸開始喜歡雷鬼樂，然後在我反應過來之前，我已經整天都在哼雷鬼的調子了。

跟著雷鬼樂搖擺

■ It's a very relaxing, beach music really. I'm not too big of a dancer, either, but I can do the swing with Reggae music.

■ 那是一種很令人放鬆，海邊的那種音樂。我也不是很會跳舞，但是我可以跟著雷鬼樂搖擺。

獨立搖滾 ❶

■ I think all my favorite songs belong to Indie Rock, so I assume that's my favorite type of music.

■ 我覺得好像我很喜歡的歌都是獨立搖滾，所以我想那應該是我最喜歡的音樂種類吧！

獨立搖滾 ❷

■ You know how sometimes when you turn on the radio, and you just connect with the tunes. I think Indie Rock is my tune.

■ 你知道有的時候你打開電台音樂，然後你就會變喜歡某一台的音樂，我想我喜歡的那台就是獨立搖滾。

紐奧良的
典藏廳 ❶

■ The best one was at the Preservation Hall in New Orleans. It's like the holy ground for all jazz fans. I had my doubts before it started because it was in a tiny and old building with no seats or air-conditioning.

■ 我聽過最棒的是在紐奧良的典藏廳。那裡就像是爵士樂迷們的聖地一樣。我在表演開始之前有我的疑慮因為那棟建築又小又舊而且又沒有座位和冷氣。

紐奧良的
典藏廳 ❷

■ But when they started to perform, I had goose bumps, and I was listeningin tears. Let's just put it that way.

■ 可是當他們開始演奏的時候，我全身起雞皮疙瘩，還含淚聽整個表演。這樣說你就懂了吧。

**紐西蘭當
背包客**

- I was backpacking in New Zealand when my CouchSurfing host took me to this family fair. It was really fun with a lot of rides and food stands.
- 我在紐西蘭當背包客的時候，我沙發衝浪的主人帶我去一個家庭園遊會。那裡真的很好玩，而且也有很多遊樂設施和小吃攤。

**西班牙公園的
地下道 ❶**

- I was walking in the underground park in Spain and that was when I came across this amazing street artist. He's a guitarist, and really all he did was just play the guitar there.
- 我在西班牙一個公園的地下道走路時，突然遇到這個超厲害的街頭藝人。他是一個吉他手，然後他真的也只是就是在彈吉他而已。

**西班牙公園的
地下道 ❷**

- But the sound was very crisp with the echoes from the underground, it became very powerful music. There were people stopping here and listening for a while, but I stayed the whole time.
- 但是吉他的聲音很清脆，而且因為在地下道有回音就讓整個音樂十分的強烈。我那時候停下來，又聽了一會兒，就走不開這個表演了。

威尼斯的嘉年華會、慕尼黑的啤酒節和印度的排燈節

 MP3 014

討厭擁擠感
❶

■ I'm not a festival person per say. I don't think I like it that much mainly because of the crowds a festival brings.

■ 我本身沒有很喜歡節慶啦。我覺得我不喜歡的原因主要是因為節慶都會有很多人。

討厭擁擠感
❷

■ If people can just keep a safe distance and mind their own business, then I might be fine with it, but that's not usually the case. Too many people just make everything worse.

■ 如果大家可以保持安全距離，或是只管他們自己的閒事的話，那我就還可以參加，可是通常都不是那樣。人太多就會把一切搞砸。

■ I'm all about it. I love everything about a festival. The smell, the people, the music, the food, and the dance...I can go on and on about this all day.

喜歡節慶 ❶

■ 我最喜歡節慶了！我喜歡關於節慶的每一件事。節慶的味道、人群、音樂、食物和跳舞…我可以一直說下去。

■ I always feel so alive when I'm in one of those events. It makes me feel like I'm a little kid again, and it's okay, too. Love it.

喜歡節慶 ❷

■ 我每次參加這類的活動時就會覺得我是活著的。它讓我覺得我好像又變成一個小孩子，而且那樣也沒關係。超棒的。

■ You know, I've been there and done that. I think it's cool to check it out, but I'm just over party scenes. I'm at that age where most of my friends hang out at coffee shops instead of clubs.

四分之一年危機

■ 你知道，我已經做過那些事了。我是覺得去看看是不錯，可是我已經不 party 了。我已經到了那個大多數的朋友都會在咖啡店而不是在夜店裡的年紀了。我想我現在應該是有四分之一年危機（25 歲）。

1 道地高分句

2 一問三答

3 話題卡回答

4 即席應答

■ I went to the Carnival of Venice, and it was such a gorgeous festival. Everyone dressed up nicely and wore these amazing masks.

■ 我去了威尼斯的嘉年華會。那個節慶真是超美的。大家都精心打扮然後還帶了很棒的面具。

■ I had to buy so many of those masks before I left Venice. There were fireworks by the canal, too. Very impressive and when can you dress up like that with so many people anyways?

■ 我在離開威尼斯之前不得不買了很多面具。在運河旁也有放煙火。超令人印象深刻的，而且你還可以去哪裡精心打扮成那樣？

■ The most impressive festival I've ever been to is the Oktoberfest in Munich. It was a pretty big event, and I always thought Oktoberfest is all about beer drinking.

■ 我去過最令我印象深刻的節慶是在慕尼黑的啤酒節。那是一個蠻大的節慶，而且我一直以為啤酒節就只是喝啤酒而已。

1 道地高分句

2 一問三答

3 話題卡回答

4 即席應答

慕尼黑的啤酒節 ❷

■ But to my surprise, there are water slides, fun rides, food stands and then there are the big tents for beers and pretzels. It was really fun to see how people dressed in traditional German outfits.

■ 可是令我很意外的是那裡有很多滑水道、遊樂設施、食物的攤販。然後你才會看到他們有設立一些大帳篷，裡面你才可以喝啤酒和吃扭結餅。看大家穿著德國傳統的服飾真的很好玩。

印度的排燈節 ❶

■ I went and celebrated the festival of lights, or Diwali, with my friends in India. It was actually the Hindu New Year, so in a way, it was their New Year celebration.

■ 我在印度跟我的朋友一起慶祝了排燈節，而那時候正是印度教的新年，所以其實也就是他們新年的慶典。

印度的排燈節 ❷

■ It was really impressive because besides the big fireworks to start with, there were candles everywhere. Every household decorated their houses, too.

■ 那個節慶很令人印象深刻因為除了一開始的時候有盛大的煙火，也有隨處可見的蠟燭。每家每戶也都會佈置他們的房子。

魔術和雜耍的表演、歌舞劇和威尼斯小型的歌劇表演

MP3 015

歌舞劇 ❶

■ I really enjoy musicals. It's live concert mixed with drama and great choreography, too. Musicals are great treats for all our senses.

■ 我最喜歡歌舞劇。因為它就是現場演唱會，加上戲劇和超棒的編舞啊！音樂劇對我們的感官是極大的享受。

歌舞劇 ❷

■ Those performers can do pretty much everything, and they have not failed me so far. A lot is going on when you are watching a musical. I love it. It is like a combination of birthday party and Christmas.

■ 那些表演者真的什麼都可以表演的出來，而且他們目前為止也沒有讓我失望。在看舞台劇的時候會覺得那個表演很豐富。我超愛的，就像是生日舞會加上聖誕節一樣。

街頭藝人

- I think the best kind of performances usually come from the street. There are so many street artists on the road, and many of them are truly talented. They rely the least on other equipment, too.
- 我覺得最好的表演通常都來自街上。在街上有那麼多的街頭藝人，而且其實他們很多人都真的很有才華！他們也是仰賴任何其他的配備最少的人。

魔術和雜耍的表演❶

- I love going to the magic and acrobatic shows. It just never gets old for me. I have loved it ever since I was little and I still do.
- 我最喜歡魔術或是雜耍的表演。我都看不膩那些。我從小就很喜歡看那些表演而且到現在都還很喜歡。

魔術和雜耍的表演❷

- Without those performances and performers, this world is going to be so dull. There is always a joyful atmosphere and full of surprises in those performances.
- 我覺得如果沒有那些表演和表演者的話，這個世界會變得很乏味。在那些表演中總是有很歡樂的氣氛而且也充滿了驚喜。

■ I told every one of my friends that if they are going to Venice, they should stop by Musica a palazzo for a small scale opera experience.

■ 我跟我每一個朋友說過如果他們有去威尼斯的話，一定要去 Musica a palazzo 體驗小型的歌劇表演。

■ However, to my surprise, Musica a palazzo offers no more than 70 seats. It's tiny, but it also means you are very close to the stage.

■ 可是讓我驚訝的是 Musica a palazzo 只有提供不超過七十個座位的表演。那裡很小，但是那也表示你也離舞台很接近。

■ Cirque du Soleil always guarantees great performances and shows. I went to every one of their shows, and I recommended all of them to my friends.

■ 太陽劇團永遠都保證有最棒的表演還有秀。我去了他們每一個表演，我也推薦我的朋友去看每一個。

太陽劇團 ❷

- It's just amazing to see how professional the whole crew is. It makes me nervous to watch them sometimes, but the performances are just very stunning and artistic ones.

- 你會很傻眼怎麼每一個表演者都那麼專業。有的時候看他們表演我會覺得很緊張，但是整個表演總是那麼美麗跟藝術。他們的表演實在是太好看了。

獅子王百老匯 ❶

- I would recommend Lion King Broadway show to all my friends. At first I thought to myself that nothing is going to beat the original animation.

- 我會推薦獅子王百老匯給我所有的朋友。一開始看之前我就想說怎麼可能可以打敗原版動畫獅子王。

獅子王百老匯 ❷

- But the show actually pulls it off! The live music, the dance, the visual effects on stage are more than perfect.

- 可是他們真的做到了！現場的音樂、舞蹈和台上的視覺效果都超完美的。

MP3 016

迪士尼樂園
❶

■ Disneyland!! It is just the best amusement ever. I've been to almost all the Disneylands in the world, and I can't say I like any particular one.

■ 迪士尼樂園！它就是最棒的遊樂園啊！我幾乎去遍全世界所有的迪士尼樂園，但是我說不出來我最喜歡哪一個。它們都有自己獨特的地方。

迪士尼樂園
❷

■ They are all unique in their own ways. Who doesn't like Disneyland really? Cinderella's castle, the carousel, and all the magic in the park. It feels like a dream come true when I'm in Disneyland.

■ 不過說真的怎麼可能會有人不喜歡迪士尼樂園？仙杜瑞拉的城堡、旋轉木馬還有園內所有的魔法。在迪士尼樂園裡就好像是夢想成真一樣！

1 道地高分句

2 一問三答

3 話題卡回答

4 即席應答

Schlitterbahn
的水上樂園

- My favorite amusement park is actually a water park called Schlitterbahn. It is hands down the best amusement park in the world. The countless water slides are all very long and fun.
- 我最喜歡的遊樂園其實是一間叫做 Schlitterbahn 的水上樂園。它真的是我認為世界上最棒的遊樂園。數不清的滑水道都很長又很好玩。

Schlitterbahn
的水上樂園

- You can carry the tubes around the park to do all kinds of slides or just float around the floating river. There are always long lines, but no one seems to care too much once they get on the ride.
- 你在園內也都可以拿著游泳圈去各式各樣的滑水道，或是只是在漂漂河上漂。雖然都要排隊很久，但是大家都是坐到之後就不會在意了。

奧蘭多的環
球影城冒險島
樂園 ❶

- Universal Studio's Island of Adventures in Orlando! It's both intriguing and exciting. Once you graduate from Disneyland, you will enjoy this place so much.
- 在奧蘭多的環球影城冒險島樂園！它又好玩又刺激。你在迪士尼樂園畢業之後，你就會很喜歡這個地方。

奧蘭多的環球影城冒險島樂園 ❶

- I only spent one day there, and I couldn't finish all the rides and exploring the park fully. I was in tears when I needed to leave.
- 我只有在那裡玩一天，可是我沒有試過全部的設施也沒有探索完整個園區。我是含淚離開那個地方的。

洛杉磯環球影城的鬼屋 ❶

- I would say my worst experience was the Haunted House at L.A. Universal Studios. Their problem was that they took everything way too seriously.
- 我要把我在遊樂園最糟的經驗是在洛杉磯環球影城的鬼屋。他們的問題就是他們太認真了啦。

洛杉磯環球影城的鬼屋 ❷

- It was a walking tour through the whole haunted house. Everything in the haunted house was as if they came out directly from a crime scene. I had nightmares and was scared to go to any haunted house after that one.
- 那是一個要走路穿過鬼屋的行程。每一個在那個鬼屋裡面的東西都好像是直接從犯罪現場搬來的。我再去玩那個鬼屋之後就做惡夢，而且還從此對鬼屋有陰影。

1
道地高分句

2
一問三答

3
話題卡回答

4
即席應答

卡在摩天輪上
❶

- I've never really had a bad experience in the amusement park although there was one time when we were stuck on the Ferris wheel for an hour.
- 我在遊樂園裡沒有什麼不好的經驗，不過有一次我在摩天輪上面卡了一個小時。

卡在摩天輪上
❷

- I didn't mind it, but it gets scary because we didn't know when we could get back to the ground. It was pretty windy up there, too. Then, I started to have flashbacks about those horrifying scenes from the scary movies.
- 我一開始是不介意，但是後來越來越可怕因為我們不知道什麼時候才可以回到陸地上。而且在上面的時候風也很大。然後我腦海就開始有一些恐怖片裡面的恐怖情節畫面。

雲霄飛車

- I got motion sickness when I was on a roller coaster ride. My best friend at the time was nice enough to sit me down at the chair nearby and listened to how dizzy I felt the whole time.
- 我坐完雲霄飛車的時候開始有點暈。我那時候最好的朋友人很好的帶我去坐在附近的椅子上，而且還全程一直聽我說我有多暈。

MP3 017

遊輪上慶祝
婚禮 ❶

■ I was on a cruise for a friend's wedding. Their wedding was a destination wedding, and the ship took everyone to Hawaii and that's where my friends had the ceremony.

■ 我有在遊輪上面慶祝我朋友的婚禮。他們的婚禮是一個度假婚禮。遊輪帶大家去夏威夷參加他們的結婚典禮。

遊輪上慶祝
婚禮 ❷

■ It was a perfect way to get everyone together and celebrate their wedding together. It was the best wedding party I've ever been to.

■ 那是一個很完美的辦法把大家聚在一起,並且一起慶祝他們的婚禮。那是我去過最棒的婚禮。

短程去阿拉斯
加的遊輪 ❶

■ I have a buddy who works for a cruise ship, so he pulled some strings and got me a ticket to a short cruise to Alaska.

■ 我有一個好朋友在遊輪上工作，於是他就動用了一些關係幫我拿到一張短程去阿拉斯加的遊輪。

短程去阿拉斯
加的遊輪 ❷

■ It was so nice and the cruise was beautiful. When we got to Alaska, we even went sports fishing. I had a blast and even if half of the time I was seasick, it was still a great experience.

■ 整個旅程很好而且那段路也十分的美麗。當我們到阿拉斯加的時候，我們還去釣魚。即使一半的行程我都在暈船，我還是玩得很開心。那是一個很棒的經驗。

雪梨的達令港
坐日落遊輪
❶

■ I went on a sunset cruise at the Darling Harbour at Sydney. It was really romantic and the sunset was beautiful. I did notice there were a lot of couples, and so it was a little bit weird.

■ 我在雪梨的時候去了達令港坐日落遊輪。我覺得很浪漫而且日落也好美。我的確是有注意到很多的情侶，所以那有點奇怪。

雪梨的達令港坐日落遊輪❶

- Other than that, the food is great, and they also have drinks on board, too. It was really nice to tour around Darling Harbour and frankly I think that's the best way!
- 除了那樣之外，食物很好吃，而且他們船上也有喝的。我覺得用遊輪觀光達令港是一個蠻棒的方式，老實説，我覺得是最棒的方式。

不太會暈船

- To my surprise, not really. I'm actually pretty good with it. So far I haven't got seasick from the cruises. I'm born to do this I guess.
- 很令我驚訝，可是我不太會暈船耶。而且其實我還蠻厲害的。到目前為止我在遊輪上都沒有暈船過。我想我就是生下來要坐遊輪的。

海浪超大

- There were times when the water was rougher than it should have been, and many people got sick. I was still in good shape though. It's pretty amazing.
- 而且有的時候海浪真的超大的，然後很多人都暈了，可是我還是很好。還蠻令人驚訝的。

暈車、暈船、暈機

■ I get car sick, seasick, and I even get sick when I'm on the plane. But I still can't pass traveling up though. Oh and by the way, the wrist band that's supposed to help you with seasickness doesn't work!

■ 我會暈車、暈船，坐飛機我也會暈。但是我還是不能放棄旅行啦。喔對了，那個手腕上在戴的防暈手環，完全沒用！

暈船經驗 ❶

■ It depends. If I have enough sleep and I have something in my stomach, I'm usually fine. Nevertheless, I had really bad experiences when I got seasick on a sailboat.

■ 要看情況耶。如果我有睡得飽，然後也有吃點東西的話，我通常都還好。但是我也有暈船很嚴重的經驗。

暈船經驗 ❷

■ Once I was on a boat. Everything was fine until I went into the tiny bathroom on the boat, and then everything went downhill from there.

■ 有一次我在船上。本來都好好的直到我去一間很小間的廁所上廁所，然後我就開始走下坡了。

1 道地高分句

2 一問三答

3 話題卡回答

4 即席應答

MP3 018

西班牙安達魯西亞的佛朗明哥裙 ❶

■ I would love to try on the Flamenco dresses from Andalucía, Spain. They are just so bright-colored and passionate. I saw a few Flamenco dancers performing at the mall.

■ 我會想要試試看西班牙安達魯西亞的佛朗明哥裙。它們是那麼的鮮艷和熱情。我有在購物中心看過一些佛朗明歌舞者表演。

西班牙安達魯西亞的佛朗明哥裙 ❷

■ then I thought their costumes are so beautiful. Hey, you know what? I'm gonna be a Flamenco Dancer this Halloween! Thanks for the inspiration! I think I can rock the outfit!

■ 然後我就在想他們的服裝都好美喔！喔你知道怎樣嗎？我今年的萬聖節要打扮成佛朗明哥舞者！謝謝你給我的靈感！我覺得我一定可以穿得很好看的！

蘇格蘭的蘇格
蘭裙 ❶

■ I want to try on the kilts from Scotland! Honestly I've never tried on a skirt in my life. When I first heard about the costume, my friends and I thought that was so ridiculous.

■ 我想要試試看蘇格蘭的蘇格蘭裙！老實說，我從來都沒穿過裙子。一開始聽到蘇格蘭裙的時候，我跟我的朋友就想說那真是太荒謬了。

蘇格蘭的蘇格
蘭裙 ❷

■ Why do men in Scotland wear skirts? However, just because of that, I really want to try it so that I can say I've tried on a kilts before. And I'm curious about how it feels to be in a skirt.

■ 蘇格蘭的男人怎麼會穿裙子啊？但是也是因為那樣，我真的很想要試試看，然後我就可以說我有穿過蘇格蘭裙了。而且其實我很好奇穿裙子是什麼感覺。

印度的紗麗
❶

■ I was in India, but I didn't get to try on a sari there. I did go to the markets, and there are a lot of sari shops there.

■ 我有去印度，可是我沒有試穿到紗麗。我有去那裡的市集，那裡有很多賣紗麗的店。

■ You can even mix and match your own fabric! I was in a hurry,so I didn't get to try on anything, but if I could go back in time, I would totally try it on!

■ 你還可以混搭不同的布料來做你的紗麗！我那時候很趕，所以我不能試穿任何一個，可是如果我可以回到當時的話，我一定會試穿的！

■ When I was in Milan last year, the first day I was there, I felt like I needed a makeover ASAP! That was the only day I dressed down.

■ 我去年在米蘭的時候，第一天到的時候，我覺得我立刻需要一個大改造。而且那是我唯一沒有什麼打扮的一天。

■ Everyone was so fashionable on the streets. I almost mistaken that I was on a runway. I was wearing a pair of flats! Flats! And I'm so tiny! Arg, so yeah, that was the time I felt like I should change the way I dressed.

■ 每個在街上的人都超時尚的。我差點以為我是在參展台上。我那時候正好穿了一雙平底鞋！平底鞋耶！我那麼小隻！哎！所以那就是我覺得我需要立刻改變我打扮方式的時候。

駝馬大衣

- I'd been very blessed to travel all summer long, following the eternal sunshine. However, on the south hemisphere, it was winter! I had to get my alpaca coat right away.
- 我整個夏天都很幸運可以在無止盡的陽光下旅行。但是在南半球的時候，就變成冬天了！我那時候必須要立刻去買駝馬的大衣。

洪都拉斯 ❶

- When I was in Honduras, I dressed in what I normally dress, a white tank top and a pair of shorts, and got weird looks from guys.
- 當我在洪都拉斯的時候，我穿著平常的穿著，一件白色背心跟短褲，然後男人們用奇怪的眼光看著我。

洪都拉斯 ❷

- They checked my whole body out unapologetically. I quickly looked around me and found out that no tourists were dressed like me. I quickly went back to the hotel and changed to less revealing dress.
- 他們是一點也不抱歉的看我全身。我立刻看看周遭的人然後發現那裡的觀光客沒有穿得像我這樣。所以我立刻回飯店換一些比較沒有那麼露的衣服。

MP3 019

食用野生動物
的經驗 ❶

■ I just threw up a little in my mouth! I would probably sue them about abusing animals or potentially poisoning the visitors.

■ 我想到就想吐！我應該會告他們虐待動物還是意圖讓他們的遊客中毒。

食用野生動物
的經驗 ❷

■ I hope they have very good reasons not because they have great proteins. I'm all upset just by thinking about it. Anyways, to answer your question, probably not. I mean never. Ever!

■ 我希望他們吃這些東西的原因不只是因為有豐富的蛋白質。我光用想的就氣起來了。好啦，所以來回答你這題，我應該不會試任何一樣，我是説，永遠都不會，永遠！

吃起來像雞肉

■ I'm intimidated, but I would probably give it a shot. They would probably taste like chicken, right? I mean as long as I'm not doing something illegal.

■ 我會怕，可是我覺得我應該會試試看。反正應該都吃起來像雞肉對吧？我的意思是說，反正只要是不違法。

他們文化的一部份

■ It would be part of their culture after all. I think I would want to experience the country in the most authentic way.

■ 這畢竟也是他們文化的一部份。我應該會想要用最道地的方式體驗這個國家。

挑食

■ I think it would be pretty unlikely. I've always been pretty picky about food already. I mean, I don't consider myself a foodie.

■ 我覺得應該是不太可能。我本來就蠻挑食的。我不是說我是美食家。

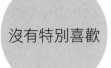

沒有特別喜歡

- But I care about what I eat. As far as I'm concerned, I'm not the biggest fan of monkeys, snakes, dogs, and insects.
- 可是我真的很在乎我吃了什麼。我個人是沒有特別喜歡吃猴子、蛇、狗還是昆蟲啦。

義大利的帕馬火腿和哈密瓜

- I tried the prosciutto with cantaloupe in Italy. I was a bit skeptical at the beginning because it was basically raw ham with melon, but when I tried it, it was the perfect marriage of foods.
- 我在義大利有吃過帕馬火腿（煙薰過很薄的火腿）和哈密瓜。一開始我很懷疑這個生火腿跟香瓜的組合，可是我一吃就發現這個組合真是太完美了。

義大利的帕馬火腿和哈密瓜

- It's savory and sweet, very juicy and simply divine. This appetizer is definitely the embodiment of "Less is more." I tried it in a couple of restaurants here, but it just wasn't quite the same.
- 又鹹又甜，而且非常多汁，反正就是很完美。這個開胃菜真的是實踐「少就是多」。我有在這裡的幾家餐廳點這個，可是就是跟在義大利吃到的那個不太一樣。

西班牙海鮮燉飯 ❶

■ I would definitely go back to Spain for their Paella. It just has everything I love. Seafood, rice, saffron spices, ...etc. I just love it. I even knew I was going to love it when I saw it.

■ 我一定會回去西班牙吃他們的西班牙海鮮燉飯。那燉飯裡面有我所有喜歡吃的東西。海鮮、飯、番紅花香料等等。我超愛的。我一開始光看到那道菜我就知道我會超愛這道菜的。

西班牙海鮮燉飯 ❷

■ The smell was just impossible to resist. And once I tried it, I knew I was hooked. I would definitely go back again and again for that.

■ 那道菜的味道是無法抵擋的。而且我一吃，我就知道我上癮了。我一定會回去很多次去吃這道菜。

澳洲的肉派

■ I love how the Aussies make their meat pies savory. There are so many great restaurants that specialize in making meat pies as well, so imagine the competition.

■ 我很喜歡澳洲人把他們的派做成鹹的！而且那裡也有很多餐廳是專賣肉派的，所以你可以想像那裡的競爭。

MP3 020

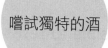

噌試獨特的酒

■ What is vacation without wine? You will be amazed at how many fine wineries there are in the world. And sometimes, you will try to get some of the most unique wines when you are traveling.

■ 度假沒有酒算什麼度假呢？你會很驚訝世界上有多少好的酒莊。而且通常在你旅行的時候，你可以噌試到很多獨特的酒。

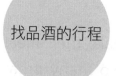

找品酒的行程

■ I always look for wine tasting tours and often end up taking lots of wine back home to add on to my wine collection at home.

■ 我都一直在找品酒的行程，而且通常在品酒之後，我都會買很多酒回家加入我的收藏。

1 道地高分句

2 一問三答

3 話題卡回答

4 即席應答

製酒

■ I used to volunteer at several wineries around the world, and it was definitely one of my most valued memories. I learned a lot and had a lot of fun doing it. There's a lot more to it than how I imagined it.

■ 我之前有在世界各地很多酒莊打工換宿，那個回憶一定是我最珍惜的之一。我學到了很多而且在打工的過程也玩得很開心。製酒比我想像的還要繁複許多。

其他管道取得酒 ❶

■ Naturally, I would love to, but I usually go to websites like Groupon or Living Social to look for good deals. It is usually not much to do with wine tasting.

■ 我當然想，可是我通常也都會上一些網站像是酷朋或是團購網站 LivingSocial 找一些便宜的。通常品酒是不會很貴啦。

其他管道取得酒 ❷

■ However, I found deals that not only include wine tasting, but you also get a free bottle of wine at the end of the wine tasting or you get some discounts. They are pretty decent wines, too!

■ 可是我都找得到很多是包含品酒，然後你品酒之後還可以拿走一瓶免費的酒，或是有些折扣買酒。而且他們也是蠻好的酒喔！

- "Scrumptious!" I went to the Volcano Winery on big Island. They have the most exotic wines I have ever tried, and they were just insanely scrumptious!
- 「超級美味！」我上次去了大島的火山酒莊。他們有我喝過最異國風的酒，而且他們超級美味的！

大島的
火山酒莊

- They have local fruit wines and honey wines that are 100% made from the island's macadamia nuts. It was a truly sensational wine tasting experience. Who would have thought wines can be so tasty!
- 他們有當地的水果酒，也有是百分之百用島上的夏威夷核果做成的蜂蜜酒。那真的是讓我很震撼的品酒經驗。誰知道酒也可以這麼美味！

夏威夷水果酒

- My last wine tasting experience was very "friendly". I was working at a winery at Mendoza in Argentina the last time I went wine tasting.
- 我上次去品酒的經驗是很「友善的」。我上次品酒的時候是我在阿根廷門多薩的一間酒莊工作的時候。

阿根廷門多薩
的一間酒莊

結識朋友

■ I met a bunch of travelers from all over the world. We started to chat, and we actually bought a few bottle of wines and enjoyed them together afterwards. I'm going to visit one of them next week.

■ 我認識了一群從世界各地來的旅行者，我們大家都開始聊天，然後後來我們還買了幾瓶酒一起享用。我下禮拜就要去拜訪他們其中一個。

雪梨的獵人谷

■ The last time I went wine tasting, I was at Hunter Valley in Sydney. I went with an empty stomach because I was running late for the tour.

■ 我上次去品酒的時候我是去雪梨的獵人谷。因為我差點就趕不上這個品酒的行程，所以我是空腹去的。

榭密雍 白葡萄酒

■ It was a very beautiful place and their famous Semillon there was just heavenly. I got tipsy very fast with both the wine and the view. It was overall a very pleasurable experience.

■ 那裡超美的，而且他們有名的榭密雍白葡萄酒真是太美好了。我很快就因為美酒和美景微醺了。整體來說那真是很開心的經驗。

能抒壓、比原價便宜、壓低價格和超出我的預算

MP3 021

喜歡購物

■ I love everything about shopping in a mall. You get your nails done, you take home beautiful clothes, and you can sit down at the food court to eat or get a cup of gourmet coffee.

■ 我喜歡購物的每件事。你可以做指甲，帶漂亮的衣服回家，你還可以在美食街吃東西或喝杯高級的咖啡。

購物能抒壓

■ There is just so much to see and try on. It is a stress-relief process for me really. Don't you just want to get out and shop a little when you are having a bad day? It just makes everything better.

■ 對我來說其實真的是一個抒壓的方式。你在心情不好的時候不會想要去買點東西嗎？購物讓每件事情都變得很美好。

1 道地高分句

2 一問三答

3 話題卡回答

4 即席應答

運動用品店

- No, not even a tiny bit. I guess I just don't find material things attractive. Nevertheless, I do have a thing for sporting goods. I guess I don't like shopping, but I do need to get necessities.

- 一點都不是。物質的東西就真的是一點都不吸引我。不過啦，運動用品店對我來說是我的死穴。我想可能是因為我不喜歡購物，但是我還是得買一些必需品啦。

特價的時候

- Sometimes. I am when there are sales. I don't mind digging out all the goodies even if it means it'll take hours. It's the result that counts.

- 有的時候是，他們特價的時候我就是。我不介意挖好貨甚至是好幾個小時也沒關係。結果最重要。

比原價便宜

- I often find goods that are way under their original prices. It's amazing how much discount you can get sometimes. Who buys with the original prices nowadays?

- 我常找到很多比原價便宜超多的東西。有的時候看到你拿到多少折扣也是蠻驚人的。現在哪有人用原價買東西啊？

在購物中心裡殺價

- I would never bargain. How can you possibly bargain in a mall? It's so not classy. I don't care about one or two more dollars really.
- 我一定不會殺價的。你怎麼可能會在購物中心裡殺價？一點都不優雅。我真的不在意多了一塊還是兩塊，真的。

壓低價格

- it's just awkward begging for a lower price. I don't know how people can do it. A cold sweat just broke out on my forehead thinking about it. No way José.
- 而且要拜託他們壓低價格就是一件蠻尷尬的事。我不懂怎麼有人可以做到。我光想我的額頭就開始冒冷汗了。絕對不可能的啦！

超出我的預算

- I'll say something like "It's a little out of my budget, but I would love to get this from you. Do you think we can work something out here?"
- 我會說：「這個有點超出我的預算，但是我真的很想跟你買。你有什麼好的辦法嗎？」。

■ And it works really well sometimes. Just be sincere I guess. If they like you, they'll give you a good price. But the key is they have to like you.

■ 這樣說有的時候真的很有用。我想就是要很誠懇吧。如果他們喜歡你的話，就會給你一個好價錢。不過重點是他們要喜歡你。

表現出誠懇的一面

■ I'll say something like if it's xxx dollars, then I'll get it. Of course you can't go crazy low. I always shop around and compare the prices first, and then give a reasonable price.

■ 我會說「如果是×××元的話，我就買了！」不過當然你不能殺太低。我通常都是先到處逛逛然後比較價錢，最後再給了一個合理的價格。

逛逛然後比較價錢

■ If you do your homework, you usually get what you want with the price you like even more! Although sometimes I'll say it's my birthday...

■ 如果你有做好功課的話，你通常會買到你喜歡的東西，而且是用你更喜歡的價錢買到的。不過有的時候我會說今天是我的生日…。

更滿意的價格購得

1　道地高分句
2　一問三答
3　話題卡回答
4　即席應答

Unit 22 美食部落客的建議、APP 軟體、餐廳的音樂

 MP3 022

餐點

■ There is no reason to eat poorly when you are on vacation. That's why usually before I go anywhere in the world, I make sure the meals are great.

■ 你在度假的時候實在沒有理由吃很差。這也就是為什麼通常在我決定要去任何地方之前,我會先確認餐點會是很棒的。

餐廳裡的體驗

■ Restaurant experience, of course, is a big part of the whole trip. Besides, asking local tour guides directly, I usually just ask the front desk of my hotels for recommendations. They haven't failed me so far. Knock on wood!

■ 在餐廳裡的體驗算是佔了旅行很大一部分。除了直接問我當地的導遊之外,我也會到飯店的櫃台請他們幫我推薦。他們目前為止都還沒讓我失望過。老天保佑!

跟著感覺走

- I usually just go with the flow and take a chance. You never know whom you are going to meet and what you might get into.
- 我通常就是跟著感覺走耶，然後就冒個險。你永遠不知道你會遇到誰或是會遇到什麼事。

很酷的小地方

- Most of the time, I meet people and they usually have something in mind. Othertimes, I just go to any restaurant that I think it is interesting. I found many cool little places this way.
- 大部分的時候，我遇到的人都會有想要去的地方。其他的時候，我就去我覺得蠻有趣的餐廳看看。我都是這樣找到一些很酷的小地方。

查美食部落客的建議

- You will be surprised by how many users it has around the globe. I read the foodie blogger's suggestions and then I Yelp those places. So far, the experiences have been more than satisfactory.
- 你如果知道全球有多少人在用的話你一定會很驚訝。我會先查美食部落客的建議，然後再用 Yelp 查查看那個地方。目前為止我都很滿意啦。

用一些 APP 軟體

■ I also like to explore APPs, there are a lot of APPs that can tell you where are some good restaurants people like around your location.

■ 我也會用一些 APP 軟體，現在有很多 APP 都可以跟你說離你很近的地方大家喜歡的餐廳在哪裡。

食物的品質

■ I think obviously what makes a restaurant great is its food. The quality of the food should be over the top and it speaks for all. All those five stars restaurants work so hard to make sure the quality of the food is great.

■ 我覺得很顯然的一個好餐廳一定要有一很好的食物啊！食物的品質應該要很好，那剩下的就沒話說了。所有五星級的飯店都為了食物的品質而努力。

創新的菜肴

■ they always have innovative dishes. One of my pet peeves is to go to a good restaurant and not be able to get good food there. It's just sad.

■ 他們也通常都會有很多創新的菜肴。我的死穴之一就是去一個好餐廳但是卻吃不到好的食物。就只會讓我覺得很悲哀。

1
道地高分句

2
一問三答

3
話題卡回答

4
即席應答

很好玩的氣氛

- I think what makes a restaurant great is its fun atmosphere. Eating in a restaurant for me is about the whole dining experience. It's not just the food that I'm going for.
- 我覺得一個好的餐廳一定要有很好玩的氣氛。我在餐廳吃飯比較在意的是吃飯整體的經驗。我不是只有為了食物而去的。

餐廳的音樂

- I'm going to the restaurant for the music, the fun crowd of people, and if the food happens to be great, too, then awesome.
- 我去是為了那個餐廳的音樂，好玩的人們，然後如果剛好食物也很好吃的話，那就太棒了。

員工在意處理的食物

- I think if the restaurant staff care about their food, it makes such a big difference. The service, the food, the place will be great and it's easy to see if the staff care about their own restaurant, too.
- 如果餐廳的員工在意他們的食物的話，那就會很不一樣。他們的服務、食物，還有整個地方都會很棒因為他們的員工在意他們自己的餐廳。

MP3 023

■ The best one I've been to is Le Louvre in Paris. The museum itself is an art piece already, not to mention the famous artworks inside. It took me a while to wait till it was my turn to see Mona Lisa.

■ 我去過最棒的博物館是在巴黎的羅浮宮。博物館本身就是一個藝術品了,更別提在裡面那些有名的藝術品。我那時候等了蠻久才換我看蒙娜麗莎的微笑。

巴黎的羅浮宮 ❶

■ It's beautiful, but I have to say it was smaller than how I had imagined it. However, I think the best way to store beautiful art is to store them in a beautiful building.

■ 它真的很美,可是我必須說它比我想像的還要小。但是我想儲存美麗藝術品最好的辦法就是把它們放在漂亮的建築物裡。

巴黎的羅浮宮 ❷

夏威夷歐胡島
的主教博物館
❶

■ However, Bishop Museum in Oahu, Hawaii is a really fun museum. It demonstrates how lava is formed and there are a lot of activities and performances at certain time of the day, such as Hula Dance performance.

■ 但是在夏威夷歐胡島的主教博物館是一個很好玩的博物館。它展示了岩漿是怎麼形成的，而且那裡不一樣的時間也都有不一樣的表演，例如草裙舞表演。

夏威夷歐胡島
的主教博物館
❷

■ I didn't get bored at that museum and I took a lot of new knowledge with me home. It was a huge museum, but I was thrilled walking around in it.

■ 我在那個博物館裡都不覺得無聊，而且也學了很多。那裡超大的，可是我在裡面十分興奮地走來走去！

義大利烏非茲
博物館 ❶

■ I thought Uffizi Gallery was an excellent in museums. It was overwhelming to see all the famous work gathered together in one museum.

■ 我覺得義大利烏非茲博物館是博物館裡面的翹楚。在一個博物館裡面看到那麼多有名的作品其實蠻震撼的。

- Michelangelo, Da Vinci, Raphael and more. I took my time walking from room to room and tried to absorb the fact that these were works that I read about from history books in class.
- 米開朗基羅、達文西、拉斐爾等等。我在每個展示間裡都慢慢地逛然後盡可能地相信在我眼前都是在歷史課本裡面讀到的那些作品。

- I heard there's a Museum of Bad Art at Somerville Mass. That's just so out of the box! Normally, we see amazing or beautiful art in a museum.
- 我有聽說一間在美國薩莫維爾市的糟糕藝術博物館。那真是太有創意了。通常我們都只會在博物館裡看見很棒或是很美的藝術。

- But in that museum, they look for bad art which has to be original as well. I'm not too sure about the point of the museum yet.
- 但是在他們這間博物館，他們要找的是原創就很糟糕的藝術。我現在還是有點不懂他們的用意。

1 道地高分句

2 一問三答

3 話題卡回答

4 即席應答

日本大阪的泡麵發明博物館

- The strangest museum I've heard is the Momofuku Ando Instant Ramen Museum in Osaka, Japan. The whole museum is decorated with instant noodles, and they also have a section where people can try to make the instant noodles.
- 我聽過最奇怪的是日本大阪的泡麵發明博物館。整間博物館都是由泡麵所佈置而成的，而且他們也有一區是人們可以來試試看怎麼製作泡麵的。

克羅埃西亞的失戀博物館 ❶

- The Museum of Broken Relationships in Croatia is by far the strangest museum I've heard. What do you do with the stuff that belongs to your past relationships?
- 在克羅埃西亞有一間失戀博物館是我目前為止聽過最奇怪的博物館。你失戀之後都怎麼處理那些屬於之前戀情的東西啊？

克羅埃西亞的失戀博物館 ❷

- I put them in a box or throw them away, but this museum is looking for remnants of a broken relationship.
- 我都把它們放到箱子裡或是丟掉，可是這間博物館都在找那些過去戀情遺留下的的東西。

109

🔊 MP3 024

印度阿格拉
的泰姬馬哈陵
❶

■ I really want to see Taj Maha in Agra, India one day! It's the mausoleum of a Persian princess who was the favorite wife of the emperor at the time.

■ 我真的很想要去在印度阿格拉的泰姬馬哈陵！那是一個當時皇帝最喜歡的妻子，一個波斯公主的陵墓。

印度阿格拉
的泰姬馬哈陵
❷

■ After she passed away, the emperor was so sad, he decided to build this for her. She still died like a princess. I really want to be there and learn about their love story after all this time.

■ 在她去世之後，皇帝就十分的傷心，並且決定要為她打造這個陵墓。她就算死也是很公主的。在過了這麼久以後，我也真的很想要去那裡了解他們的愛情故事。我真希望我死的時候也有人幫我蓋一個陵墓。

埃及的基沙大金字塔 ❶

- I really want to visit The Great Pyramids of Giza in Egypt. It's on my ultimate bucket list. I love everything about Pyramids, and there are so many movies with the theme of pyramids.
- 我真的很想要去埃及的基沙大金字塔。那一直都是在我的終極死前要完成的事的清單中。我很喜歡所有關於金字塔的事，而且也有那麼多部電影都是以金字塔為主題。

埃及的基沙大金字塔 ❷

- I still cannot believe such structures were built by men. I just want to be there and witness this wonder and mystery.
- 我還是無法想像這個建築物是人造的。我只想要去那裡目睹這個奇景還有謎。

長城 ❶

- I haven't had a chance to visit the Great Wall yet, but I really want to visit. They built the wall to keep the enemies from coming to their territory.
- 我還沒有機會去過長城，可是我真的很想去。他們當年建造這個牆是為了要避免敵人入侵他們的領土。

長城 ❷

- can you imagine the work they were doing to build the Great Wall? It's 21, 196 km long! And it's from such a long time ago!
- 你可以想像他們那時候要花多少功夫嗎？這個長城有兩萬一千一百九十六公里長耶！而且還是從那麼久以前造的！

高第建造的
聖家堂 ❶

- The most amazing building I have ever seen is the famous Sagrada Familia built by Gaudi. It's one thing to see it from a picture, but it's another when you see it in person.
- 我看過最棒的建築是鼎鼎有名的由高第建造的聖家堂。從照片看是一回事，但是真正看到又是另外一回事。

高第建造的
聖家堂 ❷

- I thought to myself Gaudi must have lost it. The building is beyond creativity. It's not like anything I've seen before.
- 我那時候在想說高第一定瘋了。這個建築物已經超越創意了。我從來沒有看到任何像這樣的建築。

馬丘比丘 ❶

- By far I have to say Machu Picchu is still the most amazing building I've ever seen, especially with the location, too! It's just amazing to be able to live all the way up in the mountain and so secluded, too.
- 我目前為止是覺得馬丘比丘是我看過最棒的建築，尤其是那個地點！真的很棒他們可以住在深山裡，而且還那麼的隱密。

馬丘比丘 ❷

- The irrigation system there is pretty cool, too. I wonder if there are more Machu Picchu deeper in the mountain. I wouldn't mind living there at all.
- 那裡的灌溉系統也很酷。我在想不知道在更深山裡有沒有更多的馬丘比丘。我一點都不介意住在那裡。

印度的蓮花廟 ❶

- I was really impressed with the Lotus Temple in India. The whole building is just extremely peaceful. The shape of the temple is a lotus.
- 我對印度的蓮花廟印象很深刻。整個建築都十分的平和。它的外型就是一個蓮花。

MP3 025

丹麥的哥本哈根 ❶

■ Yes, I was in Copenhagen, Denmark. The city really surprised me with how bike friendly it was. There are bike lanes throughout the city. I never had to share the road with other motor vehicles.

■ 有啊，我去了丹麥的哥本哈根。我真的還蠻驚訝那個城市竟然騎腳踏車那麼方便。整個城市裡都有自行車道。我從頭到尾都不用跟其他的車擠同一個車道。

丹麥的哥本哈根 ❷

■ I felt pretty safe biking around the city. I'm not the strongest in biking, but I have to say it was relatively easy to bike around in Copenhagen. I mean I wasn't whining or pouting at all!

■ 我那時候覺得在那個城市裡騎自行車是還蠻安全的。我騎腳踏車沒有很強，可是我得說在那城市騎車還蠻容易的。我都沒抱怨還是嘟嘴欸。

■ Yes, I've been to Amsterdam in the Netherlands. It was really amazing to see the biking population there. It's very common that everyone rides bikes, and rarely do people own cars.

■ 我有去荷蘭的阿姆斯特丹。在那裡騎腳踏車的人口真的很驚人。在那裡大家騎腳踏車是很正常的事，反而比較少人開車。

荷蘭的阿姆斯特丹 ❶

■ The parking lots for the bikes are jaw dropping. It was immense. I literally stood there and wowed for a minute. There are traffic lights for the bikes, bike lanes, all the basics and beyond.

■ 腳踏車的停車場也很令人掉下巴。超大的。我那時候真的是就站在那裡驚呼了一分鐘。那裡有腳踏車紅綠燈、自行車道，所有基本的還有其他的都有。

荷蘭的阿姆斯特丹 ❷

■ I was in Berlin and my Airbnb host lent me a bike to explore the city. I thought that was very nice of him, so I took the bike out and biked around the city.

■ 我在柏林的時候，我 Airbnb 的主人借了一輛腳踏車給我去探索那個城市。我那時候覺得他人很好，於是我就帶了腳踏車出去蹓躂。

柏林 ❶

115

柏林 ❷

- Berlin struck me as the top student in class, but one that dresses very nicely and is very chic. What was my point...I just lost my train of thought.
- 柏林讓我覺得他好像是一個班上頂尖的學生，但是又很會打扮很時髦。我想說的是什麼…我的思路亂掉了啦。

腳踏車觀光 ❶

- I like it, but it's not my top choice. There are some advantages of touring by bike. It's really easy to park them,and the breeze is nice.
- 我喜歡，可是那不是我最喜歡的選項。用腳踏車觀光有很多好處。很好停車，然後微風也很舒服。

腳踏車觀光 ❷

- However, on the other hand, if it's a hot day, then it'll ruin your trip. I'll just ride to the nearest coffee shop and call it a day.
- 但是，另外一方面來說，如果今天很熱的話，那就會毀了你的旅程。我應該會騎到最近的咖啡店，然後就結束今天的行程。

1 道地高分句

2 一問三答

3 話題卡回答

4 即席應答

腳踏車觀光 ❸

■ I love touring by bike if I'm given the choice. You can go wherever you go without worrying too much about traffic jams. You don't hide yourself on the bike.

■ 如果可以的話我非常喜歡用腳踏車觀光。你可以去任何地方然後也不用太擔心塞車，而且你在腳踏車上面沒辦法躲起來。

腳踏車觀光 ❹

■ Yes, I do actually. It's cheap and you can see a lot when you are on a bike, too! Of course I can't go as far as when I'm in the car, but I think a bike will do.

■ 嗯，我真的很喜歡。因為它是很便宜的方式，而且在腳踏車上你也可以看到很多。我當然是不會像在開車的時候一樣去那麼遠，但是我想腳踏車就夠了啦。

腳踏車觀光 ❺

■ It's just a very organic way to tour around the place, and really slow down to see what is around you.

■ 那是一種很有機的觀光方式，而且同時間也可以慢下來並且看看在你身邊的事物。

選擇住飯店

■ I usually just go with the hotels. Pay a little bit extra to get the peace of mind. I think it's worth it.

■ 我通常都會選擇住飯店。付多一點換來一點心安,我是覺得很值得啦。

選沙發衝浪

■ Couchsurfing for sure. I know how some people would have concerns about the safety of Couchsurfing, but the website has so many safety measures in play. It's really not bad at all.

■ 我一定是選沙發衝浪。我知道有些人會對沙發衝浪有安全的考量,但是其實它網站上有做了許多安全的措施。其實沒那麼糟。

很愛沙發衝浪

- I love Couchsurfing because that's where the magic of traveling happens. You get to mingle with your local host and possibly their friends. It, in a way, is forcing you to make friends, and I like that idea.
- 我很愛沙發衝浪，因為那就是旅行神奇的地方。你可以跟當地的主人或是主人的朋友交流。而且其實沙發衝浪有一點強迫你去交朋友，我真的很喜歡那樣。

喜歡用 Airbnb ❶

- I like to use Airbnb. It's usually a good deal if you play it right. And different from Couchsurfing, you don't always see your host.
- 我喜歡用 Airbnb. 其實你用對戰術的話，它通常都是很便宜的。而且跟沙發衝浪不同的是，你不一定會見到你的住宿主人。

喜歡用 Airbnb ❷

- Most of the time they just give you a separate room or even the whole place to yourself. I like the price and I also want my privacy.
- 大部分時候他們都會給你另外一間房間，或甚至是留整個地方給你。我喜歡它的價錢，也想要我自己的隱私。

邁阿密的四季酒店 ❶

■ I was staying at the Four Seasons Hotel in Miami and found out that a local celebrity and his family were staying next to my room.

■ 我在邁阿密的時候住在四季酒店，然後發現隔壁住的是當地的名人和他的家人。

邁阿密的四季酒店 ❷

■ I didn't really know him since I didn't really watch TV that much, but from what the housekeepers told me, he was really popular, but he was a very difficult customer.

■ 我不認識他因為我沒什麼在看電視，但飯店的管家跟我說，他在當地很受歡迎，但他真是一個大奧客。

歐洲青年旅社 ❶

■ Once I was on a hiking trip in Europe. I didn't have Internet to book my hostel, so I could only go to the hostel after I finished the hike that day.

■ 有一次我去歐洲健行旅行。我身上沒有網路可以訂青年旅社，所以我只好健行完再去青年旅社訂房間。

1 道地高分句

2 一問三答

3 話題卡回答

4 即席應答

歐洲青年旅社 ❷

■ It was after sunset, and the only hostel in the town was all booked out. They only had one private room available, but it would cost me 60 dollars. I didn't have that much budget, so sadly I had to leave.

■ 那時候已經是日落，而且鎮上唯一的一間青年旅社房間也完全被訂完了。他們只剩下一間單人房，但是一間要價六十元美金。我沒有那麼多預算，所以只好難過的要離開。

印度 ❶

■ So there are times when you cannot hide from your host from Airbnb. I went to the meeting place to get my room key from my host in India.

■ 有時候你沒辦法躲過你的 Airbnb 住宿主人。我在印度去了約好見面的地方跟住宿主人拿鑰匙。

印度 ❷

■ However, she insisted that I join her for their family reunion that evening. The next thing I knew, I was sitting in the middle of a big Indian family and taking family photos.

■ 但是，她堅持要我加入她們家晚上的家族聚會。我反應過來的時候，我就坐在一個印度大家族的中間，跟她們拍家族合照。

121

Uber、威尼斯私人導覽、越南坐嘟嘟車和佛羅里達州電動代步車

 MP3 027

選擇司機兼
導遊的服務
❶

■ I usually go with the driver guide service. I really don't feel like handling the stress of looking for directions or getting lost when I'm traveling. I just want to use the time in the most efficient way.

■ 我通常會選擇司機兼導遊的服務。我真的很不想要在旅行的時候還要煩惱找路，或是迷路。我只是想要有效率地利用時間。

選擇司機兼
導遊的服務
❷

■ If someone can drive for me and take me to the spots I'm interested in with local knowledge, it's like I have a friend in that country. In a way, I hire a local friend for my vacation.

■ 如果有人可以幫我開車，還可以帶我到我有興趣的地方去玩，那就好像是我在那個國家有一個當地的朋友一樣。其實就好像是我為了我的假期僱用了一個當地的朋友啦。

搭便車 ❶

■ I usually hitchhike when I'm traveling. You will be amazed at how many kind people there are in the world. Sometimes it only takes me 5 minutes to get a ride, but sometimes it takes a couple of hours.

■ 我在旅行的時候通常喜歡搭便車。你會很驚訝世界上有多少好人。有的時候只會花五分鐘，可是有的時候要等好幾個小時。

搭便車 ❷

■ It was hard for me to hitchhike at the beginning because I couldn't handle the rejection, but it's just silly thinking back.

■ 一開始的時候其實搭便車對我來說很難，因為我不喜歡被拒絕的感覺，但是現在回想過去我真的是很傻。

Uber ❶

■ It really depends on where I go. There are a lot of places that have metro systems. It's cheap and it's quick. Local people use it, too. If I need to go somewhere remote, I'll go with Uber.

■ 真的要看我是去哪裡。其實很多地方都有地鐵。它又便宜又快。當地人也會使用它。如果我要去很遙遠的地方的話，我就會用Uber。

Uber

- It's a new thing though, it's pretty much an app you can request rides from where you are. It's usually cheaper than a taxi, so there you go!
- 不過那個還蠻新的。其實它就是一個 APP 你可以在你所在的地方叫車。而且通常他還比計程車便宜，當然是選他囉！

威尼斯私人導覽 ❶

- I was in Venice and of course I had to try a Gondola ride, but I went with the slightly fancier one. My gondola offered a private tour and it came with the singers and the musicians.
- 我在威尼斯的時候當然要試試看貢多拉，但是我是選了比一般高級一點點的。我的貢多拉有私人導覽，而且船上還有歌手和樂手。

威尼斯私人導覽 ❷

- It was really romantic, but I didn't really have a date, so it was actually a little bit awkward. Well, it was really cool though.
- 真的很浪漫但是我那個時候沒有伴啦，所以其實有點尷尬。不過還是蠻酷的就是了。

■ I was taking the Tuk Tuk in Vietnam and it wasn't really the safest ride I took. I felt like the vehicle was about to break at any time.

■ 我在越南的時候有坐嘟嘟車，它真的不是我坐過算很安全的。我覺得那車好像隨時都會垮掉一樣。

越南坐嘟嘟車
❶

越南坐嘟嘟車
❷

■ Strangely enough, I enjoyed my ride as my driver was weaving through the traffic in the middle of Ho Chi Minh City. It was a pretty unique experience.

■ 很奇怪的是，我的司機在胡志明市中穿梭在車陣之間時，我其實是還蠻喜歡的。那是一個蠻獨特的體驗。

佛羅里達州
電動代步車

■ I was in Florida riding the Segway while I was touring around. I felt like a really lazy person from the future, but it was really awesome.

■ 我在佛羅里達州的時候有用賽格威（電動代步車）到處遊覽。我那時候覺得我真的很像是從未來來的很懶惰的人，但是那真的很棒耶！

1 道地高分句

2 一問三答

3 話題卡回答

4 即席應答

MP3 028

加勒比海旅行
❶

■ Once when I was traveling to the Caribbean, it took me two days to get there and seven days for my bags to arrive! You can only imagine my dismay. I was utterly destroyed inside.

■ 有一次我到加勒比海旅行，花了我兩天的時間才飛到目的地，但是我的行李七天才到！你可以想像我有多沮喪。我內心完全崩潰。

加勒比海旅行
❷

■ I had bought and matched up all my outfits for my Caribbean trip before I left. Also, all my toiletry and skincare products were all in the luggage.

■ 在我出發到加勒比海之前，我已經買好了衣服，也都搭配好每天要穿的了。而且，我的盥洗用品和保養品也都在行李裡。

1 道地高分句

2 一問三答

3 話題卡回答

4 即席應答

庫斯科食物
中毒 ❶

■ I was food poisoned when I was in Cusco. It was bad because I was traveling by myself, and I couldn't do anything besides puking and having diarrhea for the first few days.

■ 我在庫斯科的時候食物中毒。那時候很慘因為我只有一個人在旅行，而且我前幾天除了吐和拉肚子之外完全無法做其他事。

庫斯科食物
中毒 ❷

■ It was scary because I was too weak to go seek help of any sort. I was just sleeping, woke up to puke and then passed out again. Luckily, all the bacteria must have eventually got out of my system.

■ 那時候很可怕因為我虛弱到完全無法去求救。我就只有睡覺，醒來去吐，然後又昏睡過去。好險最後細菌總算完全脫離我的身體。

遇劫 ❶

■ My friends and I rented a car and we parked it with all the other cars by the road and we went hiking. After we were done hiking, our car was broken into.

■ 我朋友跟我租了一台車，我們停在路邊其他車旁，然後我們就去爬山了。我們回來的時候，發現有人打破我們的車子。

■ The windows were broken and our bags were stolen. I hid my wallet in the car and the thieves found it, so I had to cancel all my credit cards, but luckily I didn't have much cash in the wallet.

■ 窗戶都破了，而我們的包包都被偷了。我把我的皮夾藏在車子裡，但是小偷找到了，所以我要掛失一堆信用卡，但是好險我皮夾裡沒有很多現金。

■ Needless to say, losing my bags again would seriously be the worst thing ever. Surprisingly, this kind of thing happens so much.

■ 不用說，當然就是再弄丟我的行李一次會是最糟的。很令人傻眼的是，這很常發生耶。

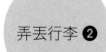

■ I did some research and wrote a complaint letter to the airlines, but apparently almost everyone has a friend that lost their luggage before.

■ 我有查了一下然後就寫了一封抱怨信給航空公司，但是好像幾乎大家都有一個朋友有弄丟過行李。

受了重傷

■ There are a lot of bad things that can happen when you are on the road. I think for me, getting seriously injured would definitely be the worst. There's nothing more important than health.

■ 你在旅行的時候有很多不好的事有可能會發生。我覺得對我來說最糟的就是受了重傷。沒有什麼事比健康更重要了。

遇到不懷好意的男生 ❶

■ For girls, I think the worst thing that could happen is guys with very bad intentions. There's really not much you can do when you are in those kinds of situations.

■ 我覺得對女生來說，最糟的就是遇到不懷好意的男生。在那些情況下你真的也沒有什麼辦法了。

遇到不懷好意的男生 ❷

■ Not to be a sexist, most guys are physically stronger than us. I personally think I'm somewhat attractive, too, so...

■ 我也不是要作性別歧視，不過大部分的男生都比女生還要強壯很多。我個人是覺得我還有點姿色，所以…。

Part 2 規劃了一問三答，除了能夠從三個人物中拓展思路並從中組織出自己的回答外，主題概述中的描述能夠有效強化本身的描述。例如在回答家鄉時，就可以使用主題描述中出現的保護區或漁村等，將這些融入回答，就可以延續描述出家鄉的特色還有什麼，改善無話可答的窘境。

Part

2

一問三答

主題概述

　　家鄉可以涵蓋的部分很廣，從地理位置上的氣候來說又可以分為熱帶（tropical）、亞熱帶（semi-tropical）。台灣最有可能產生天災的季節是颱風季（typhoon season）而颱風所產生的問題有炎熱潮濕（hot and humid）、淹水（flood）、土石流（landslide）。

　　從台灣特有的景觀來切入的話，可以介紹停紅燈時滿坑滿谷的摩托車（scooter）、市區的高樓大廈（high risers）、郊區的果園（orchard）還有田間偶然出現的墳地（cemetery）。由地方特色或美景上來說，也可以介紹斷崖（cliff）、溪流（creek）、濕地（wet land）、水庫（reservoir）、漁村（fishing village）、溫泉（hot spring）、夜市（night market），保護區（conservation area）等等。

1 道地高分句

2 一問三答

3 話題卡回答

4 即席應答

 Q 01 **Can you tell me something about your hometown?**

可以告訴有關你家鄉的一些事嗎? MP3 029

 Josh ▶ During my upbringing, I was lucky enough to be raised in Heng Chuan, a small town at the southern end of Taiwan right by the famous beach area called Kenting. Like every other kid growing up in the area, I spent a lot of time under the sun doing surfing and snorkeling. You don't get that kind of lifestyle elsewhere!

喬許 ▶ 我很幸運的我小時候在恆春長大，恆春是台灣南邊的一個小鎮，就在有名的墾丁海域旁邊。每個恆春長大的小孩從小就花很多時間在戶外衝浪和浮潛，我也不例外。別的地方可找不到這種生活方式呢!

 Instructions

· 不能只是閱讀每個人物如何回答唷！這是口說測驗，所以一定要開口說。

· 現在請跟著 CD 覆誦，同步練習「說」跟「聽」，第一次請跟著 CD 以相同語速覆誦，第二次和第三次可以逐步拉長到 CD 唸完第一句、第二句後再開始覆誦，能神奇地提升你的聽力專注力喔！

Abby ▶ I was born in Kaohsiung, the 2nd largest city located in southern Taiwan. I have always been a city girl, and I love the hustle and bustle, and Kaohsiung city offers exactly that. There are numbers of famous night markets adjacent to charming beaches nearby. Being a tropical city, summer in Kaohsiung gets quite brutal, but winter is normally very mild, nice, and pleasant.

艾比 ▶ 我在南台灣的高雄出生，高雄市台灣的第二大城市。我從小就 是個城市女孩，我喜歡熱鬧的感覺，而高雄就是這樣的地方。高雄有一些有名的夜市，也很靠近迷人的海灘。因為高雄位於熱帶，夏天可是熱得很，但是冬天通常也不太冷，很舒適怡人。

 Instructions

- 不能只是閱讀每個人物如何回答唷！這是口說測驗，所以一定要開口說。
- 現在請跟著 CD 覆誦，同步練習「說」跟「聽」，第一次請跟著 CD 以相同語速覆誦，第二次和第三次可以逐步拉長到 CD 唸完第一句、第二句後再開始覆誦，能神奇地提升你的聽力專注力喔！

Cameron ▶ I was born in Chia-yi before my family moved to Taipei. Chia-yi is a small town south of Taichung. Cha-yi is famous for the turkey on rice and the beautiful sunrise in Ali Mountain, one of the major attractions in Central Taiwan. One thing people don't realize about Chia-Yi is how cold it gets in winter because we get cold breezes from the mountains.

卡麥倫 ▶ 在我家搬來台北之前，我是在嘉義出生的。嘉義是台中南邊的一個地方。嘉義有名的火雞肉飯還有迷人的阿里山日出，那可是中台灣有名的景點。大家通常不知道嘉義的冬天非常的冷，因為有山區的寒風吹下來。

 Instructions

- 不能只是閱讀每個人物如何回答唷！這是口說測驗，所以一定要開口說。
- 現在請跟著 CD 覆誦，同步練習「說」跟「聽」，第一次請跟著 CD 以相同語速覆誦，第二次和第三次可以逐步拉長到 CD 唸完第一句、第二句後再開始覆誦，能神奇地提升你的聽力專注力喔！

Housing 房屋

主題概述

台灣早期的傳統式房屋種類有平房（single story building）、連排透天厝（town house）等，但隨著都市化等因素，其他形式的建築像是電梯大樓住宅（apartment）也開始林立，其中公寓中每單位稱為（unit），有些大樓也推出套房（studio）租售，提供給單身族。

在國外幾乎是獨棟包含含前後院的房子（cottage）和別墅（mansion）等等。有的還附有後院的戶外用餐區（alfresco），甚至於頂樓陽台（balcony）上附有省電裝置如太陽能板（solar power），有些家庭主婦甚至將廚房是否附有烤箱（oven）或屋外是否有雙車庫（double garage）也納入考量，不過最重要的還是準備頭期款（down payment），評估能府負擔房貸（mortgage）、月付金額（repayment），若是再都市工作則需考量若租賃（lease）則需要考量押金（bond）、租金（rent）金額。

What kind of housing do you have?
你家裡是住怎樣的房子？ MP3 030

Josh ▶ We have a three-bedroom apartment in a 15 story building. There is little space in the apartment itself, but we do have a large public area with an outdoor communal pool and an indoor gym. I love going down for a swim on Saturday afternoon because the hot chick from 12 B likes to hang out by the pool.

喬許 ▶ 我們家在一棟 15 樓的大樓裡，是一間三房的單位。屋子裡的空間不是很大，可是公共區域倒是蠻大的，有個公用的室外游泳池還有室內的健身房。我最喜歡星期六下午去游泳因為 12 樓 B 座的美眉都是那個時候去。

 Instructions

- 不能只是閱讀每個人物如何回答唷！這是口說測驗，所以一定要開口說。
- 現在請跟著 CD 覆誦，同步練習「說」跟「聽」，第一次請跟著 CD 以相同語速覆誦，第二次和第三次可以逐步拉長到 CD 唸完第一句、第二句後再開始覆誦，能神奇地提升你的聽力專注力喔！

Abby ▶ Currently, I am renting the top floor out from a lady who owns a 3 story town house right next to Xindian MRT station. It is quite an old building, but the rent is surprisingly cheap compared with central Taipei. The decoration of the house is very dated, and there are a few issues with the plumbing, but as long as it is not haunted, I can live with a few leaking pipes.

艾比 ▶ 目前我跟我的房東太太承租一棟三層樓透天厝的頂樓，就在新店捷運站旁邊。那是一棟很舊的房子，可是租金跟台北市中心比起來真的便宜很多。房子的裝飾很過時，而且家裡也有管線漏水的問題，可是只要沒有鬧鬼，我是不太介意滴水的問題啦。

 Instructions

- 不能只是閱讀每個人物如何回答唷！這是口說測驗，所以一定要開口說。
- 現在請跟著 CD 覆誦，同步練習「說」跟「聽」，第一次請跟著 CD 以相同語速覆誦，第二次和第三次可以逐步拉長到 CD 唸完第一句、第二句後再開始覆誦，能神奇地提升你的聽力專注力喔！

Cameron ▶ Mum and Dad worked really hard to own our flat. It is on the 5th floor, but there is no lift in the building. We are planning to move to somewhere on the ground floor because my mum's got arthritis and her knees are getting worn out. Walking up and down the stairs everyday is killing her.

卡麥倫 ▶ 我爸媽很辛苦地買下我們住的公寓，公寓位在 5 樓可是沒有電梯。我們在想是不是要找個位在一樓的地方搬，因為我媽有關節炎，她的膝蓋快不行了，每天要走樓梯爬上爬下真的要她的命。

 Instructions

· 不能只是閱讀每個人物如何回答唷！這是口說測驗，所以一定要開口說。

· 現在請跟著 CD 覆誦，同步練習「說」跟「聽」，第一次請跟著 CD 以相同語速覆誦，第二次和第三次可以逐步拉長到 CD 唸完第一句、第二句後再開始覆誦，能神奇地提升你的聽力專注力喔！

1 道地高分句

2 一問三答

3 話題卡回答

4 即席應答

Unit 03 Building 建築物

🖍 主題概述

　　建築物的種類可以從地標（landmark）說起，例如:摩天大（skyscraper）、古蹟（historical building）、教堂（church）、佛寺（temple）、巨蛋（superdome）、體育館（stadium）或是特殊的工廠，例如水泥工廠（cementfactory）或是煉油廠（oil refinery）。

　　也可以從代表國家的建築物來發想，例如總統府（presidential hall）、市政府（cityhall）等等。或是換個角度從特殊的外觀設計切入，例如:窗戶的形狀（shape）、頂樓（rooftop）的設施、戶外或高樓觀景台（viewing platform）、走道（hallway）、人造水池（water feature）等等。而選擇節能減碳（reduce carbon footprint）的建材（building material）的種類的設計也是一種趨勢。

Can you recommend an interesting building in your home country to tourists?

能推薦我你國家的一棟建築物給觀光客?

MP3 031

Josh ▶ Sure thing! It would have to be the 85 Sky Tower in Kaohsiung. It is more than just an ordinary skyscraper. It is a shape of a castle to be exact and situated in the Kaohsiung harbour. The outside architectural glass reflect the view of the harbour. It looks amazing during sunset. Nothing can really top that!

喬許 ▶ 當然可以!我會推薦高雄的 85 大樓,它跟一般的摩天大廈不同,它的外觀像一座城堡而且坐落在高雄港邊。外觀的玻璃帷幕反射著海港的景觀,日落的時候看起來真是美呆了! 沒有什麼比那更好了!

Instructions

· 不能只是閱讀每個人物如何回答唷!這是口說測驗,所以一定要開口說。

· 現在請跟著 CD 覆誦,同步練習「說」跟「聽」,第一次請跟著 CD 以相同語速覆誦,第二次和第三次可以逐步拉長到 CD 唸完第一句、第二句後再開始覆誦,能神奇地提升你的聽力專注力喔!

Abby ▶ It might not be everyone's cup of tea, but I will recommend the waste incinerator in Beitou, Taipei. The incinerator is a 150 meter tall chimney with a revolving restaurant on the roof top and a viewing platform. I recommend the visitors have a meal in the restaurant as long as they can get over the idea of having a meal on top of piles of rubbish.

艾比 ▶ 我想推薦的建築可能有些人沒辦法接受，那就是北投的垃圾焚化爐。它的外觀像個 150 公尺高的煙囪，頂樓卻有個旋轉餐廳還有觀景台。如果大家不排斥坐在滿坑滿谷的垃圾上吃的東西的話，那我會建議旋轉餐廳用個餐。

 Instructions

- 不能只是閱讀每個人物如何回答唷！這是口說測驗，所以一定要開口說。
- 現在請跟著 CD 覆誦，同步練習「說」跟「聽」，第一次請跟著 CD 以相同語速覆誦，第二次和第三次可以逐步拉長到 CD 唸完第一句、第二句後再開始覆誦，能神奇地提升你的聽力專注力喔！

Cameron ▶ Yes, the first thing to come to mind is the Lan Yang Museum located in Yi-Lan county. What makes it interesting is, it looks like a tilted building and half of it has sunken into the lake, you think you are seeing the other half that is emerged on the water. The design is so clever, and I have never seen anything else like it.

卡麥倫 ▶ 可以，我第一個想到的建築物是位在宜蘭的蘭陽博物館。它最有趣的地方是建築物本身看起來像一座半倒的建築，而其中一半沉在湖裡。你會覺得你看到的是浮出水面的一半，它的設計真的很特殊，我從來沒有看過這樣子的設計。

 ## Instructions

- 不能只是閱讀每個人物如何回答唷！這是口說測驗，所以一定要開口說。
- 現在請跟著 CD 覆誦，同步練習「說」跟「聽」，第一次請跟著 CD 以相同語速覆誦，第二次和第三次可以逐步拉長到 CD 唸完第一句、第二句後再開始覆誦，能神奇地提升你的聽力專注力喔！

主題概述

　　以種類來區分可以分成主題餐廳（theme restaurant）、庭園餐廳（outdoor café），自助餐廳（buffet restaurant/all-you-can-eat restaurant）、素食餐廳（vegetarian restaurant）、親子餐廳（family restaurant）、無菸餐廳（smoke-free restaurant）、速食餐廳（fast food restaurant）等等。跳開一般餐廳的標準來說，近年來百貨公司美食區（food court）也很受歡迎、或是夜市小吃攤（hawker foodstall）也能獲選米其林星級的榮譽。

　　點餐時在特殊時段會有不同的套餐（combo）、或是可以單點（a lar Carte/ on its own）、前菜（entrée）、主餐（main）之類。有些主詞餐廳會有特殊的座位設計，例如情人座（lover's seat）、固定式的長桌沙發座（booth）、包廂（private room）等等，包廂可能會有低消（minimum charge）的限制。

What is your favourite restaurant?
你最喜歡去哪間餐廳吃飯？ MP3 032

 Josh ▶ I love going to the buffet restaurant in Hyatt hotel. They have the best selection of seafood and good range of carvery. Their oysters are absolutely to die for! I don't go there that often because it is quite pricey, probably only for special occasions like my birthday. I think to indulge yourself once a while is pretty reasonable!

喬許 ▶ 我最喜歡去凱悅飯店吃自助餐了！他們的海鮮種類很多樣，爐烤肉塊的選擇也還不少。他們的生蠔超美味的！我是不太常去吃，因為實在還蠻貴的，大部分都是特殊節日像生日之類的才會去。偶而犒賞一下自己也不過分吧！

 Instructions

· 不能只是閱讀每個人物如何回答唷！這是口說測驗，所以一定要開口說。

· 現在請跟著 CD 覆誦，同步練習「說」跟「聽」，第一次請跟著 CD 以相同語速覆誦，第二次和第三次可以逐步拉長到 CD 唸完第一句、第二句後再開始覆誦，能神奇地提升你的聽力專注力喔！

Abby ▶ Most people might give me a hard time about the choice of food, but my favourite restaurant is actually KFC, I go there at least once a week. I know fast food is not good for you, but their fried chicken is just so irresistible! I do try to health it up by getting salad instead of chips. It makes me feel less guilty for eating junk food!

艾比 ▶ 大部分的人聽到我最喜歡的餐廳都會皺眉頭，可是我真的很喜歡肯德基，我至少一個星期去一次。我知道速食對身體不好，可是他們的炸雞真的很難抗拒！我會把薯條換成沙拉來均衡一下，這樣我也比較沒有吃垃圾食物的罪惡感。

Instructions

· 不能只是閱讀每個人物如何回答唷！這是口說測驗，所以一定要開口說。

· 現在請跟著 CD 覆誦，同步練習「說」跟「聽」，第一次請跟著 CD 以相同語速覆誦，第二次和第三次可以逐步拉長到 CD 唸完第一句、第二句後再開始覆誦，能神奇地提升你的聽力專注力喔！

Cameron ▶ I must tell you about this restaurant called Buddha's hand. Their vegetarian food is top shelf! I go there with my family when we have visitors. My favourite dish is the sweet and sour monkfish. The monk fish is crispy on the outside and soft in the centre. It is amazing! I mean, with food like that, it is actually not so bad being a vegetarian.

卡麥倫 ▶ 我一定要跟你推薦這家叫"佛手"的餐廳,他們的速食真的非常棒!我家如果有客人來的時候,都會去那裏吃飯。我最喜歡的那道菜是糖醋素魚,素魚炸的外酥內軟,真的很美味。其實如果吃的是這樣的菜色,那吃素真的一點也不痛苦。

 Instructions

· 不能只是閱讀每個人物如何回答唷!這是口說測驗,所以一定要開口說。

· 現在請跟著 CD 覆誦,同步練習「說」跟「聽」,第一次請跟著 CD 以相同語速覆誦,第二次和第三次可以逐步拉長到 CD 唸完第一句、第二句後再開始覆誦,能神奇地提升你的聽力專注力喔!

Unit
05　Park 公園

主題概述

　　台灣其實到處都有公園，一般常見的公園有，中央公園（central park）、濕地公園（wetland park）、親子公園（family park）、河岸公園（riverside park）、森林公園（forest park）、紀念公園（memorial park）、國家公園（national park）等等。

　　大部分公園裡都可以看到兒童遊樂設施（Kid's playgroud）、運動設施（exercise equipment）、人造湖（man-made lake）、草地（lawn）、花叢（meadow）。清晨，傍晚或假日也是公園人最多的時候，在公園可以從事的戶外活動有：烤肉（BBQ）、溜冰（rollerblading）、跑步（jogging）、散步（going for a walk）、野餐（picnic）、賞鳥（bird watching）、太極拳（Tai-Chi）、看日出（sun rise）等等。

Can you recommend a park for families with young kids?

你可以推薦一個適合有小孩的家庭去的公園嗎？ MP3 033

Josh ▶ I think Kenting National park is great for kids of all ages. There are natural reserves up in the hilly area for kids who like bushes and hiking. And if they are into watersports, Kenting National park is right next to the beach. Young kids can have a splash by the beach and older ones can go for snorkelling or surfing if they are adventurous.

喬許 ▶ 我覺得墾丁國家公園最適合小孩了，不管是大小孩還是小小孩。喜歡爬山健走的可以到山丘的自然公園去走走。如果喜歡水上活動的直接到墾丁國家公園的旁的海灘，小小孩可以玩玩水，大一點愛刺激的還可以去浮潛或是衝浪。

Instructions

· 不能只是閱讀每個人物如何回答唷！這是口說測驗，所以一定要開口說。現在請跟著 CD 覆誦，同步練習「說」跟「聽」，第一次請跟著 CD 以相同語速覆誦，第二次和第三次可以逐步拉長到 CD 唸完第一句、第二句後再開始覆誦，能神奇地提升你的聽力專注力喔！

149

Abby ▶ It would have to be the Central park in Kaohsiung. The park is totally designed for kids, there is a playground, a water fountain, and a small maze. The best part is the bird life there. There are lots of pigeons and ducks by the pond. I was lucky I didn't get pooed on! I think a family with young kids would really enjoy it.

艾比 ▶ 那一定是高雄的中央公園了！這個公園完全為小孩設計的，有遊樂場，噴水池還有一個小迷宮。最特別的是這裡鳥類很多，池塘附近聚集的很多鴿子還有野鴨，還好沒有鳥在我頭上大便。我覺得有小孩的家庭一定會很喜歡這裡。

 Instructions

- 不能只是閱讀每個人物如何回答唷！這是口說測驗，所以一定要開口說。
- 現在請跟著 CD 覆誦，同步練習「説」跟「聽」，第一次請跟著 CD 以相同語速覆誦，第二次和第三次可以逐步拉長到 CD 唸完第一句、第二句後再開始覆誦，能神奇地提升你的聽力專注力喔！

Cameron ▸ I would recommend Da-An Forest Park in Taipei. Here are slides, swing sets, and a large jungle gym. It is difficult to find a decent park for kids in Taipei because of the value of the land. I am glad at least the kids got a nice park to go to.

卡麥倫 ▸ 我會推薦台北的大安森林公園。有溜滑梯，盪鞦韆還有很大的攀爬設備。在台北因為寸土寸金，所以很難找到適合小孩的公園，還好至少有它們這個地方可以去。

 Instructions

· 不能只是閱讀每個人物如何回答唷！這是口說測驗，所以一定要開口說。

· 現在請跟著 CD 覆誦，同步練習「說」跟「聽」，第一次請跟著 CD 以相同語速覆誦，第二次和第三次可以逐步拉長到 CD 唸完第一句、第二句後再開始覆誦，能神奇地提升你的聽力專注力喔！

1 道地高分句

2 一問三答

3 話題卡回答

4 即席應答

151

Unit 06 Museum 博物館

主題概述

　　博物館總是給人很嚴肅的感覺，但其實博物館有很多不同的類型，例如：美術館（Art museum）、科工館（scienceand technology museum）、歷史博物館（history museum）、史前文化博物館（prehistory museum）、星象館（astronomy museum）、海洋博物館（marine scienceand technology museum）。

　　在博物館裡的展示廳（showroom）常常會舉辦不同主題（theme）的展覽（exhibition）或展示（display）。為了讓民眾對展示的主題有更深入的了解，博物館也常會有互動體驗區（interaction games），也可以預約導覽員（guide）做解說服務。博物館常常是學校的戶外教學（school excursion）的首選。大部分的博物館需要門票（admission）、成人（adult fare）與小孩的價格不同，另外還有博愛票（concession ticket）或團體折扣（group discount）。

When was the last time you visited a museum?
你上次去博物館是什麼時候？ MP3 034

Q 06

1 道地高分句

2 一問三答

3 話題卡回答

4 即席應答

Josh ▸ Only two weeks ago when my cousins came down to Kenting to visit us. We took them to National museum of Marine Biology & Aquarium in Ping Tong. We had a great time learning about different types of corals and fishes from different parts of Taiwan. I think the place is really well set up. It is both fun and educational.

喬許 ▸ 我兩個禮拜前才去過，我表弟他們來墾丁找我們時，我們帶他們到屏東的海洋生物博物館。我們學到很多跟珊瑚有關的知識，還有台灣海域不同的魚種。我覺得海生館設計得很好，讓人覺得很好玩也很有教育性。

 Instructions

· 不能只是閱讀每個人物如何回答唷！這是口說測驗，所以一定要開口說。

· 現在請跟著 CD 覆誦，同步練習「說」跟「聽」，第一次請跟著 CD 以相同語速覆誦，第二次和第三次可以逐步拉長到 CD 唸完第一句、第二句後再開始覆誦，能神奇地提升你的聽力專注力喔！

153

Abby ▶ I think it was a few years ago when I first moved to Taipei. My family and I took a trip to National Palace Museum to check out all the treasures that Chiang Kai Shek allegedly took with him to Taiwan when he lost the war with Chairman Mao.There are some really awesome things there, and my favourite is the piece of jade that looks like a piece of stewed pork.

艾比 ▶ 好像是幾年前我剛搬到台北的時候，我跟我家人到故宮去玩。去看看傳說中國共內戰蔣公撤退台灣時，從大陸運來的寶物。實在有很多稀世珍寶，可是我最喜歡的是一塊看起來像滷肉的玉石。

 Instructions

- 不能只是閱讀每個人物如何回答唷！這是口說測驗，所以一定要開口說。
- 現在請跟著 CD 覆誦，同步練習「說」跟「聽」，第一次請跟著 CD 以相同語速覆誦，第二次和第三次可以逐步拉長到 CD 唸完第一句、第二句後再開始覆誦，能神奇地提升你的聽力專注力喔！

Cameron ▶ I think the last time would be when I was on a school excursion to the National museum of Nature Science in Taichung. The memory is a bit vague, but I still remember the big dinosaur skeleton in the main entrance, I thought that was so cool when I was a kid!

卡麥倫 ▶ 我想最後一次去應該是國中時到台中科博館戶外教學的時候。我的記憶已經很模糊了，我只記得入口的地方有一個很大的恐龍骨架，我小時候覺得那很酷。

 Instructions

・ 不能只是閱讀每個人物如何回答唷！這是口說測驗，所以一定要開口說。

・ 現在請跟著 CD 覆誦，同步練習「說」跟「聽」，第一次請跟著 CD 以相同語速覆誦，第二次和第三次可以逐步拉長到 CD 唸完第一句、第二句後再開始覆誦，能神奇地提升你的聽力專注力喔！

1 道地高分句

2 一問三答

3 話題卡回答

4 即席應答

主題概述

國內外一般常見的飯店有商務旅館（business hotel）、渡假飯店（holiday resort）、膠囊旅館（capsule hotel）、青年旅館（youth hostel）、汽車旅館（Motel）。飯店裡的基本的房型可以分成單人房（single room）、雙人房（doubleroom）、家庭房（family room）、小木屋（villa）。而客人可以依情況要求兩小床（twin-share）。與房客比較有接觸的飯店的員工大概有櫃台人員（receptionist）、門房（porter /concierge）、房間清潔人員（housekeeper），大部分的飯店員工都可以接受小費（tips）。

很多房客是從硬體設備優劣來做為選擇飯店的標準，設備方面來說有登記櫃台（check in/check out counter）、大廳（lobby）、溫水泳池（heated pool）、健身房（gym）、蒸氣室（sauna room）等等。

How do you choose a hotel when you are on holiday?
你去度假的時候會選擇住怎樣的旅館?

MP3 035

Josh ▶ I always go for Youth hostel or back packer's hostel if I am on holiday. Normally, they are not far from the hustle and bustle. I am looking for people to party with and the guests there are normally looking for a good time, too! I am not picky about the facility, as long as it is clean and functional.

喬許 ▶ 我度假的時候不是選擇青年旅館就是背包客棧,通常那些旅館都離熱鬧的地方不遠。我也是想要找志同道合的人一起去跑趴玩樂,大部分的住客也都是這種心態。硬體設備如何我是不太介意,只要乾淨能用就好。

Instructions

· 不能只是閱讀每個人物如何回答唷!這是口說測驗,所以一定要開口說。

· 現在請跟著 CD 覆誦,同步練習「說」跟「聽」,第一次請跟著 CD 以相同語速覆誦,第二次和第三次可以逐步拉長到 CD 唸完第一句、第二句後再開始覆誦,能神奇地提升你的聽力專注力喔!

157

Abby ▶ I normally travel on a shoe string budget, so the cheaper the better is what I say. But I don't like to share a room with strangers, so I would look for a small hotel with maybe two or three stars. If you look hard enough, there are some really good bargains online if you book early.

艾比 ▶ 我通常預算都很低,所以越便宜越好。可是我又不喜歡跟陌生人同住一室,所以我大概都找一些小的二星或三星飯店。如果你努力一點找,通常網路上都有一些很便宜的早鳥專案。

 Instructions

- 不能只是閱讀每個人物如何回答唷!這是口說測驗,所以一定要開口說。
- 現在請跟著 CD 覆誦,同步練習「說」跟「聽」,第一次請跟著 CD 以相同語速覆誦,第二次和第三次可以逐步拉長到 CD 唸完第一句、第二句後再開始覆誦,能神奇地提升你的聽力專注力喔!

Cameron ▶ I like to spoil myself a bit when I am on holiday. I worked hard to save the money for the trip, and I just want to reward myself. I like a fancy place preferably with an outdoor pool and breakfast. There is nothing better than waking up to a breakfast buffet.

卡麥倫 ▶ 我度假的時候喜歡享受，畢竟錢是我辛苦工作賺來的，回饋一下自己有什麼不對。如果價格可以接受的話我喜歡高級一點的地方，最好要有室外游泳池還要含早餐。誰不喜歡早上起床就有豐盛的自助早餐吃。

 Instructions

· 不能只是閱讀每個人物如何回答唷！這是口說測驗，所以一定要開口說。

· 現在請跟著 CD 覆誦，同步練習「說」跟「聽」，第一次請跟著 CD 以相同語速覆誦，第二次和第三次可以逐步拉長到 CD 唸完第一句、第二句後再開始覆誦，能神奇地提升你的聽力專注力喔！

Unit 08 Sport Center 活動中心

主題概述

活動中心可以是廣義的公共活動中心（community center）租借給私人教授課程（private lessons）例如劍道（kendo）、跆拳道（taekwondo）、空手道（karate）、柔道（judo），有氧舞蹈（aerobic）。另外可以提供運動休息的場所也可以算是活動中心， 例如籃球場（basketball court）、羽球場（badminton court）、棒球場（baseball stadium），網球場（tennis court）、足球場（footballfield）、高爾夫球場（golf driving range）、游泳俱樂部（swimming club）、健身中心（fitness center）、舞蹈教室（dance studio）、瑜珈教室（yoga studio）等等。

有的活動中心是採會員制（membership only）、入會的合約上都有明細和規定（terms and conditions），中途若是不想上了很可能也無法全額退費（non-refundable）。

Do you exercise in a sport center?
你會去活動中心運動嗎？ MP3 036

Josh ▶ No, not really, because the sport center does not really offer things that I like to do. I am more an outdoor person than an indoor person. I like open water swimming and diving which are not something you can do indoors. Nothing beats the smell of the ocean and the wind blowing on my face

喬許 ▶ 沒有，並不會，因為活動中心並沒有我喜歡的運動項目，而且我喜歡自己去。我是一個很愛戶外運動的人，我喜歡到海裡游泳還有潛水，這些都不能在室內進行。我最享受大海的味道還有暖風吹在臉上的感覺了！

Instructions

· 不能只是閱讀每個人物如何回答唷！這是口說測驗，所以一定要開口說。

· 現在請跟著 CD 覆誦，同步練習「說」跟「聽」，第一次請跟著 CD 以相同語速覆誦，第二次和第三次可以逐步拉長到 CD 唸完第一句、第二句後再開始覆誦，能神奇地提升你的聽力專注力喔！

Abby ▶ I actually do, I take hip hop dance classes in China Youth Corps Center every Thursday night. The fees are affordable and facility is quite good, too. The most important thing is, the instructor is really hot, he's got a really nice six pack. I love it when he gives me the one-on-one attention and personally shows me the moves!

艾比 ▶ 其實有，我每個星期四晚上都在救國團的活動中心上嘻哈舞課。學費便宜而且設備也還不錯，最棒的是教練很帥，他的腹肌好性感。我超愛他單獨過來一對一指導教我怎麼跳！

 Instructions

- 不能只是閱讀每個人物如何回答唷！這是口說測驗，所以一定要開口說。
- 現在請跟著 CD 覆誦，同步練習「說」跟「聽」，第一次請跟著 CD 以相同語速覆誦，第二次和第三次可以逐步拉長到 CD 唸完第一句、第二句後再開始覆誦，能神奇地提升你的聽力專注力喔！

Cameron ▶ Yes, I do. Once every couple of months I will go to the baseball batting cage to practice batting. It is good fun but I can't afford to go every week, it just gets too expensive. Most of the weekend I just practice with my friends in the local school field.

卡麥倫 ▶ 有，我會去。每隔幾個月我就會去棒球打擊練習場練習擊球。是很好玩可是我沒辦法每個星期都去，實在負擔不起。大部分的周末我都是跟朋友在附近的學校操場練習。

 Instructions

· 不能只是閱讀每個人物如何回答唷！這是口說測驗，所以一定要開口説。

· 現在請跟著 CD 覆誦，同步練習「説」跟「聽」，第一次請跟著 CD 以相同語速覆誦，第二次和第三次可以逐步拉長到 CD 唸完第一句、第二句後再開始覆誦，能神奇地提升你的聽力專注力喔！

主題概述

　　戶外地點可以是觀光景點，例如民俗村（culture village）、主題樂園、鳥園（bird park）、植物園（botanic park）之類或是國家公園（national park）、沙丘（sand dune），或是住家附近的空地或廣場（square），中正紀念堂（Chiang Kai Shek Memorial Hall）、文化中心（culture centre）、動物農場（animal farm）。

　　提了地點之後也要說明為什麼喜歡特定地點的原因，可能對你來說有紀念性（significant），有特殊的風景（scenery），例如吊橋（hanging bridge）、瀑布（waterfall）之類，或是可以從事你喜歡的活動例如可以滑沙（sand boarding）、露營（camping）、採水果（fruit picking）、攀岩（rock climbing）、看夜景（check out the nightscape）、約會或家庭聚會（family gathering）。其實露天夜市也是一個選項，可以享受美食或是喜歡人聲鼎沸（hustle and bustle）的感覺。

Where is your favourite outdoor place?
你最喜歡的戶外地點是哪裡？ MP3 037

Josh ▶ There are lots of beaches in Kenting, but my favourite spot is the beach called Bai-sha which means white sandy beach in Chinese. It is a secluded area hidden among the palm trees. If you have watched the movie " Life of Pi" you would have seen the beach already, it is where Pi was washed up from the ocean.

喬許 ▶ 墾丁有很多海灘，可是我有個最愛的景點叫白砂，白砂中文的意思就是白色的沙灘。那是一個隱密的地方，被層層的椰子樹圍住。你如果看過電影「少年 Pi 的奇幻漂流」那你就知道那個地方長什麼樣子了，就是 Pi 被沖上岸的那個的地點。

 Instructions

- 不能只是閱讀每個人物如何回答唷！這是口說測驗，所以一定要開口説。
- 現在請跟著 CD 覆誦，同步練習「説」跟「聽」，第一次請跟著 CD 以相同語速覆誦，第二次和第三次可以逐步拉長到 CD 唸完第一句、第二句後再開始覆誦，能神奇地提升你的聽力專注力喔！

Abby ▶ My favourite outdoor place would have to be the rooftop of my building. It is like my secret hideout as well. I love to go up there just to chill out and do a bit of gardening to tidy up my pot plants. It calms me right down.

艾比 ▶ 我最喜歡的戶外景點就是我家的頂樓了！那也是我的私房景點，獨處的地方。如果我很想放鬆的時候我就會上頂樓澆澆花，整理一下盆栽。這使我冷靜下來。

 Instructions

- 不能只是閱讀每個人物如何回答唷！這是口說測驗，所以一定要開口說。
- 現在請跟著 CD 覆誦，同步練習「說」跟「聽」，第一次請跟著 CD 以相同語速覆誦，第二次和第三次可以逐步拉長到 CD 唸完第一句、第二句後再開始覆誦，能神奇地提升你的聽力專注力喔！

Cameron ▶ I love the hot springs in Bei-Tou, and my favourite outdoor hot spring is in this boutique hotel. Their hot spring area literately hangs off the mountain side, and you feel like you are surrounded by mountains when you are in it. I love taking my girlfriend there, it is perfect for couples, the view is unbelievable!

卡麥倫 ▶ 我喜歡北投的溫泉，而且我發現了一個泡溫泉最棒的地點，就是這間精品飯店。它的溫泉區就是真的是懸掛在山邊，在那裡你真的可以感受到群山環繞的感覺。我最喜歡帶我女朋友去那裡，很適合情人去，景色實在太美了！

 Instructions

· 不能只是閱讀每個人物如何回答唷！這是口說測驗，所以一定要開口說。

· 現在請跟著 CD 覆誦，同步練習「說」跟「聽」，第一次請跟著 CD 以相同語速覆誦，第二次和第三次可以逐步拉長到 CD 唸完第一句、第二句後再開始覆誦，能神奇地提升你的聽力專注力喔！

主題概述

　　鄰居通常充滿各式各樣不同性格的人，有的鄰居媽媽很外向（outgoing）、愛講話（chatty）、熱心（enthusiastic）、愛嘮叨（nagging），又很八卦。有些則很冷漠（keep things to themselves），文靜（quiet）、低調（lowkey），自私（selfish），古怪（weird），有潔癖的人（clean freak）就比較沒什麼來往。

　　也有那種很假（pretentious）又愛炫耀（showoff）家裡的財富或是兒女的成就，總是在比較的鄰居。以家庭背景來說，有的可能是問題家庭（dysfunctional family），或是獨居有外傭（maid）照顧的老人、做生意的老闆（bnusiness owner）、小吃攤商（hawker stall vendor）、上班族（office worker）等等，可以針對他們的職業或特性來做形容。

Do you like your neighbors?
你喜歡你的鄰居嗎? MP3 038

1 道地高分句

2 一問三答

3 話題卡回答

4 即席應答

Josh ▶ My neighbors are nice people, but sometimes I really want to avoid them. Most of them are old ladies around my mother's age, they love gossiping and are always trying to play matchmaker. They all tried to set me up with girls when I was single, I am sure if they found out I've got a steady girlfriend, they would hassle me to get married every time they see me.

喬許 ▶ 我的鄰居人都不錯可是有時候我真的想躲她們。她們大部分都是看著我長大的，跟我媽年紀差不多的太太們。她們真的很八卦而且很愛幫人做媒。我單身的時候每個人都想幫我介紹，我如果跟她們說我有女朋友了，她們一定一天到晚催我結婚。

 Instructions

- 不能只是閱讀每個人物如何回答唷！這是口說測驗，所以一定要開口說。
- 現在請跟著 CD 覆誦，同步練習「説」跟「聽」，第一次請跟著 CD 以相同語速覆誦，第二次和第三次可以逐步拉長到 CD 唸完第一句、第二句後再開始覆誦，能神奇地提升你的聽力專注力喔！

Abby ▶ I don't have much to do with my neighbors because I am always at work, and I have been moving around a bit since I moved to Taipei. I know they have a couple of young kids and they do get a bit noisy now and again, but there is no drama. I stay up late anyway, so they wouldn't keep me awake.

艾比 ▶ 我跟我鄰居不太熟，因為我大部分時間都在加班，而且我搬到台北之後也常搬家。我知道他們有兩個小孩，有時候會有點吵鬧，可是沒有什麼大問題。反正我也都很晚睡，不會吵到我。

 Instructions

· 不能只是閱讀每個人物如何回答唷！這是口說測驗，所以一定要開口說。

· 現在請跟著 CD 覆誦，同步練習「說」跟「聽」，第一次請跟著 CD 以相同語速覆誦，第二次和第三次可以逐步拉長到 CD 唸完第一句、第二句後再開始覆誦，能神奇地提升你的聽力專注力喔！

Cameron ▶ Yeah, I get along well with my neighbors. Mrs. Huang next door is my favourite because she is forever bringing us stuff. She makes the best rice dumplings. I always look forward to tasting her dumplings for dragon boat festival.

卡麥倫 ▶ 是的，我跟我鄰居們很好。尤其是隔壁的黃媽媽，我最喜歡她了。因為她常常會帶東西給我們，她包的粽子真的超好吃的！我端午節最期待的就是吃她的粽子了。

 Instructions

· 不能只是閱讀每個人物如何回答唷！這是口說測驗，所以一定要開口說。

· 現在請跟著 CD 覆誦，同步練習「說」跟「聽」，第一次請跟著 CD 以相同語速覆誦，第二次和第三次可以逐步拉長到 CD 唸完第一句、第二句後再開始覆誦，能神奇地提升你的聽力專注力喔！

✏️ **主題概述**

　　老師給人的印象很多元（diverse），可能很無趣（dull）、古板（conservative）、嚴肅（serious）、看起來很兇（mean-looking）、高高在上（superior）的或是很有熱忱（passionate）、很有活力（active）、可以讓人親近的（approachable），對學生很關愛（caring）、幽默（funny）、很聰明（witty）、很無私的（selfless）、有影響力的（influential）、有說服力的（convincing）。

　　可以從與老師的對話或是他課堂上的小故事，甚至是學校對老師的表揚獲認證（recognition）都可以讓人受到感動及啟發。

Have you ever been inspired by a teacher?

曾經有老師讓你覺得受到他的感動及啟發嗎?

MP3 039

Josh ▶ I was once told by my English teacher that I would never make it through high school because I never handed in any homework. I used to hate her, but when I got older, I am actually quite thankful for what she said because I worked twice as hard just to prove her wrong, and look at me now!

喬許 ▶ 我以前的一個英文老師跟我說我高中應該畢不了業,因為我從來不交功課。我曾經很討厭她,可是等我長大一點之後,我其實還蠻感謝她的,因為我為了證明她是錯的,我真的加倍努力,才有現在的成就。

Instructions

· 不能只是閱讀每個人物如何回答唷!這是口說測驗,所以一定要開口說。

· 現在請跟著 CD 覆誦,同步練習「說」跟「聽」,第一次請跟著 CD 以相同語速覆誦,第二次和第三次可以逐步拉長到 CD 唸完第一句、第二句後再開始覆誦,能神奇地提升你的聽力專注力喔!

Abby ▶ Most of the teachers I had just seem to take teaching as a job. I don't think they would go the extra miles to encourage students to achieve their potential, at least not to me. It is a bit unfortunate, I couldn't think of anyone that inspired me.

艾比 ▶ 我遇到的老師大部分都沒什麼熱忱，教書對他們來說好像只是一份薪水而已。我覺得他們不太會特別用心去鼓勵學生，激發他們的潛力，我遇到的都是這樣。也算我運氣不好啦！這樣來説的話，沒有唉，我沒有遇到這樣的老師。

 Instructions

· 不能只是閱讀每個人物如何回答唷！這是口説測驗，所以一定要開口説。

· 現在請跟著 CD 覆誦，同步練習「説」跟「聽」，第一次請跟著 CD 以相同語速覆誦，第二次和第三次可以逐步拉長到 CD 唸完第一句、第二句後再開始覆誦，能神奇地提升你的聽力專注力喔！

Cameron ▶ Yes, there are a few actually. I consider myself pretty lucky that I was surrounded by teachers with passion and kind words throughout my school life. I always remember when my math teacher pulled me aside and told me I should pursue my studies overseas, that is what I am always working towards.

卡麥倫 ▶ 有，其實有好幾個。我覺得我的求學生涯還蠻幸運的，我身邊的老師們都很有熱忱而且都很會講鼓勵人的話。我一直都記得，我的數學老師曾經把我拉到一邊私底下跟我說，我應該出國留學，這也是我一直追求的目標。

 Instructions

- 不能只是閱讀每個人物如何回答唷！這是口說測驗，所以一定要開口說。
- 現在請跟著 CD 覆誦，同步練習「說」跟「聽」，第一次請跟著 CD 以相同語速覆誦，第二次和第三次可以逐步拉長到 CD 唸完第一句、第二句後再開始覆誦，能神奇地提升你的聽力專注力喔！

主題概述

　　理想情人就離不開外在（appearance）和內在條件（inner beauty）了，比如說外表要高大、迷人的（charming）、斯文的（clean shaven）、粗曠的（rugged）、運動型（athletic）、很壯的（masculine）、瘦瘦的（slim）。內在條件例如: 性格（personality）、體貼（thoughtful）、溫柔（tender）、文靜的（quiet）。

　　還有一些需要相處才會發現的個人習慣，例如意見很多的（opinionated）主導/強勢的（dominating）、很有控制慾的（controlling）、聽話的（obedient）。以前的人挑老公會喜歡以家庭為重的（family oriented）、孝順的，可是如果過度的話就變成媽寶（mommy's boy）。還有 家世背景（family background）、學歷背景（education background）都會列入考慮的範圍內。

What do you look for in an ideal partner?
你心中的理想情人應該是怎麼樣的？ MP3 040

Josh ▶ I think my ideal partner would have to love outdoor sports as much as I do because I want to be able to share my passion with her. A hot beach babe would be the type of girl I normally go for, but my mother might not agree with me on that one.

喬許 ▶ 我的理想情人應該要跟我一樣熱愛戶外活動，因為我想要有一個可以分享相同興趣的伴侶。海灘辣妹是我最喜歡的型，可是我媽就不覺得她們適合我。

 Instructions

・ 不能只是閱讀每個人物如何回答唷！這是口說測驗，所以一定要開口說。

・ 現在請跟著 CD 覆誦，同步練習「說」跟「聽」，第一次請跟著 CD 以相同語速覆誦，第二次和第三次可以逐步拉長到 CD 唸完第一句、第二句後再開始覆誦，能神奇地提升你的聽力專注力喔！

1 道地高分句

2 一問三答

3 話題卡回答

4 即席應答

177

Abby ▶ I would love to meet a guy who is nice and sweet, tall and handsome with charming eyes. I don't mind his background as long as we can talk to each other and being on the same page about what we want in life. I think Orlando Bloom from Lord of the Rings would be a perfect one! I just can't resist a clean-shaven guy.

艾比 ▶ 我希望有一天我可以遇到一個溫柔體貼的男孩，最好是高大帥氣還有一雙迷人的眼睛。我不太介意他的背景如何，只要可以溝通，心靈相通，對未來的想法一樣就好。我覺得如果像魔戒中的奧蘭多布魯那就太棒了！我最喜歡斯文型的男生。

 Instructions

· 不能只是閱讀每個人物如何回答唷！這是口說測驗，所以一定要開口說。

· 現在請跟著 CD 覆誦，同步練習「說」跟「聽」，第一次請跟著 CD 以相同語速覆誦，第二次和第三次可以逐步拉長到 CD 唸完第一句、第二句後再開始覆誦，能神奇地提升你的聽力專注力喔！

Cameron ▶ I thought I would prefer a quiet person like me, but I found I am always attracted to girls who are outgoing and bubbly, I guess it is just to make up for my shortcoming. Maybe someone from a similar educational background, so we will have something in common to talk about.

卡麥倫 ▶ 我以為我自己會喜歡跟我類似的人，可是我發現我卻覺得外向活潑的女生很吸引人，應該是跟我互補吧。如果跟我有類似的教育背景的話我們就會更有話說。

 Instructions

· 不能只是閱讀每個人物如何回答唷！這是口說測驗，所以一定要開口說。

· 現在請跟著 CD 覆誦，同步練習「說」跟「聽」，第一次請跟著 CD 以相同語速覆誦，第二次和第三次可以逐步拉長到 CD 唸完第一句、第二句後再開始覆誦，能神奇地提升你的聽力專注力喔！

主題概述

　　形容朋友可以從外表，與他有關的特殊事件或他的性格和行為下手。外表，如:髮型（hairdo）、身高（height）、體型（body shape），或是臉上或身上的特徵（unique feature），例如痣（mole）、雙眼皮（double eyelid）、鼻環（nose piercing）、刺青（tattoo）。

　　也可以從你們的友誼來說起，例如願意支持你的（supportive）、心靈相通（seeeye to eye）、分不開的（inseparable）、不計較（forgiving）、興趣相同（share common interests）、一起玩（hang out）、很合得來（get along）。

Please describe a closefriend.
請形容你的一個好朋友 MP3 041

Josh ▶ It would have to be my buddy Dylan. I grew up with Dylan because he is my next door neighbor, he is like the brother I never had. We both love outdoor sports. I talk to him about everything, and he knows all my secrets!

喬許 ▶ 我想說我的麻吉狄倫，我跟狄倫從小一起長大，他是我的隔壁鄰居，我一直把他當親兄弟看。我們兩個都喜歡戶外活動，也都一直念同一所學校。我跟他無話不談，我的秘密他都知道。

 Instructions

- 不能只是閱讀每個人物如何回答唷！這是口說測驗，所以一定要開口說。

- 現在請跟著 CD 覆誦，同步練習「說」跟「聽」，第一次請跟著 CD 以相同語速覆誦，第二次和第三次可以逐步拉長到 CD 唸完第一句、第二句後再開始覆誦，能神奇地提升你的聽力專注力喔！

Abby ▶ Tina is a friend of mine, I met her at the Hip hop class. She also really enjoys dancing. We hang out a lot at the weekend because she also doesn't have a boyfriend. I did not realize she actually knows my brother until I added her as a friend on Facebook. What a small world.

艾比 ▶ 我有一個朋友叫婷娜，我在嘻哈舞課認識她的，她也很喜歡跳舞。我們週末常常一起出去，因為她也沒有男朋友。我加她臉書好友的時候才發現原來她認識我哥。這世界真小。

 Instructions

- 不能只是閱讀每個人物如何回答唷！這是口說測驗，所以一定要開口說。

- 現在請跟著 CD 覆誦，同步練習「說」跟「聽」，第一次請跟著 CD 以相同語速覆誦，第二次和第三次可以逐步拉長到 CD 唸完第一句、第二句後再開始覆誦，能神奇地提升你的聽力專注力喔！

Cameron ▶ My best friend from high school is called Ah-Hsiung. We love to play basketball together. He is tall and skinny like a stick, but his build is perfect for basketball. All the juniors go crazy for him when he is playing. He was so popular when we were in high school, and he still is now with the ladies.

卡麥倫 ▶ 我高中的好朋友叫阿雄，我們很愛一起打籃球。他又高又瘦像根竹竿一樣，可是這種身型很適合打籃球。只要他一上場全部的學妹都會為他加油，他高中時代很受歡迎，他現在還是很受女生的青睞。

 Instructions

・ 不能只是閱讀每個人物如何回答唷！這是口說測驗，所以一定要開口說。

・ 現在請跟著 CD 覆誦，同步練習「說」跟「聽」，第一次請跟著 CD 以相同語速覆誦，第二次和第三次可以逐步拉長到 CD 唸完第一句、第二句後再開始覆誦，能神奇地提升你的聽力專注力喔！

主題概述

　　除了鄰居的小孩，常接觸的小孩應該就是表弟表妹（cousins）或是姪子（nephew）姪女（niece）了。大部分的小孩天生就是天真無邪（innocent）、活潑好動（full ofbeans）、調皮（naughty）、有想像力的（good imagination）、有創造力的（creative）。但也不是每個小孩都沒有煩惱，小孩可能面臨過動（hyperactive）、過胖（overweight）、或是不停地上補習班（cram school）的問題。

　　在台灣小孩如果不是祖父母幫忙帶，就是送幼稚園（kindergarten），在幼稚園裡常做的活動除了唱歌跳舞之外，還有拼圖（puzzle）、勞作（Arts and crafts）、做早操（morning exercises）等等。

Do you like children?
你喜歡小孩嗎? 🎧 MP3 042

Josh ▶ I love kids, especially my five-year-old nephew – Jordon. Jordon is great. He loves surfing as much as I do. He is very talented. I always take him to the beach on Sundays and teach him how to surf. I can't wait for him to grow up and be my surf buddy!

喬許 ▶ 我超愛小孩的,尤其是我五歲的外甥喬丹。喬丹很棒,他跟我一樣愛衝浪,他也很有天分,我每個星期天都帶他到海邊教他衝浪。我好期待他趕快長大,可以當我的衝浪夥伴!

 Instructions

· 不能只是閱讀每個人物如何回答唷!這是口說測驗,所以一定要開口說。

· 現在請跟著 CD 覆誦,同步練習「說」跟「聽」,第一次請跟著 CD 以相同語速覆誦,第二次和第三次可以逐步拉長到 CD 唸完第一句、第二句後再開始覆誦,能神奇地提升你的聽力專注力喔!

Abby ▶ Yes, I do. I am very close to my nieces; I volunteer to pick them up from school everyday because my sister can't get off work in time. I really enjoy spending time with them. They get excited about the simplest thing. It is such a pleasure to see the smiles on their faces.

艾比 ▶ 嗯,我喜歡。我跟我的姪女們很好,因為我姊來不及下班去接他們,我都自願去接。我很喜歡跟他們在一起,他們可以因為很沒什麼的事情就很高興,我很喜歡看他們的笑臉!

 ## Instructions

· 不能只是閱讀每個人物如何回答唷!這是口說測驗,所以一定要開口說。

· 現在請跟著 CD 覆誦,同步練習「說」跟「聽」,第一次請跟著 CD 以相同語速覆誦,第二次和第三次可以逐步拉長到 CD 唸完第一句、第二句後再開始覆誦,能神奇地提升你的聽力專注力喔!

Cameron ▶ Honestly, I am a bit scared of kids actually because I don't know what to say to them, and every time I try to play with them, they just end up in tears. I tried very hard to be a popular uncle but no matter what I do, it just wouldn't work.

卡麥倫 ▶ 說真的，我其實有一點怕小孩，因為我不知道要跟他們說什麼。每次我過去跟他們玩，都會把他們弄哭。我也很想當個受歡迎的叔叔，可是就沒辦法。

 Instructions

· 不能只是閱讀每個人物如何回答唷！這是口說測驗，所以一定要開口說。

· 現在請跟著 CD 覆誦，同步練習「說」跟「聽」，第一次請跟著 CD 以相同語速覆誦，第二次和第三次可以逐步拉長到 CD 唸完第一句、第二句後再開始覆誦，能神奇地提升你的聽力專注力喔！

主題概述

　　動物可以分不同的種類（species）或品種（breed）。在台灣不容易見到大型的野生動物（wild animal），卻有不少瀕臨絕種的動物（endangered animal）。一般人接觸最多的動物除了流浪動物之外，大概就就是家庭裡的寵物（pets）了。

　　一般台灣人的家都沒有前後院，養寵物常常是缺點（disadvantage）大於優點（advantage），因為沒有足夠的空間，動物養在客廳或浴室是常有的事。 要是寵物的性格溫馴（tame）、膽小（timid） 那倒是無所謂，如果遇到兇猛（ferocious）、不受控制的（feral）的動物，就很可能被棄養（being abandoned） 。一直以來與動物相關的活動就很受歡迎，例如看野生動物旅行（safari）、餵食秀（feedingshow）。流浪動物領養（adoption）的概念也越來越普遍，所領養的動物都需要晶片植入（chip implantation）。

What is your favorite animal?
你喜歡什麼動物？ MP3 043

Josh ▶ I would love to have a pet chameleon; I think it would be really cool! They look kind of scary, and people often think chameleons are ferocious, but they are actually quite tame. They don't really bite unless they are agitated. They eat with their tongue just like frogs. I don't own one because they are just too hard to look after.

喬許 ▶ 我很想要有一隻變色龍，我覺得它很酷！他們的外型有點嚇人，讓很多人覺得變色龍很兇猛，其實他們很溫馴。除非他們被激怒了，不然不會咬人。他們跟青蛙一樣用舌頭吃昆蟲。我並沒有真的去養因為他們蠻難照顧的。

Instructions

· 不能只是閱讀每個人物如何回答唷！這是口說測驗，所以一定要開口說。

· 現在請跟著 CD 覆誦，同步練習「說」跟「聽」，第一次請跟著 CD 以相同語速覆誦，第二次和第三次可以逐步拉長到 CD 唸完第一句、第二句後再開始覆誦，能神奇地提升你的聽力專注力喔！

Abby ▶ Zebras are my favorite animals, I like the black and white stripes on them. Every time I see one I always try to figure out whether it is a white zebra with black stripes or a black zebra with white stripes. I was told a herd of zebra is called a dazzle because their pattern can actually dazzle predators' eyes when they gather in large numbers.

艾比 ▶ 我最喜歡的動物是斑馬，我喜歡他們身上的條紋。每一次我看到斑馬我都會仔細的看他到底是有黑條紋的白馬還是有白條紋的黑馬。有人跟我說一群斑馬是用 dazzle 這個字來形容，原因是他們一大群聚集在一起的時候，身上的條紋會讓掠食者眼撩亂。

 Instructions

· 不能只是閱讀每個人物如何回答唷！這是口說測驗，所以一定要開口說。

· 現在請跟著 CD 覆誦，同步練習「說」跟「聽」，第一次請跟著 CD 以相同語速覆誦，第二次和第三次可以逐步拉長到 CD 唸完第一句、第二句後再開始覆誦，能神奇地提升你的聽力專注力喔！

Cameron ▶　I love dogs. I think dogs are not only human's best friend. They are also very useful with their excellent sense of smell. Labradors are calm and friendly. They are used as guide dogs. Beagles are used in the airport to detect drugs and prohibited items. I have a lot of respect for dogs.

卡麥倫 ▶ 我喜歡狗，我覺得狗不但是人類最好的朋友，他們靈敏的嗅覺對人類的貢獻很多。就像拉不拉多既穩重又友善，他們可以當導盲犬。米格魯在機場用來偵測毒品還有違禁品。我對狗這種動物很感恩的!

 Instructions

· 不能只是閱讀每個人物如何回答唷！這是口說測驗，所以一定要開口說。

· 現在請跟著 CD 覆誦，同步練習「說」跟「聽」，第一次請跟著 CD 以相同語速覆誦，第二次和第三次可以逐步拉長到 CD 唸完第一句、第二句後再開始覆誦，能神奇地提升你的聽力專注力喔！

右側標籤：

1　道地高分句

2　一問三答

3　話題卡回答

4　即席應答

主題概述

　　所謂親戚就是大家有共同的祖先（ancestors），比較少見的稱謂（title）有曾祖父母（great grandparents）、舅公叔公（freat uncle）、姨婆（freat auntie）、繼父繼母（step father/mother）等等。親戚不免會有意見不合（disagreement）的爭執（argument）、對立（conflict）。有可能是因為遺囑（will）上遺產繼承（inheritance）、土地分配（land division）的問題。

　　遠房親戚（distant relatives）可能很少見面，見面的機會可能是因為訂婚（engagement）、結婚（tight the knot），喪事（funeral）或是健康問題（health concerns）。

Do you stay in touch with your relatives?
你跟你的親戚們會保持聯絡嗎？ MP3 044

Josh ▶ It is hard not to stay in touch with your relatives especially when you are from a small town like Heng Chuan. Most of my relatives are my neighbors, and I go to school with some of my cousins, too. I couldn't get away from them even if I wanted to!

喬許 ▶ 不跟親戚聯絡實在太難了，尤其是像我住在恆春這種小鎮。我大部分的親戚都住在附近，我跟我的表兄弟也上同一間學校。就算我不想跟他們聯絡也是會遇到。

 Instructions

· 不能只是閱讀每個人物如何回答唷！這是口說測驗，所以一定要開口說。

· 現在請跟著 CD 覆誦，同步練習「說」跟「聽」，第一次請跟著 CD 以相同語速覆誦，第二次和第三次可以逐步拉長到 CD 唸完第一句、第二句後再開始覆誦，能神奇地提升你的聽力專注力喔！

Abby ▶ Not really. I personally don't really make any effort to stay in touch with my relatives. It is more my mum's job. She is the one that calls everyone up during Chinese New Year to say hello, but sometimes you can't even find them. One of my uncles borrowed lots of money from my dad then he ran off. There is no way to contact him anyway.

艾比 ▶ 不太會，我個人是不會主動跟我的親戚聯絡，那都是我媽的事。她過年都會跟他們打個電話問好，可是有時候還找不到人呢！就像我一個叔叔跟我爸借了錢就跑路了，根本就找不到人。

 Instructions

- 不能只是閱讀每個人物如何回答唷！這是口說測驗，所以一定要開口說。
- 現在請跟著 CD 覆誦，同步練習「說」跟「聽」，第一次請跟著 CD 以相同語速覆誦，第二次和第三次可以逐步拉長到 CD 唸完第一句、第二句後再開始覆誦，能神奇地提升你的聽力專注力喔！

Cameron ▶ I am quite close to my cousins because we are all about the same age, although they live in Chia-yi still, there is Skype and LINE. I talk to them quite often.

卡麥倫 ▶ 我跟我的表兄弟們很好因為我們的年紀很接近，雖然他們還住在嘉義。可是現在有 Skype 還有 LINE 很方便，我們常常聯絡。

 Instructions

- 不能只是閱讀每個人物如何回答唷！這是口說測驗，所以一定要開口說。

- 現在請跟著 CD 覆誦，同步練習「說」跟「聽」，第一次請跟著 CD 以相同語速覆誦，第二次和第三次可以逐步拉長到 CD 唸完第一句、第二句後再開始覆誦，能神奇地提升你的聽力專注力喔！

Weather/season
天氣 / 季節

主題概述

　　春夏秋冬四季天氣的特性不同，所以可以從適合當季的活動說起。例如，春天可以去看櫻花（cherry blossom），冬天可以去拔蘿蔔（radish harvesting）。或是反過來說某季節的特性對某些活動有限制性（limitation），例如春秋兩季是過敏（allergy）的好發季，所以常需要使用抗過敏的吸入器（inha l e r ）。或是雨季潮濕，導致家裡的衣物家具常發霉（moldy），所以需要使用除濕機（dehumifier），而雨鞋（gumboots）雨衣（rain coat）不離手。

　　冬季乾冷需要擦乳液（moisturizer）來保濕，出門需要手套（gloves）、圍巾（scarf）。在家的話，暖氣機（heater）、電熱毯（electricblanket）也是必備。若以吃的方面下手，討論每個季節可以享受的季節食材（seasonal ingredient）。

What do you like to do in your favorite season?

在你最喜歡的季節裡你最喜歡做什麼事?

MP3 045

1
道地高分句

2
一問三答

3
話題卡回答

4
即席應答

Josh ▶ I love Summer; I think my skin tone says it all! I love spending time under the sun to build a nice tan. Trust me, the ladies love it! I always volunteer to do the beach watch in Summer because I get to look cool in my board shorts and show off my muscles!

喬許 ▶ 我最愛夏天,看我的膚色也知道。我喜歡在戶外曬太陽,曬成古銅色。相信我,女生都很吃這套!我夏天常常自願到海邊去當救生員,因為我可以正大光明的穿著我的海灘褲秀肌肉!

 Instructions

· 不能只是閱讀每個人物如何回答唷!這是口說測驗,所以一定要開口說。

· 現在請跟著 CD 覆誦,同步練習「說」跟「聽」,第一次請跟著 CD 以相同語速覆誦,第二次和第三次可以逐步拉長到 CD 唸完第一句、第二句後再開始覆誦,能神奇地提升你的聽力專注力喔!

Abby ▶ My favorite season is autumn because it is the best season to enjoy crabs. My favorite thing to do is to go to a seafood restaurant with my family and order seasonal made-to-order stream crabs. We will pay more to order the female crabs because the crab roe is just to die for!

艾比 ▶ 我最喜歡的季節是秋天，因為秋天的螃蟹最肥美！我最喜歡做的事就是跟我家人到海鮮餐廳去點季節限定現點現做的清蒸秋蟹。我們情願付多一點錢要母蟹，因為蟹黃蟹膏真是太美味了！

 Instructions

- 不能只是閱讀每個人物如何回答唷！這是口說測驗，所以一定要開口說。
- 現在請跟著 CD 覆誦，同步練習「說」跟「聽」，第一次請跟著 CD 以相同語速覆誦，第二次和第三次可以逐步拉長到 CD 唸完第一句、第二句後再開始覆誦，能神奇地提升你的聽力專注力喔！

Cameron ▶ I love Winter, and I love going to the hot spring then because it is just so comforting. Hotsprings are very good for your health. The proper way to do it is to soak in the hot spring first then jump into the cold one for a brief moment. Repeat that a few times, it really clears your head.

卡麥倫 ▶ 我最愛冬天了，而且我喜歡冬天去泡溫泉因為真的很療癒。其實泡溫泉對身體很好，泡溫泉正確的方式是先泡溫泉，然後簡短地泡一下冷泉，這樣重複幾次，真的讓人神清氣爽。

 Instructions

· 不能只是閱讀每個人物如何回答唷！這是口說測驗，所以一定要開口說。

· 現在請跟著 CD 覆誦，同步練習「說」跟「聽」，第一次請跟著 CD 以相同語速覆誦，第二次和第三次可以逐步拉長到 CD 唸完第一句、第二句後再開始覆誦，能神奇地提升你的聽力專注力喔！

主題概述

　　一般大家比較熟悉的國小國中科目大概有：國語（mandarin）、數學（mathematic）、英文、物理（physics）、化學（chemistry）、科學（science）、生物（biology）、法律（law）、地理（geography）、歷史（history）、體育（PE-Physical education）、美術（Art）、音樂（music）、電腦（computing）、地球科學（earth science）。

　　喜歡的課程的理由很可能是因為老師的教法或是老師本身的個人魅力，或是課程（curriculum） 的內容（content），還是本身領悟性較強，有天份（gifted）等等。

What was your favorite subject in your school days?

你求學過程中最喜歡的科目是什麼? MP3 046

Josh ▶ My favorite subject is biology. I really enjoy learning about animals, insects, and the structure of the human body. My favorite part of the class is the lab work where you get to dissect a frog to see how the muscles work. I still recall some of the girls in my class got so scared of the muscle reflex.

喬許 ▶ 我最喜歡的科目是生物,我很喜歡學跟動物、昆蟲還有人體構造有關的。課堂上我最喜歡的部分是到實驗室去解剖青蛙看肌肉的運作方式。我還記得我們班上的一些女生被肌肉的反射嚇得半死。

 Instructions

· 不能只是閱讀每個人物如何回答唷!這是口說測驗,所以一定要開口說。

· 現在請跟著 CD 覆誦,同步練習「說」跟「聽」,第一次請跟著 CD 以相同語速覆誦,第二次和第三次可以逐步拉長到 CD 唸完第一句、第二句後再開始覆誦,能神奇地提升你的聽力專注力喔!

Abby ▶ I love geography the most. My geography teacher from junior high school was really funny. He made geography really interesting. He would get us to pretend we were planning a trip to a certain area or country, and I actually learnt a lot from the class. What a brilliant way of teaching!

艾比 ▶ 我最愛上地理課了，我國中的地理老師是個很有趣的人，他讓地理變得很有趣。他會叫我們搜集要到某個地區或是國家玩的資料，我在課堂上學了很多，這種教法真的太聰明了！

 Instructions

- 不能只是閱讀每個人物如何回答唷！這是口說測驗，所以一定要開口說。

- 現在請跟著 CD 覆誦，同步練習「說」跟「聽」，第一次請跟著 CD 以相同語速覆誦，第二次和第三次可以逐步拉長到 CD 唸完第一句、第二句後再開始覆誦，能神奇地提升你的聽力專注力喔！

Cameron ▶ I really like art classes because I get to do what I like to do. Preparing for the university entry exam was a stressful time. I always look forward to art class, so I can take my mind off things. However, art class in high school doesn't really teach you much technique.

卡麥倫 ▶ 我真的很喜歡美術課,因為我可以做我喜歡的事。準備大學聯考是壓力很大的,只要到美術課我就很高興,因為我可以暫時不用想讀書的事。可是高中的美術課並不會教你什麼畫圖的技法。

 Instructions

· 不能只是閱讀每個人物如何回答唷!這是口說測驗,所以一定要開口說。

· 現在請跟著 CD 覆誦,同步練習「說」跟「聽」,第一次請跟著 CD 以相同語速覆誦,第二次和第三次可以逐步拉長到 CD 唸完第一句、第二句後再開始覆誦,能神奇地提升你的聽力專注力喔!

1 道地高分句

2 一問三答

3 話題卡回答

4 即席應答

Unit 19 Talent 才藝

主題概述

　　才藝通常大家會聯想到比較藝術性質的（artistic），例如：鋼琴（piano）、小提琴（violin）、口琴（garmonica）、長笛（flute）、吉他（guitar）、聲樂（vocal）、豎琴（harp）、古箏（chinese zither）、芭蕾舞（ballet）、爵士鼓（drums）、拉丁舞（latino dance）、國標舞（ballroom dancing）、現代舞（modern dance）、油畫（oil painting）、水彩畫（water color painting）。

　　學才藝常會有發表會（concer t）比賽之類的活動，當然也會有獎狀（merit certificate）、獎牌（medal）等等。可是相對的學才藝的學費（tuition）還有交通費可是很可觀的。

Have you ever taken any talent class
你曾經學過什麼才藝嗎？ MP3 047

Josh ▶ I actually took some Latino dance classes when I was little. I was getting pretty good at it. My speciality is the Cha Cha Cha. I didn't want to continue because I was worried about being judged by my friends. You know how 8 years old boys are like!

喬許 ▶ 其實我小時候學過拉丁舞。我的恰恰還真的跳得不錯。可是我沒有再繼續學下去因為我怕被我的朋友們笑，你知道八歲的小男生就是這樣啊。

 Instructions

- 不能只是閱讀每個人物如何回答唷！這是口說測驗，所以一定要開口説。

- 現在請跟著 CD 覆誦，同步練習「説」跟「聽」，第一次請跟著 CD 以相同語速覆誦，第二次和第三次可以逐步拉長到 CD 唸完第一句、第二句後再開始覆誦，能神奇地提升你的聽力專注力喔！

Abby ▶ I did Karate when I was in elementary school. I didn't want to do it, but my father me to be able to defend myself from bullies, and he is a firm believer in martial arts. I went along with it for a few years, but I was never any good.

艾比 ▶ 我國小的時候學過跆拳道，我不想學，可是我爸說我一定要學會保護自己，不要被霸凌。他對武術這方面是深信不疑，我順著他的意學了幾年，可是沒學到什麼。

 Instructions

- 不能只是閱讀每個人物如何回答唷！這是口說測驗，所以一定要開口說。
- 現在請跟著 CD 覆誦，同步練習「說」跟「聽」，第一次請跟著 CD 以相同語速覆誦，第二次和第三次可以逐步拉長到 CD 唸完第一句、第二句後再開始覆誦，能神奇地提升你的聽力專注力喔！

Cameron ▶ I started to learn how to do proper oil painting since I was 10 years old. I have always been artistic and gifted in painting when I was little. My parents have been very supportive, and they decided to enroll me into the oil painting class although I was the youngest student among them.

卡麥倫 ▶ 我從十歲就開始正式的學油畫，我一直都是比較有藝術細胞的，對畫畫這方面很有天賦。我父母親一直都很支持我，所以他們決定送我去油畫班，而我是全班最小的學生。

 Instructions

· 不能只是閱讀每個人物如何回答唷！這是口說測驗，所以一定要開口說。

· 現在請跟著 CD 覆誦，同步練習「説」跟「聽」，第一次請跟著 CD 以相同語速覆誦，第二次和第三次可以逐步拉長到 CD 唸完第一句、第二句後再開始覆誦，能神奇地提升你的聽力專注力喔！

Driving 開車

主題概述

開車首先要有駕照（driver's license），台灣考駕照的法定年齡（legal age）是十八歲；而大部分的人都會去駕訓班（driving School）學車，請教練（driving instructor）指導，再到監理所（Road and Traffic Authority）考照，除了筆試之外還要路考（road test）。

各國的交通規則（roadrules）不盡相同，換國際駕照（international driving permit）時要特別注意。如果出車禍，一般車險（car insurance）都會有理賠（payout），車險的保費（insurancepremium）也會因為申請理賠的紀錄而調整（adjust）。有的險種需要繳較高的自付額（out of packet expense），在國外如果要救護車（ambulance）服務也需要保險，否則自費金額很高。

Do you prefer driving or walking?
你喜歡開車還是走路？ MP3 048

Josh ▶ I think it depends on where I am going. If I am only going to the corner 7-11 to get some beer, I much prefer walking to driving since you don't have to worry about parking. The journey is too short for a car ride.

喬許 ▶ 那要看我要去哪裡，如果我只是要去轉角的 7-11 買啤酒那我走路就好了，因為我也不用擔心停車的問題，路程這麼短，根本不需要開車。

 Instructions

- 不能只是閱讀每個人物如何回答唷！這是口說測驗，所以一定要開口說。

- 現在請跟著 CD 覆誦，同步練習「說」跟「聽」，第一次請跟著 CD 以相同語速覆誦，第二次和第三次可以逐步拉長到 CD 唸完第一句、第二句後再開始覆誦，能神奇地提升你的聽力專注力喔！

1 道地高分句

2 一問三答

3 話題卡回答

4 即席應答

Abby ► I actually don't own a driver's license which leaves me with no options other than walking or taking public transport everywhere. You wouldn't want to drive in Taipei anyway. Parking is a pain in the ass to find and even if you do find a space, it will cost you an arm and a leg.

艾比 ► 　其實我連駕照都沒有，所以也沒得選擇，不是走路就是坐大眾交通工具。在台北你也不會想開車的，車位難找的要死，就算找到了也是貴得很。

 Instructions

- 不能只是閱讀每個人物如何回答唷！這是口說測驗，所以一定要開口說。
- 現在請跟著 CD 覆誦，同步練習「說」跟「聽」，第一次請跟著 CD 以相同語速覆誦，第二次和第三次可以逐步拉長到 CD 唸完第一句、第二句後再開始覆誦，能神奇地提升你的聽力專注力喔！

Cameron ▶ I prefer driving for sure because I need to visit my clients regularly at the industrial park outside of the city. I don't know any other way to get there other than driving! I know finding a place to park the car is a potential problem, but being punctural is my priority. There is no other way.

卡麥倫 ▶ 我一定選擇開車，因為我常常需要到近郊的工業區去拜訪客戶。如果不開車我還真不知道我能怎麼去。我知道找車位可能很難找，但是我不準時不行，也只能開車了。

 Instructions

· 不能只是閱讀每個人物如何回答唷！這是口說測驗，所以一定要開口說。

· 現在請跟著 CD 覆誦，同步練習「說」跟「聽」，第一次請跟著 CD 以相同語速覆誦，第二次和第三次可以逐步拉長到 CD 唸完第一句、第二句後再開始覆誦，能神奇地提升你的聽力專注力喔！

Birthday 生日

✏️ 主題概述

生日的慶祝方式，可以辦舞會慶祝，三五好友聚餐（gathering），或是跟家人切蛋糕，或是在公司跟同事慶祝，還有些人根本忙忘了。生日派對需要的物品有蛋糕、外燴（catering）、酒會點心（canapé）、汽水（soft drink）、酒類（alcoholic beverage）和調酒（cocktail）。

慶祝生日的方式: 驚喜派對（surprise par ty）、聚餐、整人/惡作劇（prank）、去夜店（go clubbing）、到海邊看日出（watch sunrise）。生日禮物（birthday present）當然也是必備，很多人乾脆直接送禮券（gift voucher），避免買了不合對方心意，還要換貨（exchange）或退貨（return）

What do you normally do for your birthday?
你通常都怎麼慶祝生日? MP3 049

1 道地高分句

2 一問三答

3 話題卡回答

4 即席應答

Josh ▶ My birthday is a big thing. My friends like to make big deal out of it. We will normally go somewhere for dinner before heading to the clubs. By the end of the night, we will be so wasted and can't even recall what we did and where we went! But it is always a night to remember.

喬許 ▶ 我的生日是件大事,我的朋友們很喜歡高調慶祝。我們通常會先去吃飯,然後再到酒吧去,我們會盡情狂飲,到最後都不知道我們到底做過什麼去過哪裡,而且絕對是不醉不歸!

Instructions

· 不能只是閱讀每個人物如何回答唷!這是口說測驗,所以一定要開口說。

· 現在請跟著 CD 覆誦,同步練習「說」跟「聽」,第一次請跟著 CD 以相同語速覆誦,第二次和第三次可以逐步拉長到 CD 唸完第一句、第二句後再開始覆誦,能神奇地提升你的聽力專注力喔!

Abby ▶ Normally, I will bring a cake to work to share with my coworkers because we get along really well. My boss doesn't normally get in until lunch time, so we are free to do what we want in the office. Some of us might go out for dinner after work, but that's about it.

艾比 ▶ 我通常會帶個蛋糕到公司跟同事一起慶生，因為我跟他們很好。而且我老闆通常午餐時間才會進公司，所以我們蠻自由的。下班後可能跟幾個同事一起吃飯，但大概就是這樣了。

 Instructions

- 不能只是閱讀每個人物如何回答唷！這是口說測驗，所以一定要開口說。
- 現在請跟著 CD 覆誦，同步練習「說」跟「聽」，第一次請跟著 CD 以相同語速覆誦，第二次和第三次可以逐步拉長到 CD 唸完第一句、第二句後再開始覆誦，能神奇地提升你的聽力專注力喔！

Cameron ▶ My mother is pretty traditional when it comes to my birthday; she insists to make me the pig knuckle noodle soup every year although she knows most likely I would have made dinner plans with my girlfriend to celebrate. However, I would always finish the noodle soup before I go out because I don't want to make her feel bad.

卡麥倫 ▶ 說到我的生日我媽是蠻傳統的，她總是堅持要煮豬腳麵線給我吃，雖然她知道我應該已經跟女朋友約了要出去吃飯慶生。我一定會先吃完她煮的麵線再出去，但那也是她老人家一番心意。

 Instructions

· 不能只是閱讀每個人物如何回答唷！這是口說測驗，所以一定要開口說。

· 現在請跟著 CD 覆誦，同步練習「說」跟「聽」，第一次請跟著 CD 以相同語速覆誦，第二次和第三次可以逐步拉長到 CD 唸完第一句、第二句後再開始覆誦，能神奇地提升你的聽力專注力喔！

主題概述

　　台灣也因為健保的不周全，所以大部分的人都有私人健康保險（private health insurance）。壽險（life insurance）、意外險（accident insurance）、車險也是非常普遍。如果發生交通意外發生時，可能需要報警留下報案紀錄（police report）以便日後保險公司做定奪。意外發生時，最忌諱慌張（panic），一定要保持冷靜（calm）。

　　如果有人受傷需要送急診（emergency），在救護人員（paramedic）抵達之前也切記不要隨便移動傷患，就怕導致骨折（fracture）或是內出血（internal bleeding）的問題更加嚴重，可能需要及時手術（operation）處理。政府也一直在提倡捐血救人（blood donation），器官捐贈（organ donation）及器官移植（organ transplant）的觀念，一般民眾也越來越能接受。

What would you do if you got into a car accident?
你不小心出車禍時會怎麼處理? MP3 050

Josh ▶ I will first check whether it is my fault or his negligence and whether we need an ambulance or not. If it is just a small bump or a scratch, I will just negotiate with the person and sort it out there and then. It gets too complicated when you get the police involved.

喬許 ▶ 我首先會判斷是我的錯還是對方的失誤,看看我們需不需要救護車。如果只是小擦撞,那我就會跟對方商議是不是能在現場賠償解決就好,叫警察來實在太麻煩了!

 Instructions

- 不能只是閱讀每個人物如何回答唷!這是口說測驗,所以一定要開口說。
- 現在請跟著 CD 覆誦,同步練習「說」跟「聽」,第一次請跟著 CD 以相同語速覆誦,第二次和第三次可以逐步拉長到 CD 唸完第一句、第二句後再開始覆誦,能神奇地提升你的聽力專注力喔!

Abby ▶ I would totally freak out! I don't have a driver's licence, so I think if I did get into an accident I would be the victim. I guess there is not much I could do, if I got hit by a car, I just hope someone would call the police and the ambulance for me!

艾比 ▶ 我真的會完全嚇壞，我沒有駕照所以我想如果我出了車禍，那我一定是被撞的那個人。我猜如果我被撞了，那我也沒有辦法做什麼事，可能要靠好心人來幫我報警還有叫救護車了。

 Instructions

- 不能只是閱讀每個人物如何回答唷！這是口說測驗，所以一定要開口說。

- 現在請跟著 CD 覆誦，同步練習「說」跟「聽」，第一次請跟著 CD 以相同語速覆誦，第二次和第三次可以逐步拉長到 CD 唸完第一句、第二句後再開始覆誦，能神奇地提升你的聽力專注力喔！

Cameron ▶ I will call the police for sure because I need the police report to show my insurance agent. I have full coverage for the car and third party insurance. I think I am pretty much covered! I just hope I don't accidently kill someone, then it would be a real nightmare.

卡麥倫 ▶ 我一定會馬上報警,因為我需要給保險公司看報案紀錄。我的車有保全險,而且還有第三人保險,我覺得我沒什麼好擔心的。我只希望我不要意外撞死人就好,那就糟糕了。

 Instructions

· 不能只是閱讀每個人物如何回答唷!這是口說測驗,所以一定要開口說。

· 現在請跟著 CD 覆誦,同步練習「說」跟「聽」,第一次請跟著 CD 以相同語速覆誦,第二次和第三次可以逐步拉長到 CD 唸完第一句、第二句後再開始覆誦,能神奇地提升你的聽力專注力喔!

主題概述

　　如果被問到工作，可以從職稱（job title）開始做介紹（introduction），可以簡單的陳述工作內容（job description），公司的規模還有公司的結構（company structure）等等。

　　再來可以講講工作的甘苦談，例如老闆不好，一天到晚要工作加班（overtime）、待命（on call），沒有加薪（pay rise）、升職（promotion），沒有績效獎金（commission）、年終紅利（bonus），壓力大（stressful）都可以談。如果是求學的話可以說明目前是哪間學校、幾年級、簡單介紹你的學歷例如主修或擅長的科目。也可以介紹擅長的課外活動及畢業後的展望。

What do you do?
你目前是做什麼的? MP3 051

Josh ▶ I graduated from university last year with a bachelor's degree in Physical training. At the moment, I am in the process of getting my application together for the master's degree in Sport Science in the University of Sydney. I hope they will offer a place to me, I can't wait to go surfing in the world famous Bondi beach!

喬許 ▶ 我去年由體育系畢業,目前我正在準備申請雪梨大學運動科學的碩士學位。希望他們會收我,我迫不及待地想去世界出名的邦代海灘衝浪!

 Instructions

· 不能只是閱讀每個人物如何回答唷!這是口說測驗,所以一定要開口說。

· 現在請跟著 CD 覆誦,同步練習「說」跟「聽」,第一次請跟著 CD 以相同語速覆誦,第二次和第三次可以逐步拉長到 CD 唸完第一句、第二句後再開始覆誦,能神奇地提升你的聽力專注力喔!

Abby ▶ I am a procurement representative in this trading company called "CandyCan". "CandyCan" specializes in importing European sweets and confectionary. The best thing about being in this industry is that you get samples for free. I literally get endless supply of the finest Belgium Chocolates.

艾比 ▶ 我是一家叫「糖罐子」的貿易公司的採購專員，「糖罐子」是專門進口歐洲的糖果糕餅。做這份工作最好的地方就是廠商會寄樣品給我，我常常收到比利時的高級巧克力呢！

 Instructions

- 不能只是閱讀每個人物如何回答唷！這是口說測驗，所以一定要開口說。
- 現在請跟著 CD 覆誦，同步練習「說」跟「聽」，第一次請跟著 CD 以相同語速覆誦，第二次和第三次可以逐步拉長到 CD 唸完第一句、第二句後再開始覆誦，能神奇地提升你的聽力專注力喔！

Cameron ▶ I am a sales engineer in a company called Sinclair. Sinclair is a production line machine supplier. My job is to look after my clients and provide them with the technical support and parts. The most annoying thing about my job is that I have to be available on the weekends, too.

卡麥倫 ▶ 我是辛克萊爾的銷售工程師，辛克萊爾是生產線機器的供應商。我的工作是照顧我的客戶，提供技術支援還有零件供應。這份工作最討厭的地方就是我週末也要待命。

 Instructions

· 不能只是閱讀每個人物如何回答唷！這是口說測驗，所以一定要開口說。

· 現在請跟著 CD 覆誦，同步練習「說」跟「聽」，第一次請跟著 CD 以相同語速覆誦，第二次和第三次可以逐步拉長到 CD 唸完第一句、第二句後再開始覆誦，能神奇地提升你的聽力專注力喔！

✏️ 主題概述

旅遊不只是出國旅行，國內當天來回，兩天一夜的微旅行也算。現在因為廉價航空（budget airline）的普遍，出國自助旅行（self-guided tour）的人數眾多。訂房網站，訂票網站盛行，訂房訂票需要填寫基本的個人資料（personal detail），須以信用卡（credit card）付款。修改（amendment）日期或取消（cancellation）需要收取手續費（administrationfees），有些則無法取消。

廉價航空的票價通常只含手提行李（carry-on luggage），機艙行李（check-in luggage）則需要另外付費，乘客也需付費選擇靠走道（aisleseat）或是靠窗（window seat）的位置，餐點（meal）也不包含在內。出國記得確認違禁品（prohibited items）的項目，表格上要確實申報（declare）以免受罰。

Do you travel a lot?
你常去旅行嗎？ MP3 052

Josh ▸ I did a fair bit of travel in Taiwan with my classmates I have been to most of the famous tourist attractions in Taiwan. The most memorable trip was my surfing competition in Taidong last year. I was so close to winning a prize.

喬許 ▸ 我以前常跟我的同學在台灣到處跑，台灣大大小小的旅遊勝地我大概都去過，可是記憶最深刻的還是我到台東參加衝浪比賽那一次，我差一點就有獎可以拿。

Instructions

· 不能只是閱讀每個人物如何回答唷！這是口說測驗，所以一定要開口說。

· 現在請跟著 CD 覆誦，同步練習「說」跟「聽」，第一次請跟著 CD 以相同語速覆誦，第二次和第三次可以逐步拉長到 CD 唸完第一句、第二句後再開始覆誦，能神奇地提升你的聽力專注力喔！

Abby ▶ I don't often go on big trips because it is hard to take time off work. I do like to go overseas, and I have been to Japan and Korea. Sometimes I will go out of my way to visit a place recommended by travel books. But I found most of the time, those places are not as good as how it is described in the book.

艾比 ▶ 我不太常有機會去很久，因為我的工作很難請假。我是蠻喜歡出國的，我去過日本跟韓國。有時候我會特別去旅遊書上介紹過的地方看看，可是我發現那些地方實在沒有書上說的那麼好。

 Instructions

· 不能只是閱讀每個人物如何回答唷！這是口說測驗，所以一定要開口說。

· 現在請跟著 CD 覆誦，同步練習「說」跟「聽」，第一次請跟著 CD 以相同語速覆誦，第二次和第三次可以逐步拉長到 CD 唸完第一句、第二句後再開始覆誦，能神奇地提升你的聽力專注力喔！

1 道地高分句

2 一問三答

3 話題卡回答

4 即席應答

 Cameron ▶ Other than going to the hot springs in Yang Ming mountain, I don't think I travel a lot. I do prefer to hang around the city. Maybe I will go to a different part of the town and try a new café or a new restaurant. That is probably as adventurous as I get.

卡麥倫 ▶ 除了到陽明山泡溫泉之外，我好像沒機會到處去。我其實也比較喜歡在市區晃。偶爾我會到平時很少去的區域去走走，試試看沒去過的咖啡店或是餐廳，這樣對我來說就算是旅行了。

 ## Instructions

· 不能只是閱讀每個人物如何回答唷！這是口說測驗，所以一定要開口說。

· 現在請跟著 CD 覆誦，同步練習「說」跟「聽」，第一次請跟著 CD 以相同語速覆誦，第二次和第三次可以逐步拉長到 CD 唸完第一句、第二句後再開始覆誦，能神奇地提升你的聽力專注力喔！

Sport event 運動比賽

✏️ **主題概述**

　　大型的運動比賽有奧運（Olympic games）、亞運（Asian games）。或是台灣職棒大聯盟（Taiwan MajorLeague）、美國職棒大聯盟（US Major League）、小聯盟（Minor League）、日本職棒（Nippon ProfessionalBaseball）、摔角（Professional Wrestling）、相撲（Sumo Wrestling）、美國籃球（NBA）等等。

　　一般學校的運動會（Sports carnival）、舞蹈比賽（Dance competition）、游泳比賽（Swimming competition），也都是運動比賽。運動比賽的勝負分為金牌得主（Gold Medalist）、銀牌得主（Silver medalist）、銅牌得主（Bronze medalist）。

Do you like to watch sports events live?
你喜歡看運動比賽的實況轉播嗎? MP3 053

Josh ▶ Absolutely! Nothing is more exciting than a live sports event. I would go to the stadium if I could, but I don't live in New York, so there is no way that I can watch the Yankees play in person. Live TV broadcasting is the next best thing! I normally watch the games with my friends in the house.

喬許 ▶ 那當然! 沒有什麼比看現場比賽更刺激的了! 如果可以的話,我當然想去體育館看現場,可是我又不住在紐約,沒有辦法現場看洋基隊比賽,能有實況轉播就很不錯了! 我通常會到我朋友家跟他一起看。

💬 Instructions

• 不能只是閱讀每個人物如何回答唷! 這是口說測驗,所以一定要開口說。

• 現在請跟著 CD 覆誦,同步練習「說」跟「聽」,第一次請跟著 CD 以相同語速覆誦,第二次和第三次可以逐步拉長到 CD 唸完第一句、第二句後再開始覆誦,能神奇地提升你的聽力專注力喔!

Abby ▶ Well, I am not a sports person, watching a sport event live would be a torture for me. I don't get excited like the fans. I mean if it is an important sports event like the Olympic, I would be curious about whether Taiwan has won a match, but I wouldn't stay up the whole night just to watch it live.

艾比 ▶ 這個嘛，我不是很愛運動的人，看現場的運動比賽簡直就是要我的命，我不像運動迷們心情跟著起伏。如果是重要的比賽像奧運之類的，我當然會關心台灣是贏還是輸，可是我絕對不會熬夜來看實況轉播。

 Instructions

- 不能只是閱讀每個人物如何回答唷！這是口說測驗，所以一定要開口說。
- 現在請跟著 CD 覆誦，同步練習「說」跟「聽」，第一次請跟著 CD 以相同語速覆誦，第二次和第三次可以逐步拉長到 CD 唸完第一句、第二句後再開始覆誦，能神奇地提升你的聽力專注力喔！

Cameron ▶ I do like to watch live sports events, but most of the time I've got work the next day, so I don't have the luxury to stay up late to watch the games. If I knew the game was going to be on in the early evening, then I would make an effort to watch it live.

卡麥倫 ▶ 我喜歡看實況轉播可是大部分的時間我隔天都要工作，所以不太可能有這個閒暇時間不睡覺來看比賽的。如果我知道轉播的時間是在下班時間以後的話，那我就會看轉播。

 Instructions

- 不能只是閱讀每個人物如何回答唷！這是口說測驗，所以一定要開口說。
- 現在請跟著 CD 覆誦，同步練習「說」跟「聽」，第一次請跟著 CD 以相同語速覆誦，第二次和第三次可以逐步拉長到 CD 唸完第一句、第二句後再開始覆誦，能神奇地提升你的聽力專注力喔！

Weekend/Free time
周末 / 休閒

主題概述

　　週末是很多人唯一可以休息的時候，有的人喜歡趁這個機會運動，逛街，做平常沒機會做的事。有人喜歡趁這個機會休息（chill out）、補眠（sleep in）、追劇（watch soaps）、陪家人（spend t ime wi th fami l y）、做家事（dochores）、去做臉（go to the day spa）、去兜風（go for a drive）、洗衣服（do laundry）、看漫畫（read comicbooks）、上課進修（take classes）、發呆（zone out）等等。

　　週末很多人選擇外出旅遊，　如果出外旅遊住房是旺季（high season），住房價格會偏高，而且觀光區（tourist attractions）人滿為患；淡季（low season）去反而比較有度假的品質。

What do you normally do in your free time?
你有空的時候通常會做什麼? MP3 054

Josh ▶ If the weather is good, then I will be at the beach, but if the weather is not right, then I will be at home playing video games! Video games are so addictive, so I lose track of time so easily. I can keep playing the whole night, if my mother didn't come and stop me.

喬許 ▶ 如果天氣不錯的話,那我就會去海邊,可是如果天氣不好,那我就會在家打電動。電玩這種東西真的很容易讓人上癮,我一開始打就會忘了時間,如果我媽沒有來叫我的話,我可以一直打下去。

Instructions

- 不能只是閱讀每個人物如何回答唷!這是口說測驗,所以一定要開口說。
- 現在請跟著 CD 覆誦,同步練習「說」跟「聽」,第一次請跟著 CD 以相同語速覆誦,第二次和第三次可以逐步拉長到 CD 唸完第一句、第二句後再開始覆誦,能神奇地提升你的聽力專注力喔!

233

Abby ▶ I will go shopping if I am free the whole day on the weekends. But if I only have an hour here and there, I watch Korean soaps instead. I stream them on-line, and I normally watch one or two episodes then I have to force myself to turn it off. Otherwise, I would run out of internet data in no time!

艾比 ▶ 如果我週末整天有空的話我就會去逛街,可是如果我只有零散的一兩個小時,那我就會上網下載韓劇。我通常只會看個一兩集就強迫關機,不然下載的容量很快就用完了。

 Instructions

- 不能只是閱讀每個人物如何回答唷!這是口說測驗,所以一定要開口說。

- 現在請跟著 CD 覆誦,同步練習「說」跟「聽」,第一次請跟著 CD 以相同語速覆誦,第二次和第三次可以逐步拉長到 CD 唸完第一句、第二句後再開始覆誦,能神奇地提升你的聽力專注力喔!

Cameron ▶ Juggling between my girlfriend and my jobs is really tiring. My favorite thing to do in my spare time is actually doing nothing, just chilling out or catching up on sleeps.

卡麥倫 ▶ 平常要陪女朋友又要上班真的很累。我有空的時候最喜歡就是懶在那裡什麼都不做，不然就是補眠。

 Instructions

- 不能只是閱讀每個人物如何回答唷！這是口說測驗，所以一定要開口說。
- 現在請跟著 CD 覆誦，同步練習「說」跟「聽」，第一次請跟著 CD 以相同語速覆誦，第二次和第三次可以逐步拉長到 CD 唸完第一句、第二句後再開始覆誦，能神奇地提升你的聽力專注力喔！

Unit
27 Colour 顏色

主題概述

　　彩虹的色調大家比較不熟的應該是靛色（indigo）與紫色（violet），還有一般常用卻不熟悉的顏色有: 米白（beige）、蒂芬妮藍（turquoise）、深藍（navy blue）、酒紅色（burgundy）。

　　顏色帶給人的感覺不同，深色通常令人覺得穩重（mature）、神秘（mysterious）、高貴（elegant）、嚴肅（solemn）。淺色則令人感覺輕鬆（relaxed）、活潑（upbeat）、正面（positive）、明亮（bright）、純真（naive）等等。

Do you prefer to wear dark colors or light colors?

你比較喜歡穿深色或是淺色的衣服? 🎧 MP3 055

Josh ▶ I prefer to wear light colors, such as white or bright green. I spend a lot of time sun-bathing to get the tan I want, and I like to wear something that would complement my skin tone. I think light colors represent my personality as well. I am energetic and always positive.

喬許 ▶ 我喜歡穿淺色的衣服,像白色或是很亮的綠色之類。我好不容易才把我的皮膚曬成我想要的膚色,我當然要選擇可以襯托我膚色的顏色。我覺得淺色也很可以代表我的個性,我一直都是很有活力而且很正面的。

 Instructions

· 不能只是閱讀每個人物如何回答唷!這是口說測驗,所以一定要開口說。

· 現在請跟著 CD 覆誦,同步練習「說」跟「聽」,第一次請跟著 CD 以相同語速覆誦,第二次和第三次可以逐步拉長到 CD 唸完第一句、第二句後再開始覆誦,能神奇地提升你的聽力專注力喔!

Abby ▶ I think it depends what kind of mood I am in. If I don't have any formal things to attend to that day, I prefer to wear a light color. But if I have a formal meeting or something important on, then I prefer to wear a dark color just to look more professional.

艾比 ▶ 我覺得要看心情，如果我今天沒有什麼重要的事要處理，那我就想穿淺色的，可是如果我有會要開或是有重要的事，那我會選擇深色，這樣看起來比較專業。

 Instructions

- 不能只是閱讀每個人物如何回答唷！這是口說測驗，所以一定要開口說。
- 現在請跟著 CD 覆誦，同步練習「説」跟「聽」，第一次請跟著 CD 以相同語速覆誦，第二次和第三次可以逐步拉長到 CD 唸完第一句、第二句後再開始覆誦，能神奇地提升你的聽力專注力喔！

Cameron ▶ I would prefer to wear dark colors because I need to visit my clients in the factory, and it is very likely to get grease or dirt on my shirt. If I wear a dark color shirt, I can hide the stains pretty well, but with a light color shirt, you can spot the stain from miles away. That's what I try to avoid.

卡麥倫 ▶ 我會喜歡穿深色，因為我常需要到廠房裡見客戶，廠房裡到處都是油汙，常會弄到衣服。所以如果我穿深色的，那污漬就看不太出來。如果換成是淺色衣服的話，那遠遠的就可以看到汙漬，我會盡量避免。

 Instructions

- 不能只是閱讀每個人物如何回答唷！這是口說測驗，所以一定要開口說。
- 現在請跟著 CD 覆誦，同步練習「說」跟「聽」，第一次請跟著 CD 以相同語速覆誦，第二次和第三次可以逐步拉長到 CD 唸完第一句、第二句後再開始覆誦，能神奇地提升你的聽力專注力喔！

1 道地高分句

2 一問三答

3 話題卡回答

4 即席應答

239

主題概述

　　電腦的設備不斷地推陳出新，常見的電腦設備有螢幕（monitor）、主機（mother board）、鍵盤（keyboard）、無線滑鼠（optical Mouse）、印表機（printer）、掃描機（scanner）等等。每個需要使用電腦的理由不同，電腦的功能（functions）除了可以上網購物（onlineshopping）、打作業（assignment）、打線上遊戲（playonline games）、聊天室（online chatroom）、線上論壇（online forum）、找資料（doing research）、下載節目（streaming）等等。

　　電腦的種類也不侷限在桌上型電腦（desk top）、筆記型電腦（lap top），近年來平板電腦（tablet）、智慧型手機（smartphone）都很受歡迎，同時也具電腦的功能性。

How often do you use a computer?
你用電腦的機會多嗎? 🎧 MP3 056

Josh ▶ I had to use a computer almost everyday while I was a student, but since I graduated last year I have been spending lots of time at the beach. My computer is sitting on my desk gathering dusts as we speak. I hardly touch it now, and I check all my emails on my smartphone anyway.

喬許 ▶ 我還沒畢業之前我很常用電腦,可是去年畢業之後我大部分的時間都在海邊,我的電腦現在就丟在桌子上埋在厚厚的灰塵底下。我現在很少開電腦,我都用智慧型手機來看電子郵件。

 Instructions

· 不能只是閱讀每個人物如何回答唷!這是口說測驗,所以一定要開口說。

· 現在請跟著 CD 覆誦,同步練習「說」跟「聽」,第一次請跟著 CD 以相同語速覆誦,第二次和第三次可以逐步拉長到 CD 唸完第一句、第二句後再開始覆誦,能神奇地提升你的聽力專注力喔!

Abby ▶ I use a computer everyday at work for the correspondence between the company and our overseas suppliers. I will be in so much trouble, if the internet is not working because all emails would not come through properly. I can't live without the computer. I stream all my Korean soaps online with my laptop, too.

艾比 ▶ 我在公司每天都要用電腦跟國外供應商們連絡。如果網路當掉的話我就糟了，因為不知道是不是每封郵件都有收到。我沒有電腦就會活不下去了，因為我的手提電腦是拿來下載韓劇用的。

 Instructions

- 不能只是閱讀每個人物如何回答唷！這是口說測驗，所以一定要開口說。
- 現在請跟著 CD 覆誦，同步練習「說」跟「聽」，第一次請跟著 CD 以相同語速覆誦，第二次和第三次可以逐步拉長到 CD 唸完第一句、第二句後再開始覆誦，能神奇地提升你的聽力專注力喔！

Cameron ▶ I don't use the desktop often but rely on my smartphone a lot because I am out and about visiting clients all the time. I do have to input the orders into the computer just for record keeping once every couple of days.

卡麥倫 ▶ 我不常用我的桌上型電腦,可是我很常用智慧型手機,因為我幾乎都在外面見客戶。我大概每隔幾天就要開電腦一次來輸入這幾天的訂單。

 Instructions

· 不能只是閱讀每個人物如何回答唷!這是口說測驗,所以一定要開口說。

· 現在請跟著 CD 覆誦,同步練習「說」跟「聽」,第一次請跟著 CD 以相同語速覆誦,第二次和第三次可以逐步拉長到 CD 唸完第一句、第二句後再開始覆誦,能神奇地提升你的聽力專注力喔!

1 道地高分句

2 一問三答

3 話題卡回答

4 即席應答

主題概述

電影的種類可以簡單分為喜劇（comedy）、驚悚片（thriller）、愛情片（romance）、劇情片（drama）、動作片（action）、科幻片（Si-Fi）、歷史片（historical）、動畫電影（animation movie）等等。票房好的電影（blockbuster）受歡迎的原因可以是因為劇情（storyline）好笑（Hilarious）、感人（Touching）、刺激（exciting）、令人意想不到的（unpredictable）等等。

票房不好的原因可能是令觀眾覺得無聊或是劇情太誇張（exaggerating）、不合情理（doesn't make sense）、太肉麻/老套（too corny）、或是故事內容太過悲情（too depressing）。

244

1

道地高分句

2

一問三答

3

話題卡回答

4

即席應答

What kind of movie do you like the most?
你最喜歡看哪一類型的電影? MP3 057

Josh ▶ I like to have a good laugh, so comedy is always my go-to. My favorite is the "Hangover". It is about a group of friends deciding to go to Vegas to celebrate stag night. They accidently got drugged, so they had no recollection of what actually happened the night before. All they know is the groom is missing, and they have to find him in time for the wedding. It is hilarious, you've got to watch it.

喬許 ▶ 我覺得人生就是要開心所以看電影我也喜歡看喜劇。我最喜歡的騙子就是「醉後大丈夫」。這部片子是在講有關一群朋友決定到拉斯維加斯去慶祝單身的最後一夜,但是他們卻意外地被下藥,完全不記得前晚發生過什麼事。他們只知道新郎不見了一定要把他在婚禮前及時找回來。故事內容超搞笑的,大推!

Instructions

• 不能只是閱讀每個人物如何回答唷!這是口說測驗,所以一定要開口說。現在請跟著 CD 覆誦,同步練習「說」跟「聽」,第一次請跟著 CD 以相同語速覆誦,第二次和第三次可以逐步拉長到 CD 唸完第一句、第二句後再開始覆誦,能神奇地提升你的聽力專注力喔!

245

Abby ▶ I love girly movies, a sweet love story would be ideal. I also prefer a happy ending because most of the love stories in real life do not have fairytale endings. I think movies should not be too close to reality because life is hard enough as it is, why watch something that reminds you of how terrible life can be!

艾比 ▶ 我喜歡浪漫愛情片，最好就是很甜蜜的故事。我也喜歡皆大歡喜的結局，因為現實生活中很難真的有童話故事般的愛情。我覺得生活既然都那麼苦悶了，電影劇情就不應該太寫實，不然看了心情更糟。

 Instructions

- 不能只是閱讀每個人物如何回答唷！這是口說測驗，所以一定要開口說。
- 現在請跟著 CD 覆誦，同步練習「說」跟「聽」，第一次請跟著 CD 以相同語速覆誦，第二次和第三次可以逐步拉長到 CD 唸完第一句、第二句後再開始覆誦，能神奇地提升你的聽力專注力喔！

Cameron ▶ I am a big fan of special effects and science fiction; I cannot resist the Si-Fi movies, such as "Starwars" and "Avatar." I think watching movies is a way to escape from reality, I always try to imagine I am one of the characters while I am watching the movie.

卡麥倫 ▶ 我超愛看有特效的故事，像「星際大戰」或是「阿凡達」那種科幻片我一定會去看。我覺得看電影就是要有想像空間，我總是一邊看一邊幻想我是電影裡的主題人物。

 Instructions

· 不能只是閱讀每個人物如何回答唷！這是口說測驗，所以一定要開口說。

· 現在請跟著 CD 覆誦，同步練習「說」跟「聽」，第一次請跟著 CD 以相同語速覆誦，第二次和第三次可以逐步拉長到 CD 唸完第一句、第二句後再開始覆誦，能神奇地提升你的聽力專注力喔！

247

主題概述

　　在台灣最普遍的交通工具應該就是機車（scooter），有轎車的人口也不佔少數，以車款（make and model）來區別可以分為房車（sedan）、掀背車（hatchback）、休旅車（station wagon）、小貨車（ute）、多功能休旅車（SUV）。

　　若是以大眾交通工具（public transportation）來說的話，除了公車之外，還有捷運（MRT/subway）、火車（train）、輕軌列車（light rail）、渡輪（ferry）和九人或十二人座的小巴（mini van）。也有頂級的交通工具，例如私人飛機（private jet）、直升機（helicopter）、私人遊艇（privateyacht）等等。現在環保（environmental friendly）意識抬頭，腳踏車（push bike）也重新受到重視。

Do you own a vehicle?
你有沒有自己的交通工具? MP3 058

Josh ▶ Yes, I do. I have a scooter, and in southern Taiwan that is all you need. There is not a lot of traffic in Heng Chuan, and unless you are going out of the town; otherwise, you don't really need a car. Scooters are perfect because they have very good fuel economy, and you don't need to worry about parking.

喬許 ▶ 有，我有。我有一台機車。在南台灣機車就很夠用了。在恆春也沒有車潮，除非你要到別的縣市去，不然你也不需要開車。機車就最適合了，又省油又不用擔心停車的問題。

 Instructions

· 不能只是閱讀每個人物如何回答唷！這是口說測驗，所以一定要開口說。

· 現在請跟著 CD 覆誦，同步練習「說」跟「聽」，第一次請跟著 CD 以相同語速覆誦，第二次和第三次可以逐步拉長到 CD 唸完第一句、第二句後再開始覆誦，能神奇地提升你的聽力專注力喔！

Abby ▶ Well, I don't own a car or a scooter, but I do have a push bike for my exercise routine on the weekends. Personally, I think there is no need to own a vehicle when you live in a city like Taipei. Owning a vehicle is more a hassle than a convenience when parking costs more than food!

艾比 ▶ 嗯，我沒有房車也沒有機車，可是我有一台腳踏車，是我用來周末假日健身用的。以我個人來說，我覺得我並不需要有車，尤其是住在像台北市這種地方。有車其實弊多於利，停車費比便當的錢都還貴呢!

 Instructions

· 不能只是閱讀每個人物如何回答唷！這是口說測驗，所以一定要開口說。

· 現在請跟著 CD 覆誦，同步練習「說」跟「聽」，第一次請跟著 CD 以相同語速覆誦，第二次和第三次可以逐步拉長到 CD 唸完第一句、第二句後再開始覆誦，能神奇地提升你的聽力專注力喔！

Cameron ▶ Yeah, I've got a small car. It is a 2014 Mitsubishi Coltplus. I drive to work everyday, and all I need is a small car which is good on fuel. I bought it secondhand from a car yard, but it comes with 6 months warranty. I bought it a year ago, and it hasn't caused any problems.

卡麥倫 ▶ 有的，我有一台小車。是 2014 年的三菱 Colt plus 車款。我每天都需要開車上班，所以省油的小車最適合我。我是在二手車場買的，還有含六個月的保固。我買了一年了，到現在都沒什麼問題。

 Instructions

- 不能只是閱讀每個人物如何回答唷！這是口說測驗，所以一定要開口說。

- 現在請跟著 CD 覆誦，同步練習「說」跟「聽」，第一次請跟著 CD 以相同語速覆誦，第二次和第三次可以逐步拉長到 CD 唸完第一句、第二句後再開始覆誦，能神奇地提升你的聽力專注力喔！

主題概述

　　歌曲除了情歌之外還有鄉村音樂（Country music）、重金屬（Heavy Metal）、沙發音樂（Lounge music）、拉丁情歌（Latino love songs）、流行歌（Pop music）、非主流音樂（Alternative）、饒舌樂（Rap）、個人的喜好不同（Each to their own）。

　　以情歌來説，旋律（Melody）與歌詞（Lyric）常常很令人感動（Moving）、有時充滿了祝福（Blessing），有時是分手（Breakup）時離別（Separation）後又重聚（Reunited）。或是有第三者（Seeing someone else），被欺騙（Deceiving）後無奈（Nothing I can do）的心情，或是心碎了（Heartbroken），對對方充滿恨意（Hatred）等等。

Do you like to listen to love songs?

你喜歡聽情歌嗎？ MP3 059

Josh ▶ Love songs are not my cup of tea. I find most of the love songs are just corny and predictable. Either you like that girl but the girl doesn't love you back, or you are happily in love with someone. I am not ready to settle down with anyone just yet I guess that's why I can't really relate to it.

喬許 ▶ 情歌呢，真的不是我的菜。我覺得大部分的情歌都很老套又一成不變，不是你愛那個女孩而那個女孩不愛你，就是目前戀愛 ING。我目前還不想定下來，可能是這樣我對情歌真的沒什麼感覺。

Instructions

- 不能只是閱讀每個人物如何回答唷！這是口說測驗，所以一定要開口說。

- 現在請跟著 CD 覆誦，同步練習「說」跟「聽」，第一次請跟著 CD 以相同語速覆誦，第二次和第三次可以逐步拉長到 CD 唸完第一句、第二句後再開始覆誦，能神奇地提升你的聽力專注力喔！

Abby ▶ I love the love songs because I always imagine I will meet my Mr. Right one day and live happily ever after just like what the lyrics say. Obviously, my Mr. Right is still waiting to be found, but listening to love songs keeps me positive about finding true love one day.

艾比 ▶ 我很喜歡聽情歌，因為我總是幻想著有一天我會遇到我的真命天子，過得幸福美滿，就像歌詞裡寫的一樣。雖然我的真命天子目前還沒出現，可是聽著情歌會讓我對未來充滿希望，我相信我總有一天會找到他的！

 Instructions

· 不能只是閱讀每個人物如何回答唷！這是口說測驗，所以一定要開口說。

· 現在請跟著 CD 覆誦，同步練習「說」跟「聽」，第一次請跟著 CD 以相同語速覆誦，第二次和第三次可以逐步拉長到 CD 唸完第一句、第二句後再開始覆誦，能神奇地提升你的聽力專注力喔！

Cameron ▶ I don't mind love songs because some of them really touch my heart especially when my ex-girlfriend decided to walk out on me a couple of years ago. I was very upset because we were almost engaged. Sad love songs did save me from misery.

卡麥倫 ▶ 我不介意聽情歌，因為有些歌我覺得寫得很好，很有共鳴。尤其是幾年前我剛跟我前女友分手的時候，我很低潮，因為我們差一點就訂婚了。聽傷心的情歌來抒發心情，我也慢慢走出來了。

 Instructions

· 不能只是閱讀每個人物如何回答唷！這是口說測驗，所以一定要開口說。

· 現在請跟著 CD 覆誦，同步練習「說」跟「聽」，第一次請跟著 CD 以相同語速覆誦，第二次和第三次可以逐步拉長到 CD 唸完第一句、第二句後再開始覆誦，能神奇地提升你的聽力專注力喔！

主題概述

　　以輸出的方式照片可以分為紙本照片（hardcopy）、相簿（album）、電子版（soft copy）、無框畫（canvas）等等，色調上可以做調整，像 黑白（black and white）、彩色（colored）、復古（retro）色調。照片的主題可以是人物寫真（portrait）、風景（scenery）、夜景（night view）、戶外全景（landscape）、網拍商品（merchandise）。相框（photo frame）及護貝（lamination）逐漸地失去重要性，因為越來越多人選擇用電腦來儲存照片，因為修圖（airbrush）很方便。

　　而底片（negatives）這種東西也快要被數位單眼相機（digital SLR）取代了。有些人會特別將照片剪貼成冊做成具有紀念性的剪貼簿（scrapbooking）。

Do you prefer to take photos of others or being in the photo?

你比較喜歡照相還是幫人拍照? MP3 060

Josh ▶ Well, I spend a lot of time and effort making sure I look the way I am, of course I would like to show off my looks as much as I can. I update my Facebook profile photo everyday with my daily selfie! Some people might think I love myself a bit too much, but I love being in photos.

喬許 ▶ 嗯,我花了很多時間與精力來維持我的外表,我當然想曝光率高一點啊!我每天都會上傳自拍照更新臉書的大頭照,有些人覺得我實在太自戀了,可是我真的很喜歡看到我自己的照片。

 Instructions

· 不能只是閱讀每個人物如何回答唷!這是口說測驗,所以一定要開口說。

· 現在請跟著 CD 覆誦,同步練習「說」跟「聽」,第一次請跟著 CD 以相同語速覆誦,第二次和第三次可以逐步拉長到 CD 唸完第一句、第二句後再開始覆誦,能神奇地提升你的聽力專注力喔!

Abby ▶ Taking photos to me is like creating memories for different occasions. I cherish every moment with my friends and family, and I like to be in the photos with them. I like to print the photos out and look at them from time to time. People always remember who is in the photo, but no one remembers who took the photo!

艾比 ▶ 我覺得照片是用來留下回憶用的，我很珍惜跟家人朋友在一起的時刻，所以我喜歡跟他們一起出現在照片中。我會把照片都洗出來，偶爾會拿出來翻閱。大家都只會記得照片中的人，不會有人記得照片是誰照的！

 Instructions

- 不能只是閱讀每個人物如何回答唷！這是口說測驗，所以一定要開口說。
- 現在請跟著 CD 覆誦，同步練習「說」跟「聽」，第一次請跟著 CD 以相同語速覆誦，第二次和第三次可以逐步拉長到 CD 唸完第一句、第二句後再開始覆誦，能神奇地提升你的聽力專注力喔！

Cameron ▶ I don't like being in the photos because I think I am not photogenic at all. To be honest, I think I look terrible in most of my photos although my mother says I look good. I much prefer being the photographer instead. I think taking photos of nice plates of food is much more fun than taking photos of myself.

卡麥倫 ▶ 我不喜歡出現在照片中，因為我很不上相。雖然我媽都說照片很好看，可是說真的我覺得我每張照片都很醜，所以我情願當幕後的攝影師，我覺得拍食物都比拍我自己來得有趣。

 Instructions

- 不能只是閱讀每個人物如何回答唷！這是口說測驗，所以一定要開口說。

- 現在請跟著 CD 覆誦，同步練習「說」跟「聽」，第一次請跟著 CD 以相同語速覆誦，第二次和第三次可以逐步拉長到 CD 唸完第一句、第二句後再開始覆誦，能神奇地提升你的聽力專注力喔！

✏️ **主題概述**

　　打開電視就可以發現電視節目的類型琳瑯滿目，在國外很常見的是實境秀（reality TV）在台灣最受歡的可能就是綜藝節目（variety shows）了，或是以選秀為主的歌唱比賽（singingcompetition）、舞蹈比賽（dancing competition）。與時事相關的新聞節目（News channel）、政論節目（political commentary shows）、談話型節目（talk shows）、紀錄片（documentary）也很受歡迎。

　　另外還有 MTV 台、運動比賽轉播（live sports channel）、美食節目（food shows）、烹調節目（cooking shows）、卡通（cartoons）兒童節目（kids shows）、電視購物（shopping channels）、連續劇（soaps）、布袋戲（Taiwanese puppet show）、歌仔戲（Taiwanese opera）、電影台（Movie channel）、電視影集（TV series）等等。

What is your favorite TV program?

你最喜歡看什麼電視節目？ 🎧 MP3 061

Josh ▶ I love to watch American TV series. My favorite show is "Friends". It is not the latest series, but it is a classic all-time favorite. It is all about love triangles and friendships among 6 friends. The storyline is funny and easy to follow. The best thing is, I picked up a lot of slang from watching the series.

喬許 ▶ 我很愛看美國的電視影集，我最喜歡的是「六人行」。這不是最新的，但卻是最經典，最受人喜歡的一套影集。內容是有關這六個好友之間的感情糾結還有誠摯的友誼。劇情很好笑，也很容易看懂。最棒的是看了這個影集我還學到很多英文的俗語。

 Instructions

· 不能只是閱讀每個人物如何回答唷！這是口說測驗，所以一定要開口說。

· 現在請跟著 CD 覆誦，同步練習「說」跟「聽」，第一次請跟著 CD 以相同語速覆誦，第二次和第三次可以逐步拉長到 CD 唸完第一句、第二句後再開始覆誦，能神奇地提升你的聽力專注力喔！

261

Abby ▶ My favorite program on TV is actually the shopping channel. I know they are just sales presentations, but I like to know what is the in thing at the moment. If I saw something I like, I would order the product because they offer 10 days free trial and guarantee your money back. There is no risk of wasting money, other than the hassle of arranging for return collection.

艾比 ▶ 我最喜歡的電視節目其實是購物頻道，我知道那不過就是賣東西而已，可是看一下現在在流行什麼也好。如果我看到我喜歡的東西，我也是會買，因為它有十天鑑賞期，還保證退款，我覺得沒什麼浪費錢的風險，只是要安排退貨比較麻煩而已。

 Instructions

- 不能只是閱讀每個人物如何回答唷！這是口説測驗，所以一定要開口説。
- 現在請跟著 CD 覆誦，同步練習「説」跟「聽」，第一次請跟著 CD 以相同語速覆誦，第二次和第三次可以逐步拉長到 CD 唸完第一句、第二句後再開始覆誦，能神奇地提升你的聽力專注力喔！

Cameron ▶ I like to watch the News channel because I think the Taiwanese News channel is quite entertaining. The news coverage not only includes serious stuff like suicide bombing, but also funny stories like where would be the best spot for Pokemon Go! I watch news everyday, so I won't run out of conversation topics with my clients.

卡麥倫 ▶ 我喜歡看新聞台因為我覺得台灣的新聞台很有娛樂性。新聞裡不只有像人肉炸彈這種嚴肅的新聞事件，還會告訴你寶可夢要去哪裡抓比較好。我每天都會看新聞，這樣我才有話題可以跟客戶聊天。

 Instructions

· 不能只是閱讀每個人物如何回答唷！這是口說測驗，所以一定要開口說。

· 現在請跟著 CD 覆誦，同步練習「說」跟「聽」，第一次請跟著 CD 以相同語速覆誦，第二次和第三次可以逐步拉長到 CD 唸完第一句、第二句後再開始覆誦，能神奇地提升你的聽力專注力喔！

1 道地高分句

2 一問三答

3 話題卡回答

4 即席應答

Fashion/Clothing
時尚 / 服飾

主題概述

　　以男裝的衣服款式來說有西裝外套（jacket）、襯衫（shirt）、西裝褲（paints）、短褲（shorts）、涼鞋（sandal）、球鞋（sneakers）、拖鞋（flip flop）等等。比較特別的女裝則有細肩帶上衣（singlet）、無袖上衣（tan top）、無肩帶上衣（tube top）等等。

　　衣服的剪裁有: 合身款（loose fit）、貼身款（slim fit）。衣服的布料（material）也有很多選擇，例如棉布（cotton）、羊毛（wool）、雪紡紗（chiffon）、燈心絨（corduroy）。提到衣著就不能忘了飾品，常見的配件有手環（bracelet）、項鍊（necklace）。

What type of clothes do you normally wear?
你平常的穿著打扮是怎樣？ MP3 062

Josh ▶ I pretty much wear T-shirt and board shorts everyday because I don't need to worry about dressing up for work. The weather in Heng Chuan is always hot and humid, even the winter is really mild. All you need is a long sleeve jacket. I do have a wind breaker for my scooter ride. I don't think I own a lot of thick winter clothing.

喬許 ▶ 我幾乎每天都是 T 恤加海灘褲，因為我不需要去上班要穿什麼。而且恆春的天氣又濕又熱，就算冬天也不是太冷，大概加件長袖夾克就可以。要騎機車的時候我會穿風衣，我其實沒什麼冬天的衣服。

 Instructions

- 不能只是閱讀每個人物如何回答唷！這是口說測驗，所以一定要開口說。
- 現在請跟著 CD 覆誦，同步練習「說」跟「聽」，第一次請跟著 CD 以相同語速覆誦，第二次和第三次可以逐步拉長到 CD 唸完第一句、第二句後再開始覆誦，能神奇地提升你的聽力專注力喔！

Abby ▶ I normally wear a dress to work on week days, but on the weekends I like to wear something more casual, maybe shorts and a singlet. If the weather is a bit windy then, I will put on jeans and a slim fit jacket. I like wearing high heels because it just looks sexy.

艾比 ▶ 如果是要上班的時候我通常是穿洋裝，可是週末的話我就穿得隨便一點，大概是細肩帶上衣加熱褲。如果風有點大的話，我就換牛仔長褲還有合身的夾克。我還喜歡配高跟鞋因為我覺得看起來很性感。

 Instructions

- 不能只是閱讀每個人物如何回答唷！這是口説測驗，所以一定要開口説。
- 現在請跟著 CD 覆誦，同步練習「説」跟「聽」，第一次請跟著 CD 以相同語速覆誦，第二次和第三次可以逐步拉長到 CD 唸完第一句、第二句後再開始覆誦，能神奇地提升你的聽力專注力喔！

266

Cameron ▶ Business shirt with workpants is my standard outfit because I need to look professional for work. If I need to go and visit clients, then I might put on a tie. I don't often wear a jacket because it is too warm in Taiwan. I get really sweaty if I wear one.

卡麥倫 ▶ 我的標準穿著就是襯衫加西裝褲，因為上班的關係，需要穿得正式一點。如果我還需要去見客戶的話，那我會再加條領帶。我通常不會穿西裝外套，因為台灣的天氣實在太熱了，我如果穿的話會汗流浹背。

 Instructions

· 不能只是閱讀每個人物如何回答唷！這是口說測驗，所以一定要開口說。

· 現在請跟著 CD 覆誦，同步練習「說」跟「聽」，第一次請跟著 CD 以相同語速覆誦，第二次和第三次可以逐步拉長到 CD 唸完第一句、第二句後再開始覆誦，能神奇地提升你的聽力專注力喔！

主題概述

　　在台灣早餐店常見早餐種類有蛋餅（omelette pancake）、煎餃/鍋貼（pot sticker）、蒸餃（steam dumplings）、蘿蔔糕（radish cake）、捲餅（wraps）等等。中式午餐晚餐的選擇如也不少，例如火鍋（hot pot/ steamboat）、乾麵（dry noodles）、餛飩湯（wonton soup）、便當（bento box），米糕（sticky rice）、碗粿（rice cake）。喜歡西餐的還有義大利麵（pasta）、千層麵（lasagne）、牛排（steak）、羊排（lamp chops）、豬排（pork chops）等等。

　　不管喜歡吃什麼，衛生（hygienic）才是最重要的，要是吃了肚子不舒服（It doesn't agree with me）或是食物中毒（food poisoning）、拉肚子（diarrhea）的話，就算再美味下次也不會再光臨。

What is your favorite food?
你最喜歡吃什麼東西? MP3 063

Josh ▶ I love to go to this hawkers' food stall right by Heng Chuan bus terminal because they got the best oyster omelette. They get the freshly harvested oysters from Tong Kang everyday, and they have a secret recipe for their omelette sauce. I go there at least once a week.

喬許 ▶ 我最喜歡恆春車站旁邊的小吃的蚵仔煎,他們的蚵仔煎最棒了!他們每天都從東港運來現撈的鮮蚵,再加上他們的特殊醬料,我至少一個星期要去報到一次。

 Instructions

· 不能只是閱讀每個人物如何回答唷!這是口說測驗,所以一定要開口說。

· 現在請跟著 CD 覆誦,同步練習「說」跟「聽」,第一次請跟著 CD 以相同語速覆誦,第二次和第三次可以逐步拉長到 CD 唸完第一句、第二句後再開始覆誦,能神奇地提升你的聽力專注力喔!

269

Abby ▶ I actually really like fried chicken and chips. I know they are not the healthiest choices for food but they are just so tasty. Most of the time my diet is pretty healthy. I eat plenty of fresh fruit and vegetables but when I feel like a midnight snack, that is the first thing that comes to mind.

艾比 ▶ 我其實很喜歡吃炸雞跟薯條，我知道這很不健康可是他們真的很美味。我大部分都吃得很健康，我吃很多新鮮蔬菜跟水果。可是如果有半夜嘴巴有點饞的時候，我第一個想吃的就是炸雞跟薯條。

 Instructions

· 不能只是閱讀每個人物如何回答唷！這是口說測驗，所以一定要開口說。

· 現在請跟著 CD 覆誦，同步練習「說」跟「聽」，第一次請跟著 CD 以相同語速覆誦，第二次和第三次可以逐步拉長到 CD 唸完第一句、第二句後再開始覆誦，能神奇地提升你的聽力專注力喔！

Cameron ▶ My favorite food is dumplings. I like them whether they are fried, steamed, or boiled. My favorite flavor is the pork and chive one. It goes really well with a bit of soy sauce and vinegar dipping sauce. Some people like to add fresh ginger to the sauce, but I just find it too strong.

卡麥倫 ▶ 我最喜歡吃餃類了，不管是煎餃、蒸餃還是水餃我都喜歡。我最愛的口味是豬肉韭菜，這跟油醋醬油沾醬很搭。有些人喜歡加一點新鮮的薑絲，可是我覺得這樣味道太濃了。

 Instructions

· 不能只是閱讀每個人物如何回答唷！這是口說測驗，所以一定要開口說。

· 現在請跟著 CD 覆誦，同步練習「說」跟「聽」，第一次請跟著 CD 以相同語速覆誦，第二次和第三次可以逐步拉長到 CD 唸完第一句、第二句後再開始覆誦，能神奇地提升你的聽力專注力喔！

主題概述

　　小時候玩遊戲的機會最多，常見的遊戲有拔河（tug-ofwar）、老師說（simon says）跳房子（hopscotch）、捉迷藏（hide and seek）、抓鬼（tag）、猜拳（paper, scissors,stone）、跳繩（jump rope）、紅綠燈（red light, green light）、打彈珠（marbles）等等。

　　長大玩遊戲的機會可能是學校聯誼的破冰遊戲（ice breaking games）或是公司訓練的團隊建立遊戲（team bonding games）、夜店遊戲真心話大冒險（truth and dare）等等。既然是遊戲就有輸贏，比分數（score）高低，或是平手（it is a tight），輸的一方要接受處罰（punishment）。

Q 36

What was your favorite game when you were little?

你小時候最喜歡的遊戲是什麼? 🎧 MP3 064

Josh ▶ My favorite game was hide and seek. I used to play it with all the kids from the neighborhood in front of the temple. I was pretty good at the game. I loved to hide right behind the big banyan tree, and the funny thing is that no one seems to know to look there!

喬許 ▶ 我以前最喜歡玩躲貓貓了，我常常跟鄰居的小孩們在廟口玩。我還蠻厲害的，我最喜歡躲在大榕樹的後面，很奇怪就沒人會去那裏找。

 Instructions

· 不能只是閱讀每個人物如何回答唷！這是口說測驗，所以一定要開口說。

· 現在請跟著 CD 覆誦，同步練習「說」跟「聽」，第一次請跟著 CD 以相同語速覆誦，第二次和第三次可以逐步拉長到 CD 唸完第一句、第二句後再開始覆誦，能神奇地提升你的聽力專注力喔！

Abby ▶ When I was little, I loved to play tea parties with my sister, we would bring out all the bears and dollies and pretend they were guests in our castle. We would dress them up as princesses and feed them imaginary cake or biscuits. It sounds silly now, but I loved it when I was a kid.

艾比 ▶ 我小時候最喜歡跟我妹妹玩家家酒，我們還會把小熊跟娃娃都拿出來把他們當成來訪我們城堡的客人，我們還會幫他們穿衣服，扮成公主，再請他們吃假裝的蛋糕還有餅乾。現在說起來好像很蠢，可是我小時候真的超愛的！

 Instructions

- 不能只是閱讀每個人物如何回答唷！這是口說測驗，所以一定要開口說。
- 現在請跟著 CD 覆誦，同步練習「說」跟「聽」，第一次請跟著 CD 以相同語速覆誦，第二次和第三次可以逐步拉長到 CD 唸完第一句、第二句後再開始覆誦，能神奇地提升你的聽力專注力喔！

Cameron ▶ I always carried marbles with me when I was little. I was obsessed about playing marbles, I took them everywhere with me. I still remember playing marbles with my classmates during recess at school everyday. I had a whole collection of them, big ones and little ones, you name it.

卡麥倫 ▶ 我小時候隨身都會帶著彈珠，我真的很迷打彈珠這回事，無論到哪裡都堅持要帶著。我還記得每天只要下課鐘聲響，我就會跟同學去玩彈珠。我蒐集了很多彈珠，有大的有小的，只要你說的出來我幾乎都有。

 Instructions

· 不能只是閱讀每個人物如何回答唷！這是口說測驗，所以一定要開口說。

· 現在請跟著 CD 覆誦，同步練習「說」跟「聽」，第一次請跟著 CD 以相同語速覆誦，第二次和第三次可以逐步拉長到 CD 唸完第一句、第二句後再開始覆誦，能神奇地提升你的聽力專注力喔！

這個 part 是雅思口說的第二部分，需要針對一個話題做兩分鐘左右的論述，除了書中的拓展話題和提供的參考答案外，也請構思出自己遇到相同問題會想要表達的答案，因為背誦答案很容易跟其他人重複且會因為緊張而忘詞。這個部分其實是拿分關鍵，所以一定要認真準備且把官方題目出現的雅思題目都練習過再應考。

Part

3

話題卡回答

✏️ 話題拓展

- ⊙ 新聞一：停車留言 Message on the windscreen
- ⊙ 新聞二：為了救小孩殺了大猩猩 Kill the gorilla to save the kid
- ⊙ 新聞三：日本的猴子愛泡溫泉 Hot spring monkeys
- ⊙ 新聞四：小孩不見了 Missing kid
- ⊙ 新聞五：載大熊回家 The giant Teddy
- ⊙ 新聞六：新加坡的再生水 Newater
- ⊙ 新聞七：川普選總統 Trump runs for president
- ⊙ 新聞八：世界末日的預言 Armageddon

Describe a story you heard or read about in the news that made an impression.
請描述一段讓你印象深刻的新聞故事

印度能吃的餐具 Edible cutlery 🎧 MP3 065

I read this story in the newspaper once. This Indian inventor created an edible spoon which is made of a combination of millet, rice, and wheat. It looks just like a normal wooden spoon, but it is totally biodegradable.

我曾經在報紙上讀到，有一個印度的發明家，他用小米、白米還有麥子混和做出了可以吃的湯匙。那個湯匙看起來跟一般的木湯匙沒兩樣，可是卻是可以腐化分解的。

He first got this idea from knowing how much plastic cutlery is wasted each year and it just keeps piling up. Plastic does not degrade in a natural environment, plus, it is not as safe as we thought because plastic is a chemical complex. Toxic substances will be released into food when the conditions are right, such as high temperatures or contact with oil.Therefore, an edible one would be just the solution.

他靈感的來源是發現原來一年裡面被丟棄的塑膠餐具這麼的多，而且數量每一年不停地增加。塑膠在自然環境裡面不會

腐化分解而且塑膠也不是我們想像中的那麼安全，因為那是種化學合成物，毒素會藉由高溫或是跟油質接觸時而溶解到食物裡。所以發明可以吃的湯匙就是最好的解決辦法了。

His edible spoons even come in different flavors to compliment different dishes that you can choose from: plain, sweet or savory. I think it is really clever! However, his business did not take off rapidly. Although he has the perfect recipe and idea to make the edible cutlery, the cost of the making it is so much higher than making plastic cutlery. India is known as a poor country; the majority of the population cannot afford edible cutlery.

他的湯匙還有分不同口味來搭配不同的食物，有原味、甜的或是鹹的，我覺得實在很酷！可是他的生意並沒有大展鴻圖，雖然他有很棒的配方和想法來做出可以吃的餐具，可是他卻沒有辦法把這個餐具做的跟塑膠餐具一樣便宜。在大家印象裡，印度是一個蠻窮苦的國家，大部分的人口負擔不起可以吃的餐具。

He would have to market his environmental friendly product to a different consumer group. I think he should promote the idea in the western countries where there is more environmental awareness. It might make his business more sustainable.

　　他必須要另外找客戶群。我覺得他應該到西方國家去推廣，他們也比較有環保意識。這樣他生意才可能可以持續下去。

 Instructions

- 不能只是閱讀每個人物如何回答唷！這是口說測驗，所以一定要開口說。
- 現在請跟著 CD 覆誦，同步練習「說」跟「聽」，第一次請跟著 CD 以相同語速覆誦，第二次和第三次可以逐步拉長到 CD 唸完第一句、第二句後再開始覆誦，能神奇地提升你的聽力專注力喔！

話題拓展

- 湖泊一：嘉明湖 Chia-Ming Lake
- 湖泊二：曾文水庫 Tseng-Wen Reservoir
- 湖泊三：日月潭 Sun-Moon Lake
- 湖泊四：大學池 University lake
- 湖泊/河川五：碧潭 Bitan scenic area
- 湖泊/河川六：蓮池潭 Lotus Lake
- 湖泊/河川七：大豹溪 Dabao River
- 湖泊/河川八：愛河 Love River

Describe a lake or river that you have visited or wish to visit.

請描述一個你曾去過或是想去的湖泊或河川

水漾森林 Mystery swampy forest 🎧 MP3 066

There is this secret location in Chai-Yi County in Ali Mountain that not many people know about. There is this beautiful dammed lake that was caused by the 921 earthquake. What's special about this lake is, the trees were trapped in the flood slowly losing their leaves and dying eventually, and all the dead tree trucks stick out of the lakes like the telephone poles. It looks amazing with the blue sky and the reflection of the lake. People call this place "Mystery swampy forest."

在 921 大地震後，嘉義縣阿里山鄉出現了一個秘境，一座因為地震阻斷溪流而產生的堰塞湖，這個湖特別的地方是，湖裡原有的樹因為泡在水裡而死亡，只留下一根根像電線桿的樹幹從水中竄出，配合藍天及湖水的倒影，大家稱這個地方為水漾森林。

Around 10 years while the club members of mountain hiking were planning a trip to the "Mystery swampy forest." I was very tempted, but unfortunately it was only open to club members, so I missed out on the opportunity.

大概是十年前我還在念大學的時候，登山社的同學計畫要到水漾森林去。我很有興趣可是因為只有開放給社員，所以我就錯過了。

I was told you have to be fit to be able to make it because it would take 5-6 hours on foot in the winding mountain trail and occasionally there are vertical climbs. I am quite a small person, and I doubt if I would be able to carry all the gear with me and walk such a long way. I know the view would probably be worth it, but the moment I think I have to walk another 5-6 hours to get back. The reality starts to sink in.

有人告訴我要去水漾森林需要很有體力，因為大概要走 5-6 小時的山路，還有垂直的攀爬。我不算高大，我懷疑我真的有辦法背那麼重的行囊走那麼遠嗎？ 我知道美景應該很值得看，可是一想到回程又是 5-6 個小時，我就怕了。

I watched a documentary about it not long ago, and it was saying the water level there is dropping dramatically. I do wish I could visit the lake before it disappears completely.

　　偶而不久前我看了一段紀錄片，説水漾森林的水位急速減少，我希望在它完全消失之前有機會去看。

 ## Instructions

- 不能只是閱讀每個人物如何回答唷！這是口説測驗，所以一定要開口説。
- 現在請跟著 CD 覆誦，同步練習「説」跟「聽」，第一次請跟著 CD 以相同語速覆誦，第二次和第三次可以逐步拉長到 CD 唸完第一句、第二句後再開始覆誦，能神奇地提升你的聽力專注力喔！

電器：智慧型手機

話題拓展

- 電器一：電視 Television
- 電器二：洗衣機 Washing machine
- 電器三：電鍋 Rice cooker
- 電器四：冰箱 Refrigerator
- 電器五：吹風機 Hair dryer
- 電器六：吸塵器 Vacuum
- 電器七：電腦 computer
- 電器八：行動電源 Power bank

Please describe a piece of electronic equipment which made your life easier.
請描述一樣讓你生活更便利的電器

智慧型手機 Smartphone

Where shall I start with my smartphone? A smartphone is everything in one！It is a phone, a camera, a calculator, a computer and so much more！I was not a smartphone user until pretty late. I was a bit resentful about learning new technology.

　　我該從何說起呢？智慧型手機簡直是集所有優點於一身，它是手機，也是相機，計算機還是台電腦呢！還有其他數不清的功能。我不是一開始就是個智慧型手機的支持者，剛開始我也很排斥新科技。

Before I got my first smartphone, I didn't understand why people get addicted to their phones, but now I can't live without my phone. I have to check my emails when I am out and about for work.I had to bring my laptop with me everywhere I went before, but all I need now is my smartphone. If I want to scan some information to share with my coworker, all I have to do is take a photo with my smartphone, then send it as an attachment in my email. This is definitely revolutionary！

在我拿到第一支智慧型手機之前，我不懂為什麼有人會對手機上癮，可是我現在真的不能沒有我的手機。我在外面出差時需要不斷地察看電子郵件，以前我到哪裡都一定要帶我的筆記型電腦，現在我只需要我的手機，就算我需要掃描文件給我的同事看，我也只要拿手機照張相，然後用郵件附件傳出去。這真是太劃時代了！

My favorite function is skype. I can check on my boyfriend all the time. If I wasn't sure whether he is telling me the truth, I will get him to put skype on, so I can see where he is. Who would have thought this is what I use Skype for !

我最喜歡的功能其實是 Skype 視訊，我隨時隨地都可以查我男朋友在哪裡。如果我覺得他沒有講實話，我就叫他開視訊，讓我看看他在哪裡。

But the thing is, convenience does not come cheap. I spent about 1000 NTD a month in phone bills; otherwise, I would not have enough data to do all I want to do. Luckily, I am not obsessed about having to have the latest model; otherwise, it would cost more !

　　沒有人想到視訊可以這樣用吧！可是科技的方便性真的不便宜，我一個月大概要花台幣一千元來繳電話費，不然我的網路容量不夠從事我所想做的事。還好我是不堅持一定要最新款的手機，不然開銷會更大！

 ## Instructions

- 不能只是閱讀每個人物如何回答唷！這是口說測驗，所以一定要開口說。
- 現在請跟著 CD 覆誦，同步練習「說」跟「聽」，第一次請跟著 CD 以相同語速覆誦，第二次和第三次可以逐步拉長到 CD 唸完第一句、第二句後再開始覆誦，能神奇地提升你的聽力專注力喔！

Unit 04　重要的決定：唸哪個科系

話題拓展

- 決定一：升學或就業 Work or study
- 決定二：出國留學 Study aboard
- 決定三：買房子 Buying a house
- 決定四：投資理財 Investment
- 決定五：分手 The break up
- 決定六：結婚 Marriage
- 決定七：辭職 Resignation
- 決定八：北上找工作 Heading north

Please describe an important decision in your life.
請描述一個你人生中重要的決定

念哪個科系 Choosing a major　🎧 MP3 068

I had a hard time making the decision about the major I'm going to take, knowing it would have a major impact on my career life in the future.

選科系的時候我實在很難下決定，因為我知道這會影響我未來工作的方向。

I always liked dancing and I always dreamed of being a professional dancer one day I have been taking dance classes since I was little, and I was pretty talented, too. But when I started to look at the reality, I was not confident that I could make a living as a dancer. I know I am a good dancer and with more training, I would be an outstanding one！

我一直都很喜歡跳舞，也想像有一天可以當個專業舞者，我從小就學舞，而且也蠻有天份的。可是當我想到實際面的時候，我實在沒把握當舞者可以填飽肚子。我知道我跳得很好，如果透過適當的訓練我會變得更傑出。

However, I think the reality of being a part of the entertainment business is pretty cruel. I am not the tallest or the finest looking dancer on the dance floor. I guess it kind of limited my opportunities. It was a painful decision, but I decided to do commerce instead. I think commerce fits in this society better, and I also believe the salary of business related position would be able to support the lifestyle I want. I gave in to reality !

可是娛樂業的現實面是很殘忍的，放眼看過去我也不是最高挑最漂亮的舞者，我看我還是算了。下這個決定實在很痛苦，可是我決定要念商科。因為商科的性質比較容易被這個社會接受。而且我也相信從商的薪水可以達到我想要的生活型態。我向現實屈服了。

I don't mind being in the accounting firm, and I don't regret what I chose. But somehow I always wonder, if I ever did take up dancing, where would I be today ? Maybe I would be performing in Broadway or being part of a dancing company touring the world ! You just never know !

我不介意現在在會計公司的職務，我也不後悔我的選擇，可是我偶而會幻想如果我當初選擇舞蹈系的話，現在會在哪

裡？ 我可能會在百老匯表演，搞不好會跟知名舞團去世界巡迴
表演！ 真的很難說呢！

 Instructions

· 不能只是閱讀每個人物如何回答唷！這是口說測驗，所以一定
　要開口說。
· 現在請跟著 CD 覆誦，同步練習「說」跟「聽」，第一次請跟著
　CD 以相同語速覆誦，第二次和第三次可以逐步拉長到 CD 唸完
　第一句、第二句後再開始覆誦，能神奇地提升你的聽力專注力
　喔！

音樂：韓國流行音樂

話題拓展

- ⊙ 音樂一：交響樂 Symphony Orchestra
- ⊙ 音樂二：沙發音樂 Lounge music
- ⊙ 音樂三：雷鬼音樂 Reggae
- ⊙ 音樂四：爵士樂 Jazz
- ⊙ 音樂五：英文經典情歌 English classic love songs
- ⊙ 音樂六：國語流行歌曲 Chinese pop music
- ⊙ 音樂七：嘻哈舞曲 Hip Hop
- ⊙ 音樂八：拉丁情歌 Latino love songs

What music do you like to listen to ?
請描述你喜歡聽的音樂類型

韓國流行音樂 K Pop

MP3 069

My favourite music would be K Pop. I think they have the best boy bands and girl bands in the world！Their songs are really catchy. You don't have to know Korean to know how to sing along for a few sentences, like "Gangnam style" by Psy and "No body" by the Wonder girls.

我最喜歡的音樂就是韓國流行音樂，我覺得他們的男子和女子樂團真是世界第一！他們的歌曲很容易琅琅上口，就算你不會韓文也可以跟著唱幾句，就像江南大叔的 Gangnamstyle 還有 Wonderg i r l s 唱的 Nobody。

I once watched this documentary about the inside of forming a Korean pop band. Not only do they want the band to be popular in Korea, their ultimate goal is to make Korean Pop music an international success.

我曾經看過一段有關韓國團體的秘辛，他們的目標不只是要在韓國成功，最終目標是要把韓國流行音樂推向世界。

To achieve that, the record companies have to make sure they have got the best cards in hand. Apparently, every single component is carefully thought out and executed, when it comes to a team member selection, training and most importantly, the song selection. How to make people who do not understand Korean to like Korean songs is one big challenge, if you pay attention to those popular Korean songs, you will notice they all have part of it in English. Apparently, hundreds of songs are discarded for every one song that is selected. This is how much effort they put in to make sure the song is right.

為了要達成這個目標，唱片公司必須要好好計畫，並確認每個步驟都做得正確。尤其是選擇團員，嚴格的訓練還有最重要的是歌曲的選擇。要如何讓不懂韓文的人唱韓國歌曲可是個大挑戰，如果你仔細聽，你會發現他們的歌裡面都一定會有一段英文。而且他們是從幾百首歌中挑出一首歌，這就是他們對歌曲選擇的用心。

I think K Pop is the whole package, the team members are expected to look a certain way too. So many fans are willing to go under the knife just to enhance their look to look more like their favourite pop star. I must say K pop does wonders to people !

　　我覺得 K Pop 是一種文化，所有的團員看起來都有種特定的樣子，讓很多歌迷更是不顧一切的去動刀，就為了讓自己看起來像喜歡的歌手。我只能說韓國天團還有讓人變美的神奇力量呢！

 Instructions

- 不能只是閱讀每個人物如何回答唷！這是口說測驗，所以一定要開口說。
- 現在請跟著 CD 覆誦，同步練習「說」跟「聽」，第一次請跟著 CD 以相同語速覆誦，第二次和第三次可以逐步拉長到 CD 唸完第一句、第二句後再開始覆誦，能神奇地提升你的聽力專注力喔！

話題拓展

- 國家一：英國 UK
- 國家二：法國 France
- 國家三：義大利 Italy
- 國家四：帛琉 Palau
- 國家五：日本 Japan
- 國家六：阿拉伯聯合大公國 United Arab Emirates (UAE)
- 國家七：祕魯 Peru
- 國家八：美國 United States of America (USA)

Please tell me a countryyou would like to visit, andwhy ?

請描述一個你想去的國家，還有為什麼想去？

澳洲 Australia

I would love to visit Australia, maybe move there for a bit to do working holidays. I was told if you tried hard enough, you could really save a lot of money within a year.

我會很想去澳洲，可以的話去當背包客一陣子也不錯。我聽說如果你努力一點的話，你一年之內就可以存不少錢。

I have been planning for it since I graduated from university. But I haven't quite worked up the courage to go over on my own yet. I would prefer to travel with a partner, so we can look out for each other, but so far I still haven't found someone who would like to go together.

我從大學畢業就開始有這個想法，可是我一直還沒有勇氣自己去。我會希望有同伴可以一起去，大家互相照顧，可是到現在我還沒找到志同道合的人。

Australia is a big country compared with Taiwan. Most

of its population and attractions are in the east coast. Some of the famous attractions are: Uluru, Sydney opera house, Gold Coast, and so on. And what I want to do the most is to take a diving tour in the world famous Great Barrier Reef.

跟台灣比起來的話，澳洲是個大國。大部分的人口和觀光勝地都在東岸，知名景點有:艾爾斯岩，雪梨歌劇院，黃金海岸等等。而我最想要做的事就是到大堡礁潛水，我聽了很多有關大堡礁的事，在那裡你可參加潛水一日遊。

I heard so much about it, apparently you can join this tour which takes you out diving for a day to a few famous spots and you might get to swim alongside this friendly fish called Big Willy. I am also very interested in all the native animals there, such as kangaroos, koalas, and wombats.

他們會帶你到幾個潛水的景點，如果運氣好的話還可能遇到一隻叫大威利的魚，他會游過來跟你玩。我也很想去看當地的動物，就像袋鼠、無尾熊，還有袋熊。

I was told it is likely to see kangaroos in the wild especially during dusk when they are out looking for food. That is just something you need to go to experience yourself. I am not sure whether my trip would eventually happen because you have to go before you turn 30, and the clock is ticking.

我聽說在郊外常常可以看到野生袋鼠，尤其是傍晚他們出來覓食的時候，我覺得這真的是要自己來體驗才會了解那種感覺。我不知道我到底會不會去，因為條件是你三十歲生日前要出發，我也快三十了。

 ## Instructions

· 不能只是閱讀每個人物如何回答唷！這是口說測驗，所以一定要開口說。

· 現在請跟著 CD 覆誦，同步練習「說」跟「聽」，第一次請跟著 CD 以相同語速覆誦，第二次和第三次可以逐步拉長到 CD 唸完第一句、第二句後再開始覆誦，能神奇地提升你的聽力專注力喔！

話題拓展

⊙ 廣告一：樂透彩券 Lottery
⊙ 廣告二：汽車廣告 Peugeot
⊙ 廣告三：蠻牛廣告 Taiwanese Red bull
⊙ 廣告四：報紙的贈品廣告 Newspaper
⊙ 廣告五：海尼根 Heineke
⊙ 廣告六：福斯汽車 Volkswagen
⊙ 廣告七：電話簿付費廣告 Yellow pages
⊙ 廣告八：貸款公司 Mortgage broker

Please describe a TV commercial that you think it is interesting.
請描述一段你覺得有趣的廣告

眼鏡公司廣告 SpecSaver

MP3 071

This commercial was created for a glasses company called SpecSaver in Australia. They were aiming to differentiate themselves as being more affordable than the others.

這個廣告是澳洲一家叫 SpecSaver 眼鏡公司的電視廣告。他們的訴求就是要以價格將他們與其他競爭者區隔開來。

One day, a son came to his elderly mother's house to visit her, and they are having tea and cake in the kitchen with the view of her garden. He noticed that she was wearing a new pair of glasses. He commented on how nice those glasses were, and it must have cost her a lot of money. She then replied and said, No, the insurance would cover it. Then the son started to question how expensive the lenses must be. She replied: It is 25% off on all lenses. I went to SpecSaver and don't you worry I am not spending your inheritance.

有一天兒子回家看媽媽，跟媽媽在廚房喝下午茶一邊聊

天，他家的廚房看出去就是花園。他注意到他媽媽配了一副新的眼鏡，他稱讚那副眼鏡很好看，一定很貴吧！他媽媽回答：沒有，保險都有給付。兒子又說：那鏡片也一定要不少錢吧？媽媽回答：鏡片也都有打七五折，放心啦兒子，我不會隨便把你的遺產給花掉，我是去 SpecSaver 配的！

The son acted relaxed and said to her, Good！ Then his mother said something that made him really worried. She looked through the window and said to him: Don't you worry, I am leaving them all to Dereck. He turned his head then saw this hot, sexy and topless guy trimming the trees for his mother. The look on his face is priceless！ He was in such shock. I think this commercial is simple but clever. The ending caught everyone by surprise.

兒子聽了就放心地說，那很好！結果沒想到他媽媽說你別擔心，我全部都要留給德瑞克！兒子轉頭順著他媽媽的視線看過去，沒想到看到一個沒穿上衣的性感猛男正在幫他媽修剪花園裡的樹枝。他真的臉都綠了！完全嚇傻了！我覺得這個廣告拍得很淺顯易懂，結尾更是在大家的意料之外。

Viewers got the idea how competitive their price is straight away, but at the same time the commercial does not make SpecSaver seem like a cheap place. It still looks quite classy. I think that is why this commercial left an impression.

　　觀眾看完就知道他們眼鏡的價錢很有競爭力，而且同時也不覺得 SpecSaver 是一間很廉價的公司，還是蠻有品味的。這應該是我對這個廣告印象深刻的原因。

💬 Instructions

- 不能只是閱讀每個人物如何回答唷！這是口說測驗，所以一定要開口說。
- 現在請跟著 CD 覆誦，同步練習「説」跟「聽」，第一次請跟著 CD 以相同語速覆誦，第二次和第三次可以逐步拉長到 CD 唸完第一句、第二句後再開始覆誦，能神奇地提升你的聽力專注力喔！

幫助：世界展望會

✏️ 話題拓展

- ⊙ 經驗一：喜憨兒基金會 Children Are Us foundation
- ⊙ 經驗二：幫忙募款 Fundraising
- ⊙ 經驗三：請人讓座給孕婦 Priority seat
- ⊙ 經驗四：撿到手機歸還 Return the cellphone
- ⊙ 經驗五：當義工 Volunteering
- ⊙ 經驗六：參加淨灘活動 Clean the beach campaign
- ⊙ 經驗七：叫人起床 Wake up call
- ⊙ 經驗八：機車意外 Scooter accident

Please describe a situation when you h elped someone.

請描述一段你曾經幫助別人的經驗

🖊 世界展望會 World Vision　　🎧 MP3 072

Ever since I got my first stable job, I said to myself that I want to do something for someone and pay it forward. I happened to see the campaign for World Vision and how they help out poor kids around the world.

　自從我有第一份穩定的工作開始，我就跟我自己說要做些有意義可以回饋社會的事。我剛好看到世界展望會的幫助世界貧童的廣告，所以決定加入成為資助人。

I decided to sign up with them as a sponsor. It does not cost much, only 7 hundred dollars a month, and it can change someone else's life completely. I think I can afford that！The kid that was assigned to me is a five-year-old boy from Kenya. His name is Aton, and he has 5 other siblings.

　一個月才台幣 700 元就可以完全改變另一個人的生活，那我真的花得起這個錢。我分到的兒童是一位五歲的非洲肯亞男童，他叫做阿堂，他的家有其他五個兄弟姊妹。

His parents do simple farming trying to support the family but with the weather conditions, what they get in return is not very much, and is totally not sustainable. With my sponsorship, not only does Aton get the education that he needs, but also there will be a regular food hamper delivered to his family. I think I help more than just one person. I have been doing it for over 10 years now, and I don't think I would ever stop being a sponsor.

他爸媽只能種植一點簡單的東西來維生，可是因為氣候的關係收成很差，根本不可靠。因為有我的資助金，阿堂不只可以去上學，他們家也固定會收到糧食包。我覺得受惠的不只是他而已。我已經資助他十年了，我覺得我會一直資助下去。

I was just wondering what happens once Aton turns 18, does that mean he wouldn't need the sponsorship anymore? I guess they might give me another kid to sponsor since there are so many kids in need especially in third world countries. I really think it is meaningful to be a sponsor like that. I hope there will be more people who feel the same.

　　我只是在想如果等阿堂滿 18 歲之後，展望會就不再資助他嗎？我猜他們應該會分另一個小孩給我吧，畢竟在第三世界國家需要資助的小孩是數以萬計。我覺得當資助人是很有意義的事，我希望會有越來越多的人跟我有同感。

 Instructions

- 不能只是閱讀每個人物如何回答唷！這是口說測驗，所以一定要開口說。
- 現在請跟著 CD 覆誦，同步練習「說」跟「聽」，第一次請跟著 CD 以相同語速覆誦，第二次和第三次可以逐步拉長到 CD 唸完第一句、第二句後再開始覆誦，能神奇地提升你的聽力專注力喔！

Unit 09 汙染：輻射汙染

話題拓展

- 汙染一：水汙染 Water pollution
- 污染二：土地汙染 Soil pollution
- 污染三：光害汙染 Light pollution
- 汙染四：噪音汙染 Noise pollution
- 汙染五：垃圾汙染 Solid waste pollution
- 汙染六：外來物種汙染 Invasive species pollution
- 汙染七：視覺汙染 Visual pollution
- 汙染八：空氣汙染 Air pollution

Please describe a pollution problem you are facing or might be facing in your area.
請描述一項你目前居住地區可能或是正面臨的汙染問題

輻射汙染 Radioactive pollution　MP3 073

I never used to think radioactive pollution could affect our life so much. It was a foreign concept to me until the Tsunami hit Japan a few years back which damaged a nuclear power plant in Fukushima, and caused the radiation to leak out.

我以前從來不覺得輻射污染會對我們的生活帶來這麼大的影響，一直到幾年前日本海嘯使福島核電廠受損，造成輻射外洩之前，輻射污染對我來說是一個很陌生的名詞。

Fresh Japanese produce was one of the top-selling items you can get in the market, and people were willing to pay top dollar for. I personally love their apples and seafood, but I haven't been buying them for a long time since the disaster happened. I am really wary about the residue from the radiation although all exporters claimed they have passed the radiation check and quality controls. But no one can guarantee that it is 100 percent safe to eat. Maybe you would not see the effect until later in your life.

從前，日本的農產品是市場上最高等級的東西，大家都願意花大錢去買。我最喜歡他們的蘋果還有海鮮了，可是自從海嘯之後我已經很久沒買了，因為我很擔心輻射的殘留。雖然出口商都保證他們的產品都有通過輻射還有品質的檢測。可是沒有人敢保證百分百的安全，可能要很久以後才看的到結果。

As much as I love the produce, I decided to seek alternatives. Being so close to Japan, I don't even know whether our seafood is radiation-free because some of the species would travel to Taiwanese water through currents.

雖然我真的很愛吃，可是我還是決定找其他替代產品。我們離日本這麼近，我也不敢確定我們的海鮮沒有輻射汙染，因為有些魚種是會透過洋流到台灣海域的！

This really makes me think twice about opening up more nuclear power plants in Taiwan. If we have a disaster occurring in a high population density area, one could not escape from it. The direct contact with the radiation would make us sick, too. Maybe we need to seek alternative energy sources.

　　這不禁讓我想到台灣核電廠的安全，如果這種災害發生在台灣人口稠密的地區，那可是會無一倖免的！直接受到輻射的接觸可是會讓人生病的，可能尋找替代能源會比較好。

 Instructions

- 不能只是閱讀每個人物如何回答唷！這是口說測驗，所以一定要開口說。
- 現在請跟著 CD 覆誦，同步練習「説」跟「聽」，第一次請跟著 CD 以相同語速覆誦，第二次和第三次可以逐步拉長到 CD 唸完第一句、第二句後再開始覆誦，能神奇地提升你的聽力專注力喔！

國家的問題：
詐騙集團問題

話題拓展

⊙ 問題一：社會福利問題 Social welfare
⊙ 問題二：食安問題 Food safety
⊙ 問題三：教育問題 Education
⊙ 問題四：低薪問題 Low average income
⊙ 問題五：房價問題 Housing affordability
⊙ 問題六：治安問題 Crime and safety
⊙ 問題七：國安問題 Boarder security
⊙ 問題八：天然災害問題 Nature disaster

Please describe a possible problem your country might be facing.
請描述一項目前你的國家可能面臨的問題

詐騙集團問題 Scam syndicate 　🎧 MP3 074

For some reason scam syndicates are everywhere in Taiwan. I would say almost every single one of us would have an encounter with them at one point or another. It is so common that the government would advertise on TV to warn people to not believe what people told you over phone easily.

不知道為什麼在台灣詐騙集團真的很猖獗，我敢說幾乎每一個人都有遇過。就連政府都意識到要在電視上宣導不要輕易地相信電話中的人。

The thing is, they sound so convincing, even when they are pretending they work for tax office or other government departments. They are very professional and well-trained. I remember one time I received this call to notify me that I won a big lump sum of money but in order to claim the money, I have to first transfer them the 20% tax. I knew immediately it is a scam, and I didn't fall for it.

事實是，詐騙集團都很能言善道，就連裝成政府部門的員工都那麼的專業，訓練有素。我記得有一次我接到電話說我中獎得了一大筆錢，可是要先匯百分之 20 的稅金給他們才可以把獎金給我。這一聽就知道是詐騙，我才沒有上當呢！

However, there are still people falling for the traps and losing their lifesavings. A lot of scam syndicates have their headquarters based overseas to avoid police investigation. In some cases, the police are able to catch the scapegoat of the syndicate, which is the person who is hired by the syndicate to collect the money in public.

可是還是有很多人連畢生積蓄都被騙光了。很多詐騙集團的總部都設在海外以逃避偵查。有時候警方抓到的只是代罪羔羊，不過是集團聘僱的車手，負責出面領錢而已。

However, it is difficult to bring the chief of the syndicate to justice because they are always behind the scenes. I must give the police some credit because not long ago they busted an international scam syndicate who was scamming bank ATM systems in Taiwan. I was very impressed they not only caught some of the people but also retrieved most of the money which is unheard of !

　　很難將集團的首腦定罪因為他們都藏在幕後。但我也必須要給警方一點讚賞，因為不久前他們偵破一個國際犯罪集團專門在台灣破解銀行的提款機系統，他們不但抓到幾個人，居然還有辦法把部分的錢追回來，實在太猛了！

 ## Instructions

- 不能只是閱讀每個人物如何回答唷！這是口說測驗，所以一定要開口說。
- 現在請跟著 CD 覆誦，同步練習「說」跟「聽」，第一次請跟著 CD 以相同語速覆誦，第二次和第三次可以逐步拉長到 CD 唸完第一句、第二句後再開始覆誦，能神奇地提升你的聽力專注力喔！

Unit 11 書籍：人生不設限

話題拓展

- 書籍一：哈利波特 Harry Potter
- 書籍二：賈伯斯傳 Steve Jobs
- 書籍三：富爸爸窮爸爸 Rich dad Poor dad
- 書籍四：行銷妙招 Sales psychology
- 書籍五：印度廚房 World kitchen- Indian
- 書籍六：壹週刊 Next Magazine (Tabloid)
- 書籍七：第一次自助旅行就上手 Self-guided travel for first timers
- 書籍八：面對父母老去的勇氣 How to care for your parents when they are aging

Please tell me about a book or a magazine you like.
請描述一本你喜歡的書籍或是雜誌

人生不設限 Life without limits by Nick Vujicic 🎧 MP3 075

Speaking of Nick Vujicic who is the author of this book, I believe most of us have heard about him. He was born without limbs which is a rare form of disability. The book "Life without limits" is a reflection on his life, you can imagine being born with such a severe deformity, his life would not be smooth.

說到這本書的作者力克胡哲，應該沒有人不認識，他出生就沒有四肢，是一種罕見的病例。人生不設限這本書是他人生的回顧，可以想見他一生下來就有這麼嚴重的缺陷，他的人生一定充滿挫折。

I am not surprised he did attempt to end his life a few times since he was still a child. I feel really bad for him being forced to deal with teasing and scorn and bullied so badly at school, I mean I am a normal kid, but I still get teased about being fat or ugly. You know what kids are like at school. It does take him quite sometime to realize that he needs to change his attitude if he still wants to live and he needs to turn his life around.

聽到他說小時候就有好幾次試著結束自己的生命，其實我並不驚訝。我覺得很難過他求學過程中被迫面對了多少輕蔑苛薄的言語還有欺負他的人。你也知道小孩就是這樣，我算是個正常人，都會有人說我肥或是醜了，何況是他。他也是花了不少時間才體會到如果他還想活下去，他需要改變現狀，他需要改變他對生命的態度。

My favorite quote in the book is: "Life without limbs or life without limits" and he did just that！ He knows he can't sit around to wait for the miracle to happen for him, or he needs to turn himself into a miracle. How does he do that？

書裡我最喜歡的一句話是「到底要相信自己沒有手腳還是要相信自己潛力無限」他決定相信後者，既然等不到奇蹟出現，就把自己變成一個奇蹟吧！他是怎麼做到的呢？

First, he needs to learn to accept his condition and like who he is. Once he knows he needs to love and respect himself, he is fearless and driven to success. He is such an inspiration. I feel stronger and more confident towards things that I was too scared to try before. This book is highly recommended.

　　首先他要接受自己的缺陷，當他學會愛自己，尊重自己之後，他就沒有什麼好擔心的了，可以盡全力去做到最好。他的書很鼓勵人心，充滿了正面能量，看了之後我覺得我更有信心去面對我之前很恐懼的事。我很推薦大家去看這本書。

 ## Instructions

· 不能只是閱讀每個人物如何回答唷！這是口說測驗，所以一定要開口說。

· 現在請跟著 CD 覆誦，同步練習「說」跟「聽」，第一次請跟著 CD 以相同語速覆誦，第二次和第三次可以逐步拉長到 CD 唸完第一句、第二句後再開始覆誦，能神奇地提升你的聽力專注力喔！

1 道地高分句

2 一問三答

3 話題卡回答

4 即席應答

Unit 12　難忘的情境：求婚

話題拓展

- 情境一：畢業典禮 Graduation
- 情境二：三分球 Three-point shot
- 情境三：上台表演出糗 School performance
- 情境四：被女生拒絕 The rejection
- 情境五：上廁所忘了鎖門 Lock that door
- 情境六：偶像見面會 Meet and greet
- 情境七：面對面 Face to face
- 情境八：男友出軌 The cheater

Please describe an unforgettable moment in your life.
請描述一個人生中難忘的情境

求婚 The proposal

MP3 076

1 道地高分句

2 一問三答

3 話題卡回答

4 即席應答

I must say my proposal is an unforgettable moment in my life. I have been seeing my girlfriend for a bit more than 3 years, and I decided to ask her to marry me early this year.

說到難忘的情境，那應該就是我的求婚記了。我跟我的女朋友交往了三年多，今年年初我決定要跟她求婚。

I have been thinking what would be the best way to do it. I decided to take her to the lounge bar she's always liked and ask her there. I wanted to surprise her, but I was getting more and more nervous when the time was approaching. The plan was, once we got seated, I would take out the ring and then ask her.

我一直在想該怎麼開口，我決定帶她到她喜歡的沙發酒吧，在那裡跟她求婚。我想要給她個驚喜，可是時間越接近我就越緊張。我的計畫是等我們坐下來之後，我就把戒指拿出來。

I went ahead and made the reservation at the lounge, but the weather was really bad that day. It trained so much that it took us along time to get there. She was a bit upset about why I insisted that we have to go out in such a bad weather. Once we got to the lounge, I was so nervous, and I just got up and went to the toilet. I was trying to work up my courage, but I didn't realize I must have been in the toilet for a long time. She even sent a waiter in to check on me.

我就照計畫去訂位，沒想到那天天氣很糟，雨下得很大，我們搞了半天才到。她有點不高興為什麼這種天氣我還要堅持出門。我實在太緊張了，我們一到我就說要去廁所。我躲在廁所裡穩定我緊張的情緒，可是我應該是待了太久，她還叫服務生進來看看我有沒有事。

I finally got back to the table, but the ring stuck in my pocket and I couldn't get it out. Then she already figured out what I was about to do. She burst into tears, and then yelled "I do ! "Although it didn't turn out as planned, it was still an unforgettable moment.

　　我終於走回到座位上了，可是這個時候戒指卻卡在口袋拿不出來！看到這裡她已經猜到我要做什麼，沒想到她居然哭了出來大聲說"我願意！"雖然跟我計畫的不一樣，可是還是真是個難忘的情境。

 Instructions

・ 不能只是閱讀每個人物如何回答唷！這是口說測驗，所以一定要開口說。

・ 現在請跟著 CD 覆誦，同步練習「說」跟「聽」，第一次請跟著 CD 以相同語速覆誦，第二次和第三次可以逐步拉長到 CD 唸完第一句、第二句後再開始覆誦，能神奇地提升你的聽力專注力喔！

話題拓展

- ⊙ 人物一：史努比 Snoopy
- ⊙ 人物二：藍色小精靈 Smurf
- ⊙ 人物三：多啦 A 夢 Doraemon
- ⊙ 人物四：白雪公主 Snow White
- ⊙ 人物五：雪寶 Olaf
- ⊙ 人物六：佩佩豬 Peppa pig
- ⊙ 人物七：超人 Superman
- ⊙ 人物八：櫻木花道 Sakuragi

Please describe a character that you like from a cartoon or story.
請描述一個你喜歡的卡通或事故中的人物

海底總動員的多莉 Dory　　　⊙ MP3 077

I love Dory from Finding Nemo. Finding Nemo is a story about a clown fish which accidently got caught by humans and his father searched everywhere he could trying to find him. The father clown fish named Marlin runs into Dory who helps him along the way to find his son.

我最喜歡《海底總動員》裡面的多莉，海底總動員是一個有關一隻小丑魚被人類抓走，而他的爸爸不停地搜尋只想找到他。這隻爸爸小丑魚叫馬林，他在途中遇到一隻叫多莉的魚，多莉沿途幫助他找他的兒子。

The duo went on an adventure across the 5 seas and finally found his son in Sydney, Australia. Dory is this blue fish with yellow fins, she suffers from short-term memory loss, but she never takes it as a problem！I guess her memory is just too short to remember it anyway！

這個兩人拍檔展開了橫跨五大洋的歷險記，到最後終於在澳洲雪梨找到他的兒子。多莉是一隻藍色帶有黃色鰭的魚，她

常常只有短期失憶症，可是她從來不覺得這是個問題。我想也是，因為她根本記不得她有記憶的問題！

Most people would think she is just a forgetful and careless fish. But I see her differently. I think she is the eternal optimist, she is always so happy and excited about things. Her level of excitement is like she experiences things for the first time. I guess she is, because she can't remember she has done it before. Same as the frustration and disappointments, she doesn't hold things against anyone because she can't remember what they have said or done to her any way.

大部分的人會覺得她是一隻健忘又粗心的魚，。可是我不這麼想，我倒覺得她是終極的樂觀者！她對每件事總是那麼的正面，積極的去面對。她對每件事的興奮程度就好像她從來沒做過這回事，我想也是，因為她不記得她有做過。同樣的，不高興或是失望的事她也忘得快，她對人沒有敵意，因為她早忘了別人是怎麼對她。

I guess it is probably not a bad thing to forget things that bother you after all. There is a sequel coming out about finding Dory this time. I am looking forward to seeing what happens after they found Nemo and how she got lost. I am sure it will be a great story！

我覺得忘記不好的事其實是件好事。海底總動員的續集要上映了，這次是有關尋找多莉的事。我很期待想知道他們找到尼莫之後多莉是怎樣不見的，這故事一定會很有趣。

 Instructions

- 不能只是閱讀每個人物如何回答唷！這是口說測驗，所以一定要開口說。
- 現在請跟著 CD 覆誦，同步練習「說」跟「聽」，第一次請跟著 CD 以相同語速覆誦，第二次和第三次可以逐步拉長到 CD 唸完第一句、第二句後再開始覆誦，能神奇地提升你的聽力專注力喔！

話題拓展

- 名人一：歐巴馬 Barack Obama
- 名人二：周杰倫 Jay Chou
- 名人三：林志玲 Chi-Ling Lin
- 名人四：林書豪 Jeremy Lin
- 名人五：成龍 Jacky Chan
- 名人六：郭台銘 Terry Guo
- 名人七：希拉蕊 Hillary Clinton
- 名人八：王雪紅 Cher Wang

Please tell me about a famous person that you admire.
請描述一個你欣賞的名人

傑米奧利佛 Jamie Oliver

MP3 078

Jamie Oliver is someone I really look up to. There are lots of famous chefs in the world, but I think his belief makes him stand out from the rest.

傑米奧利佛一直是我很欣賞的一個人，這世界上有很多出名的廚師，可是我覺得傑米的信念讓他與眾不同。

I think he is doing a lot of charity work through his ability to cook and understanding of food. He knows everyone likes to eat, but not everyone knows how to eat well or what is good for them. He just wants to promote the idea of eating good food to avoid being overweight.

我認為他是用廚藝的天分還有對食材的了解來做公益。他了解大家都喜歡吃美食，可是並不是每個人都清楚怎麼樣吃才是對健康有益。他想要推廣吃好的食物而不是讓人會肥胖的食物。

He wants to help to rectify the problem of being

overweight in the UK when he noticed the number of people suffering obesity in the UK is skyrocketing. He soon realized that, the most effective way to rectify the problem is to educate the future generation to stop the trend of being obese. He initiated a program to visit school canteens to inspire the food provider to offer nutritious food instead of the junk food to the kids.

他注意到英國過重的人口年年遞增，而他想拯救肥胖的問題。他腦筋動得很快，他發現最有效的方法就是從教育下手，讓下一代不要加入肥胖的趨勢。他發起了到學校去拜訪福利社的食品供應商，讓他們避免提供垃圾食物，盡量提供有營養的食物。

By the same token, he wants to take this opportunity to educate kids about what type of food is good for them. I think Jamie Oliver is trying to change the world with his own power and wanting to make an impact on people's perception of food which is a wonderful thing to do. I know it is impossible to change things overnight, but at least he is raising awareness and trying to reach out to his viewers.

　　他也順便趁這個機會教育學生，讓他們了解什麼叫做好的食物。我覺得傑米奧利佛是想用他的力量來改變人們對食物的觀念，我覺得這是件很值得讚揚的事。我了解改變需要時間，他現在開始提倡這個觀念至少可以影響到他觀眾群的層面。

 Instructions

- 不能只是閱讀每個人物如何回答唷！這是口說測驗，所以一定要開口說。
- 現在請跟著 CD 覆誦，同步練習「說」跟「聽」，第一次請跟著 CD 以相同語速覆誦，第二次和第三次可以逐步拉長到 CD 唸完第一句、第二句後再開始覆誦，能神奇地提升你的聽力專注力喔！

話題拓展

⊙ 名人一：歐巴馬 Barack Obama
⊙ 名人二：周杰倫 Jay Chou
⊙ 名人三：林志玲 Chi-Ling Lin
⊙ 名人四：林書豪 Jeremy Lin
⊙ 名人五：成龍 Jacky Chan
⊙ 名人六：郭台銘 Terry Guo
⊙ 名人七：希拉蕊 Hillary Clinton
⊙ 名人八：王雪紅 Cher Wang

Please describe a festival which is important to you.
請描述一個對你來說重要的節慶

🖊 清明節 Tomb sweeping day　⊚ MP3 079

1 道地高分句

2 一問三答

3 話題卡回答

4 即席應答

I would say Tomb sweeping day is quite an event in my family because we still have a few ancestors' plots in the cemetery where we go and pay our respects. One of the Tomb sweeping day traditions is to bring spring rolls as offerings.

清明節對我家來説還算是件大事，因為我們家還有幾門祖先的墓要去掃。清明節的其中一個傳統是要拜春捲。

My aunt will always prepare lots of food in her house, and the family will gather there for a big spring roll making spree before we head off to the cemetery. This is probably the only chance for me to catch up with my cousins and relatives from my father's side as well.

我嬸嬸總是會準備很多材料，大家會先在她們家集合做春捲，做完再出發到墓園去。這也是一年中難得的機會可以見到爸爸那邊的表兄妹還有親戚。

So Tomb sweeping is also a social occasion for us. Other than the spring rolls, we also need to have the gardening tools to get rid of the overgrown weeds, and also some ceremonial items, such as ghost money, incense sticks, and a set of colorful paper strips. We first do the general tidy up, and then we will put out offerings and set up the altar. When everyone is ready, we will light the incense sticks and burn the ghost money to greet our ancestors, to let them know their family is here to pay the respect and pray for good fortune.

所以清明也是家族聚會。等我們做完春捲後,除了要準備園藝的工具來除掉高大的雜草,還需要帶祭拜用的東西,像紙錢、香,還有一疊彩色的壓墓紙。我們首先會環境整理,再來把供品供桌弄好。等大家都差不多了,就點香燒紙錢向祖先膜拜,跟祖先說子孫們來看你們了,祈求祖先保佑。

The colorful paper strips are the final step of the ritual, they will be spread out evenly on the tomb and we will pin them down with rocks. It is kind of spooky because you have to literally walk on top of where the coffin is buried top to place paper strips. The colorful strips served as the decoration to show the others that this tomb is properly looked after by their family.

　　壓墓紙是最後一道步驟，我們會把彩色的紙用石頭一張張分別地壓在整個墳墓上，其實有一點恐怖因為你在埋葬棺材的上方走來走去。壓墓紙算是一種裝飾，好讓別人知道這家的子孫有在照顧自己的祖墳。

 Instructions

- 不能只是閱讀每個人物如何回答唷！這是口說測驗，所以一定要開口說。
- 現在請跟著 CD 覆誦，同步練習「說」跟「聽」，第一次請跟著 CD 以相同語速覆誦，第二次和第三次可以逐步拉長到 CD 唸完第一句、第二句後再開始覆誦，能神奇地提升你的聽力專注力喔！

part 4 為雅思口說考試中的 part 3，有時候會覺得不太好回答，因為有些話題我們很少仔細去想過，而且考官也會針對類似的問題抽絲剝繭地詢問你。可以將這個 part 收錄的話題為依據，構思自己的理由並將理由都列出來，作為自己答題的依據，才可以避免答一兩句又不知道該接什麼話的困境。

Part

4

即席應答

What makes a good leader?
優秀的領袖應該具備什麼條件 MP3 080

I believe a good leader should be strong and tough because sometimes the decisions he makes might not be acceptable to everyone. I also believe he needs to be able to listen to his people, and gather the information to make the most sensible decision.

我覺得一個好的領袖需要堅強也必須嚴格，因為有時候他們做出的決定並不是每個人都可以接受。我也相信他必須要能考慮人民的意見，綜合資訊而做出最適當的決策。

I understand the outcome might not be as expected everytime, but he should own up to his mistakes instead of pointing fingers at others. Furthermore, integrity is also a key element, too. Because being a leader, he would be presented with a lot of temptations. It could be money, expensive presents or women even. If he doesn't have an integrity, I am afraid he will lose his way sooner than you think.

　　我了解當然有時候結果不如預期，可是他也要有擔當的承認他的失誤而不是推託給別人。除此之外，清廉也是很重要的一部分，因為當你是個領袖想想看會有多少誘惑送上門。有可能是金錢、貴重的禮物，甚至是女人。如果他沒有清廉的心，那他很快就會迷失方向。

 ## Instructions

- 不能只是閱讀每個人物如何回答唷！這是口說測驗，所以一定要開口説。
- 現在請跟著 CD 覆誦，同步練習「說」跟「聽」，第一次請跟著 CD 以相同語速覆誦，第二次和第三次可以逐步拉長到 CD 唸完第一句、第二句後再開始覆誦，能神奇地提升你的聽力專注力喔！

Who is the leader in your family?
在你家是誰做主？ 🎧 MP3 081

My family is a bit unconventional. I would say I am the leader by name, but my mother is the one who wears the pants. My mother registered me as the head of the family since my dad passed away. She just wanted me to inherit what is left from my dad. My mother has never been a dominating person. She does not like to be put under the spot light, so she pushes me forward. My mother would actually ask my opinion when she couldn't come to a decision.

　　我的家庭不是很傳統。我可以說我是掛名的領袖，可是我媽其實才是作主的人。在我爸過世之後我媽把我登記為一家之主，我知道她只是想讓我繼承爸爸留下來的一切。我媽從來不是個專橫的人，她完全不喜歡出風頭，所以家裡的事情都派我去處理。

I really appreciate how much support my mother gave me, especially being a single mother like her. She has always been the unofficial leader in my mind and always will be.

我媽下不了決定時還真的會來問我想怎麼做。我真的很感謝她那麼的支持我,當個單親媽媽不簡單呢。她一直都是我心裡不過名的領袖,也永遠都會是。

💬 Instructions

- 不能只是閱讀每個人物如何回答唷!這是口說測驗,所以一定要開口說。
- 現在請跟著 CD 覆誦,同步練習「說」跟「聽」,第一次請跟著 CD 以相同語速覆誦,第二次和第三次可以逐步拉長到 CD 唸完第一句、第二句後再開始覆誦,能神奇地提升你的聽力專注力喔!

Do you think it is difficult to meet people as you get older?
你覺得長大之後是不是比較難交朋友?

🎧 MP3 082

I don't think it is much more difficult. I would say how you meet people is definitely different. When I was younger, I met all my friends through schools or neighborhood.

我覺得好像沒有比較難,可是我覺得交朋友的方式不同了。我年輕的時候,我的朋友全部都是學校的同學或是鄰居。

But as I get older, especially after I entered the workforce, I realized that my co-workers are my new circle of friends. I still meet new people other than people I work with, but most of them are either my clients or suppliers from work. I am lucky enough to actually turn the business relationship into friendship with a few of my clients who are friends of mine now. I see them outside of work as well, we hang out now and again.

　　可是我長大了之後，　尤其是進了職場，我發現我新的朋友圈就是我的同事們，除了同事我還是有交到新的朋友，大部分不是我的客戶就是我的供應商。我算是蠻幸運地可以把工作的關係昇華成友誼，我有幾個客戶現在是我的好朋友，我們私下也會約出來，有空就見個面。

 ## Instructions

· 不能只是閱讀每個人物如何回答唷！這是口說測驗，所以一定要開口說。

· 現在請跟著 CD 覆誦，同步練習「說」跟「聽」，第一次請跟著 CD 以相同語速覆誦，第二次和第三次可以逐步拉長到 CD 唸完第一句、第二句後再開始覆誦，能神奇地提升你的聽力專注力喔！

Q 02 Do you think friendship would last forever?
你覺得友誼一定會歷久不衰嗎? 🎧 MP3 083

This is a hard question to answer. I would love to say yes, but deep down I know it doesn't. I think friendship is a two waystreet. Unless your friend also feels the same way and wants to keep the relationship going. Otherwise, it can end pretty quickly after not seeing that person for a while. I had this friend, she was always my best friend while we were growing up. We even went to high school together.

這是個很難回答的問題,我很想說是的,可是我心裡知道其實不會。我覺得友誼是雙向的,除非你的朋友也有同感,會主動地想持續下去,不然其實一陣子沒見很快大家就失去聯絡了。我有一個青梅竹馬的朋友從小一起長大, 還念同一所高中。

I always imagined she would be part of my life even after I got married and had a baby. But for some reason, we just stopped talking to each other after graduation. I guess we were both waiting for each other to initiate and make the first move.

　　我總是想說我結婚生小孩的時候她一定會在我身邊。可是很奇怪的是我們畢業後就漸漸不再找對方了，我猜是因為我們兩個都在等對方先主動聯絡。

 Instructions

- 不能只是閱讀每個人物如何回答唷！這是口說測驗，所以一定要開口説。
- 現在請跟著 CD 覆誦，同步練習「説」跟「聽」，第一次請跟著 CD 以相同語速覆誦，第二次和第三次可以逐步拉長到 CD 唸完第一句、第二句後再開始覆誦，能神奇地提升你的聽力專注力喔！

Is Food safety becoming an increasingly serious problem in our lives?
食安問題逐漸變成我們生活中一個嚴重的問題了嗎? MP3 084

I never thought food safety would even become a problem in the first place because food to me, is something that is safe to eat. Then after watching the news in the past couple of years, I was shocked by how much toxin we have been fed by those heartless, profit-driven food manufacturers.

我從來沒有想過食品安全會成為一個問題,因為對我來說所謂食品都是安全無虞的,可以吃的東西。但是在看過這幾年的新聞事件之後,我無法想像我們到底被那些沒有良心,只愛錢的商人們騙著吃進了多少毒素。

It makes me wonder how much more there is to be

discovered. I really think law enforcement should take some responsibility, too. The current food safety regulation is full of flaws, and the inadequate punishment and sentence length do not reflect the seriousness of their crimes. The food manufacturers often walk out clean which is very disappointing.

　　我在想還不知道有多少事件要爆發呢！我覺得執法者也要負點責任，目前的食品安全法規充滿漏洞，罰則根本不成比例，還有罰則太輕，根本無法反映出罪行影響的層面有多廣泛。食品製造商也常常無罪釋放，這太令人失望了。

 Instructions

- 不能只是閱讀每個人物如何回答唷！這是口說測驗，所以一定要開口說。
- 現在請跟著 CD 覆誦，同步練習「說」跟「聽」，第一次請跟著 CD 以相同語速覆誦，第二次和第三次可以逐步拉長到 CD 唸完第一句、第二句後再開始覆誦，能神奇地提升你的聽力專注力喔！

What do you think of organic food?
你對有機食品有什麼想法? 🎧 MP3 085

Q 02

Some people believe it is better for you and also better for the environment because organic farming follows a strict set of guideline on what pesticide and fertilizers are allowed to be used. I don't know whether it is necessarily better for the health, but what really concerns me is the rising price of groceries.

　　有些人覺得有機食品對身體比較好，也比較環保，因為有機耕種必須遵守嚴格的規定標準，尤其是農藥還有肥料種類的選用。我是不太曉得到底對身體是不是比較好，可是我的顧慮是物價的飆漲。

Organic food can cost up to 2-3 times more compared with food that was produced under the conventional methods. I would love to support the idea of organic farming, but I just don't think I can afford it unless my salary goes up to 2-3 times as well. Most of us grow up eating conventional farmed food, and it doesn't seem to do us any harm.

　　有機食品的價格通常是一般傳統耕種食品的 2-3 倍。我是很想支持有機耕種，可是我覺得除非我的薪水也漲 2-3 倍，不然我根本負擔不起。大部分的人都是吃傳統耕種食物長大的，好像也沒什麼不妥。

 Instructions

· 不能只是閱讀每個人物如何回答唷！這是口說測驗，所以一定要開口說。

· 現在請跟著 CD 覆誦，同步練習「說」跟「聽」，第一次請跟著 CD 以相同語速覆誦，第二次和第三次可以逐步拉長到 CD 唸完第一句、第二句後再開始覆誦，能神奇地提升你的聽力專注力喔！

1 道地高分句

2 一問三答

3 話題卡回答

4 即席應答

Q 01

What can schools do to help students to be more prepared in the next stage of their lives?
學校教育對於學生面對未來的人生可以提供怎樣的幫助？ MP3 086

I think Taiwanese schools tend to focus on academic performance rather than industrial related training and knowledge. I chose to do vocational training school instead where they provide more hands-on training than textbook learning. I still articulated to university after I graduated. I do think I have a better idea of what I want to achieve in the future compared with my friends who came through the conventional high school system.

我覺得台灣的學校都傾向專注在學業成績而不注重產業相關的訓練或是知識。我反而選擇職業學校，因為他們會提供實際產業相關的訓練而不是死讀書。我到最後還是上了大學，可

是我覺得我比我那些就讀傳統高中的同學們更有想法。

I chose to join the workforce instead of pursuing further studies because I actually felt I was ready to start working, and there is no need for me to obtain a master's degree to do the things I want to do. I think vocational training definitely helped me to know what I want to do.

我後來選擇不去念碩士，而是直接就業，因為我覺得我準備好要工作了，而我想做的工作並不需要碩士學歷。我覺得是因為念職校的關係讓我知道我要什麼。

 Instructions

· 不能只是閱讀每個人物如何回答唷！這是口說測驗，所以一定要開口說。

· 現在請跟著 CD 覆誦，同步練習「說」跟「聽」，第一次請跟著 CD 以相同語速覆誦，第二次和第三次可以逐步拉長到 CD 唸完第一句、第二句後再開始覆誦，能神奇地提升你的聽力專注力喔！

Q 02 Do you think people are offered more opportunity in life if they have a qualification?

你同意學歷可以幫你打開更多機會的大門嗎？

🎧 MP3 087

Yes, I totally agree. I think qualification is a ticket of entry to all kinds of opportunities. It is something that makes you stand out from all those candidates who apply for the same job. How does the employer know who is best suited for the job before they even meet you？

是的！我完全同意，我覺得學歷是一張讓你通往很多機會的門票。學歷會讓你在一群申請同一份工作的應徵者中一枝獨秀。老闆在還沒見到你本人之前怎麼會知道你適合這份工作呢？

To be good on paper is definitely an advantage to push you through to the next round which is the interview. But, how well you can impress the selection panel and whether you get the job, that's another question. When I apply for jobs, I often get called for the interview, but I don't always get that job. That's what

354

makes me realise if it wasn't for the qualification, I might not even make it that far.

　　所以有好的學經歷真的可以幫你爭取到面試的機會，可是你能不能讓考官們喜歡你，或者能不能得到那份工作，這又是另一個問題了。說到應徵工作，我常常都會有面試的機會，雖然有時候我面試的表現並不好，這更是讓我深刻了解如果沒有學歷可能根本連面試的機會都沒有!

 ## Instructions

- 不能只是閱讀每個人物如何回答唷！這是口說測驗，所以一定要開口說。
- 現在請跟著 CD 覆誦，同步練習「說」跟「聽」，第一次請跟著 CD 以相同語速覆誦，第二次和第三次可以逐步拉長到 CD 唸完第一句、第二句後再開始覆誦，能神奇地提升你的聽力專注力喔！

Q 01

Who needs to learn how to cook? Men or women?
你覺得誰應該學煮飯，男人還是女人？

MP3 088

I know society expects women to take up the role of cooking in a household, but I personally believe men need to learn how to cook. Growing up as a girl I was coached by my mother to learn how to cook since day one, but my brother got away with doing most of the household duties. He was laughing at that time, but once we moved out of home, he quickly realised he doesn't even know how to do his laundry because my mother has always done it for him.

　　我知道這個社會都期待女人來擔起煮飯的責任，可是我個人覺得男人才需要學煮飯。我是個女孩，而女孩們從小就會被媽媽帶在身邊學煮飯，可是反觀我哥哥幾乎什麼家事都不用做，他那時候可是爽得很。可是等我們搬出去的時候，他很快

就發現他連衣服都不會洗，因為我媽從小幫他做到大。

When it comes to cooking, I believe most men do not have a clue about basic cooking skills. I don't expect them to turn out to be Michelin chefs, but to know how to make a few stir-fried dishes would do them good.

談到煮飯，我相信大部分男生可能連最基本的煮飯技巧都不懂，我是不期待他們煮得像米其林主廚一樣好，可是會炒幾道菜對他們來說應該受用無窮。

 Instructions

· 不能只是閱讀每個人物如何回答唷！這是口說測驗，所以一定要開口說。

· 現在請跟著 CD 覆誦，同步練習「說」跟「聽」，第一次請跟著 CD 以相同語速覆誦，第二次和第三次可以逐步拉長到 CD 唸完第一句、第二句後再開始覆誦，能神奇地提升你的聽力專注力喔！

What do you think of arranged marriage?

你對媒妁之言的婚姻有什麼感覺? MP3 089

I think the arranged marriage here is not as strict as the arranged marriage in countries like India, a place where you might not even know the person who you will be married to. In Taiwan, It is more like meeting the potential life partner through a mutual friend or a professional matchmaker.

我覺得在台灣的媒妁之言的婚姻不像其他國家如同印度一樣的嚴格,在那裏你可能完全不認識你將要嫁娶的人。在這裡比較像透過共同的朋友或是專業媒婆認識人。

Although you still get the family involvement, but you do have a say in deciding who you would like to marry. I don't have anything against it as long as the couples are genuinely happy with each other and they both want to spend their lives together. I would hate to see an arranged marriage when one was forced to marry someone that he or she is not willing to commit to.

　　雖然這裡也會牽涉到家人的意見可是畢竟是你的婚姻，你還是有發表意見的空間。我是不反對相親結婚，只要兩方面都是真心地想跟對方共度一生，我最不想看到的是其中有一方是被逼或是對這個決定有疑慮的。

 Instructions

- 不能只是閱讀每個人物如何回答唷！這是口說測驗，所以一定要開口説。
- 現在請跟著 CD 覆誦，同步練習「説」跟「聽」，第一次請跟著 CD 以相同語速覆誦，第二次和第三次可以逐步拉長到 CD 唸完第一句、第二句後再開始覆誦，能神奇地提升你的聽力專注力喔！

Q 01 Do you think wearing traditional costume is important?
你覺得穿傳統服裝很重要嗎? MP3 090

I think it is important to keep the culture alive as much as possible, but a lot of traditions have become unpractical in the modern days. I think wearing traditional costume is one of the things that is disappearing fast because wearing a Chi-Pao is not fashionable, and not practical at all. I mean, how do you ride a scooter when you are wearing a Chi-Pao？

我覺得能夠盡量保持傳統是一件很重要的事，但是很多傳統到現在已經變得不合時宜。 我覺得穿傳統服裝是一件非常容易被淘汰的事，因為説真的穿旗袍真的沒有流行感，而且也非常不實穿。你看，如果穿旗袍你要怎麼騎機車呢？

For that very reason, I think Vietnam has done a great

job because their costumeis actually practical, and it looks beautiful on the bike, too！That's why the traditional costume is still very popular in Vietnam. I think if the designers can incorporate Chi-Pao with clothing of western design, it might make Chi-Pao more popular which might help us to keep the costume alive.

　　從這個觀點來看的話，我覺得越南的傳統服裝就很棒，因為不只實穿而且就騎車來看還更美！所以在越南穿傳統服裝的人還是很多。我覺得如果服裝設計師能夠把旗袍跟西式的服裝做結合，那旗袍的接受度會更高，這樣就更能延續傳統。

 Instructions

· 不能只是閱讀每個人物如何回答唷！這是口說測驗，所以一定要開口說。

· 現在請跟著 CD 覆誦，同步練習「說」跟「聽」，第一次請跟著 CD 以相同語速覆誦，第二次和第三次可以逐步拉長到 CD 唸完第一句、第二句後再開始覆誦，能神奇地提升你的聽力專注力喔！

What are the traditions that you still practice at home? Why?

你們家有什麼傳統？為什麼要維持這個傳統？

MP3 091

One of the traditions is that we always stay up until midnight on Chinese New Year's eve and light fireworks with my dad. In the old days, people believe the sound of the fireworks scares the monster away, which is the reason why we celebrate Chinese New Year.

我家其中的一個傳統是，我們除夕的時候都會守夜到午夜，然後跟我爸爸一起放鞭炮。傳說鞭炮的聲音會把年獸嚇走，這也是我們慶祝新年的由來。

I love this tradition not because it is to do with Chinese New Year, but because we get to bond with my dad, and we are always so looking forward to doing it together. Another traditionis to do with birthdays, my mother insists to make us pig knuckle noodle soup for our birthday. It is a tradition she grew up with. It just reminds her of our grandma.

1　道地高分句

2　一問三答

3　話題卡回答

4　即席應答

可是我喜歡這個傳統的原因並不是因為過年，而是可以跟我爸爸一起玩的回憶，我們總是既期待又興奮。另一個傳統是有關生日，我媽堅持我們生日一定要吃豬腳麵線，這是她從小到大的傳統，她總是會想起我的外婆。

 Instructions

- 不能只是閱讀每個人物如何回答唷！這是口說測驗，所以一定要開口說。

- 現在請跟著 CD 覆誦，同步練習「說」跟「聽」，第一次請跟著 CD 以相同語速覆誦，第二次和第三次可以逐步拉長到 CD 唸完第一句、第二句後再開始覆誦，能神奇地提升你的聽力專注力喔！

Sport event 運動競賽

 Q 01

Do you think the Olympic is different now compared with ancient Olympic games?
你覺得原始的奧運跟現今奧運有何不同**?**
MP3 092

That's for sure, I believe the ancient Olympic games had a lot to do with their religion's beliefs and the importance of how it brings peace to all the Greek countries during the game. I believe it is a lot more spiritual compared with the modern Olympic games. The intention of participating countries which take parts in the games, definitely evolved.

絕對是，古代的奧運跟宗教神話很有關係，而且最難得的是奧運期間希臘所有的參賽小國都能和平相處。我覺得古代的奧運比較有神聖的感覺，而且現在參賽國的動機已和原始的奧運不同。

Nowadays, the countries are head over heels fighting for the opportunity to host the games. I believe it is all about bringing in profit for the local business and boosting the tourism industry. For the athletes, I think it didn't change that much. All they wanted is to win regardless what century it is. I think the modern Olympic is very commercially orientated.

對於參賽國來説，所有的國家都爭著要當奧運的主辦國，我相信都是為了增加國家當地商業及觀光業的收入。對於運動員來説，應該沒有改變太多，因為無論如何運動員都是想拿金牌。我覺得現代的奧運非常的商業化。

 Instructions

- 不能只是閱讀每個人物如何回答唷！這是口説測驗，所以一定要開口説。
- 現在請跟著 CD 覆誦，同步練習「説」跟「聽」，第一次請跟著 CD 以相同語速覆誦，第二次和第三次可以逐步拉長到 CD 唸完第一句、第二句後再開始覆誦，能神奇地提升你的聽力專注力喔！

What do you think of betting on sports events?

你對運動彩券有何感想? MP3 093

I am not a big fan of gambling, and I would never bet on anything, let alone sports events. I believe anything with human involvement gets trickier when money gets involved, too. When an athlete did not perform as expected, it is hard to tell whether he just had a bad day or he was manipulated by someone.

我一直以來就不喜歡賭博,我從來沒有賭過什麼,更別說是體育活動。我覺得任何與人有關的活動一旦跟錢扯上關係就變得很複雜。當運動員今天表現不好的時候,很難判斷出他到底是單純的情況不好還是他被人控制。

I used to really enjoy watching baseball matches, but ever since a whole bunch of baseball players got caught by foul play a few years ago, it really damaged the purity of baseball games. Some of players even got felony conviction and was sent to jail which terminated their career as professional players. I think betting onsports events should not even be legal.

　　我以前很愛看棒球賽，可是自從一大群球員被爆出打假球的案子，這真的把棒球賽的單純性給毀了。其中一些球員還被定罪抓去關，球員生涯也因此斷了。我覺得運動彩券根本不應該合法。

 Instructions

- 不能只是閱讀每個人物如何回答唷！這是口說測驗，所以一定要開口說。
- 現在請跟著 CD 覆誦，同步練習「說」跟「聽」，第一次請跟著 CD 以相同語速覆誦，第二次和第三次可以逐步拉長到 CD 唸完第一句、第二句後再開始覆誦，能神奇地提升你的聽力專注力喔！

Q 01

In what way have advertisements changed in the past 10 years.
過去十年裡廣告有怎樣的轉變? MP3 094

I think advertisements evolved rapidly over the past 10 years due to the popularity of the smartphone. It is almost impossible to avoid advertisements these days because they are literally everywhere. In the old days, they were mostly on TV, magazines, and even on my scooter when I only walked away for a few hours ! But nowadays, they are on my Facebook, LINE, and Wechat, they follow me wherever I go. Not only that, I think the presentation of the advertisement has become more technology orientated as well.

我覺得廣告因為智慧型手機的普遍性,在過去十年裡轉變很大。現在幾乎睜開眼睛就可以看到廣告,因為真的到處都是。以前廣告大部分是在電視、雜誌或是機車上也有,就算我只不過離開幾個小時。反觀現在,臉書、LINE 或是微信上都有廣告。廣告好像追著我不放。不只這樣,我覺得呈現的方式也越來越高科技。

In order to draw viewers' attention, graphic designers use a lot of computer animation to make the advertisement stand out and make an impression on the viewer's mind. I think technology plays an important part in the advertisement evolution.

為了要引起觀眾的注意，視覺設計師會用很多電腦動畫來讓廣告引人注目，讓觀眾留下深刻印象。我覺得科技對廣告的轉變影響很大。

 ## Instructions

- 不能只是閱讀每個人物如何回答唷！這是口說測驗，所以一定要開口說。
- 現在請跟著 CD 覆誦，同步練習「說」跟「聽」，第一次請跟著 CD 以相同語速覆誦，第二次和第三次可以逐步拉長到 CD 唸完第一句、第二句後再開始覆誦，能神奇地提升你的聽力專注力喔！

Q 02 How do the advertisements influence you on purchasing an item?
廣告對於你決定購買某樣物品時有怎樣的影響? MP3 095

I think influence is not a big enough word, I would say advertisements actually brainwash the viewers and detect what they buy. I'd like to pay attention to the latest product and the easiest way is look at the advertisements, Some of the advertisements are very cleverly done, after I watched them, I actually felt the urge to rush out of the door to buy it and try it out !

我覺得用影響來形容還不夠貼切，應該要說廣告直接幫你洗腦而且控制你的選擇。我喜歡注意現在有什麼新產品，而最容易的方式就是看廣告，有些廣告拍得很好，我看了之後會很想衝出門去買那個產品來試試看！

Although sometimes the products I bought did not demonstrate the desired result, I felt deceived, but there is nothing I can do ! The advertisement is feeding the information to me, and I was convinced, that's all I can say.

　　雖然有時候有些產品實在是沒有廣告上講的神奇，我會覺得被騙，可是那也無可奈何。我只能說廣告知道我想聽什麼，而且真的講到我的心坎裡。

 Instructions

· 不能只是閱讀每個人物如何回答唷！這是口說測驗，所以一定要開口說。

· 現在請跟著 CD 覆誦，同步練習「說」跟「聽」，第一次請跟著 CD 以相同語速覆誦，第二次和第三次可以逐步拉長到 CD 唸完第一句、第二句後再開始覆誦，能神奇地提升你的聽力專注力喔！

Q 01 **Do you think using social media poses danger in our lives?**
你覺得使用社群網站對我們的生活有什麼潛在的危險嗎？ MP3 096

I think it is potentially dangerous because you have no idea who else has access to your profile other than your friends. What worries me the most is those people who like to update their location and activities in real time, it actually reveals more information than you think. I know there is a privacy set-ting function, but not everybody knows how it works.

我覺得真的是有潛在的危險，因為你不知道除了你的朋友們，還有誰在看你的資料。其實最令人擔心的是那些喜歡即時上傳更新他們的所在地，還有從事的活動的人，這可是把你的行蹤都洩漏出去！我知道你可以更改隱私設定，可是不是每個人都知道怎麼改。

I was really surprised to find when someone shared your photo on Facebook, all his or her friends can see it, too. You just never know whether there is a predator out there waiting for his chance.

當我發現原來如果有人分享你的照片，你朋友的朋友們也都看的到，我很驚訝！你真不知道是不是有壞人在等待機會害你。

Instructions

- 不能只是閱讀每個人物如何回答唷！這是口說測驗，所以一定要開口說。

- 現在請跟著 CD 覆誦，同步練習「說」跟「聽」，第一次請跟著 CD 以相同語速覆誦，第二次和第三次可以逐步拉長到 CD 唸完第一句、第二句後再開始覆誦，能神奇地提升你的聽力專注力喔！

What do you think of people who do not use social media?
你對於不用社群網站的人有什麼感想?
🎧 MP3 097

I understand life is all about choices and social media might not be everyone's cup of tea. I do respect their choice, but honestly, people choosing not to use social media are likely to lose touch with most people in their lives. Almost everybody owns a smartphone nowadays, and people with smartphones tend to use social media to communicate instead of the conventional phone calls. Even my 70-year-old grandmother can use Skype to call me !

　　我了解生活中充滿的選擇而且不是每個人都喜歡用社群網站。我尊重他們的選擇可是說真的如果他們選擇不用社群網站,很可能他們會漸漸地跟周邊的人們失去聯絡,因為現在大家都有智慧型手機,而且大家反而不用傳統的方式打電話,都用社群網站在聯絡。連我七十歲的奶奶都會用 Skype 打電話給我!

I often wonder what is the reason that makes them resentful about using social media and refuse to keep up with rest of the population. I guess they are not firm believers of selfies either; otherwise, I am sure they will be all over it.

　　我總是在想是什麼原因讓人排斥使用社群網站而且情願跟其他人脫節。我覺得他們一定是不喜歡自拍，不然再多社群網站也不夠用！

Instructions

- 不能只是閱讀每個人物如何回答唷！這是口說測驗，所以一定要開口說。
- 現在請跟著 CD 覆誦，同步練習「說」跟「聽」，第一次請跟著 CD 以相同語速覆誦，第二次和第三次可以逐步拉長到 CD 唸完第一句、第二句後再開始覆誦，能神奇地提升你的聽力專注力喔！

1 道地高分句

2 一問三答

3 話題卡回答

4 即席應答

Unit 10 Accident 意外

Q 01

Do you believe most accidents happen at home?

你覺得大部分的意外都是在家裡發生的嗎?

MP3 098

Well, I think minor accidents tend to happen at home like small cuts on the finger or bumps on the head, but I must say things can go bad pretty quickly at home, especially when you have a young kid at home who needs adult supervision at all times. They could drown in the bath in a blink of an eye, while the mother goes to answer the door.

嗯，我覺得小意外大部分都是在家裡發生，就像不小心切到手，或是撞到頭。可是我必須要承認在家也可能出大事，尤其是家裡有小小孩需要大人不停看著的。媽媽可能走開去應門而已，一瞬間他們就在澡盆淹死了。

However, I do believe most horrific accidents happened outside of the house where we have less control of the surroundings, such as car accidents or shark attacks. I know people are more alert when they are out, but they also have less control of whether the car next to them is going to hit them！

可是我相信大部分可怕的意外都是在戶外發生的，因為我們無法控制大環境，就像出車禍或是被鯊魚攻擊。我知道大家出門在外都會比較小心，可是就算小心也沒辦法控制旁邊的車要來撞他。

 Instructions

- 不能只是閱讀每個人物如何回答唷！這是口說測驗，所以一定要開口說。
- 現在請跟著 CD 覆誦，同步練習「說」跟「聽」，第一次請跟著 CD 以相同語速覆誦，第二次和第三次可以逐步拉長到 CD 唸完第一句、第二句後再開始覆誦，能神奇地提升你的聽力專注力喔！

1 道地高分句

2 一問三答

3 話題卡回答

4 即席應答

Do you think your government is fully prepared to deal with a catastrophic disaster?

你覺得你的政府有能力處理重大災難嗎?

🎧 MP3 099

Well, I don't think anyone can say they are fully prepared to deal with a catastrophic disaster because disasters always happen when you are least expecting them. And when you get caught off guard, sometimes you just panic and forgot how you are supposed to react in the practice run.

嗯，我不認為有人敢出來說他們有能力處理任何的重大災難，因為災難總是在人們沒有準備的時候發生。而當你毫無心理準備的時候，有時候你就慌了，根本忘了練習的時候是應該怎麼樣處理。

According to past records, our politicians were not ready to deal with any kind of disaster at all. They were hopeless！Those who were supposed to be working on the rescue plan were not even aware there was a disaster！The rescue was always delayed and not well-planned. Things have improved, but in a very slow fashion. Therefore, I wouldn't say the government is ready. All I can say, is there is definitely room for improvement.

從以前的紀錄看來，我們的一些官員是完全沒辦法處理任何災難，他們真的很沒用！那些應該坐鎮指揮救援的人都還沒發現有災難正在發生。救援行動總是不夠迅速而且不夠周詳。現在是有好一點，可是進步的速度太慢。所以我不敢說政府準備好了，我只能說進步的空間還很大。

 ## Instructions

· 不能只是閱讀每個人物如何回答唷！這是口說測驗，所以一定要開口說。
· 現在請跟著 CD 覆誦，同步練習「說」跟「聽」，第一次請跟著 CD 以相同語速覆誦，第二次和第三次可以逐步拉長到 CD 唸完第一句、第二句後再開始覆誦，能神奇地提升你的聽力專注力喔！

1 道地高分句

2 一問三答

3 話題卡回答

4 即席應答

How do you pick the perfect present for someone?
你是怎樣決定哪樣禮物最適合某個人?

MP3 100

I think first I will observe the person's lifestyle and see if there is anything that he or she might need or something suits his or her lifestyle. Or I will try to have a conversation with the person and try to find out what he or she likes without giving too much away.

首先我會先觀察那個人的生活型態,再看看他是不是需要什麼東西,還是有某樣東西他生活中會用得上的。不然我會試著在不讓他知道的形況下,跟他聊聊他喜歡什麼東西。

If they seem to have everything they need, and I couldn't work out what they want then I will organise a surprise instead, like taking them to a restaurant and prearrange with the restaurant for the staff to jump out and sing a song for him or something.I think a memorable moment is the best gift that anyone can ask for ! It doesn't have to be something tangible.

　　如果他什麼都不缺的話，而且我也猜不出他要什麼的話，那我就會安排一個驚喜給他，就像先跟餐廳串通好，然後再帶他去餐廳，再請服務生出來幫他唱首歌之類的。我覺得難忘的回憶就是最好的禮物，有錢也買不到！好的禮物不見得一定要是實體的東西。

 ## Instructions

· 不能只是閱讀每個人物如何回答唷！這是口說測驗，所以一定要開口說。

· 現在請跟著 CD 覆誦，同步練習「說」跟「聽」，第一次請跟著 CD 以相同語速覆誦，第二次和第三次可以逐步拉長到 CD 唸完第一句、第二句後再開始覆誦，能神奇地提升你的聽力專注力喔！

Q 02 Are there special customs regarding giving and receiving presents in your country?
在你的國家有什麼送禮的習俗還是禁忌嗎?

🎧 MP3 101

Yes, there are. Most of the customs are based on the rhythm of the Chinese words which could sound like either bringing a good fortune or cursing to the person who receives the present. For Example, you would never give someone a wall clock as a present because it sounds like attending someone's funeral in Mandarin.

有的,大部分的習俗跟禁忌都是跟中文的押韻有關,不是聽起來像吉祥話,就是好像詛咒收禮物的人壞事會發生。舉個例子來說,你不能送時鐘給人當禮物,因為中文聽來很像是送終。

Another interesting one is, never give an umbrella to your partner because it sounds like you will be breaking up with him or her. Taiwanese believes if a pregnant woman handles sharp objects, such as needles and scissors it would cause miscarriage. I know this is purely based on superstitious reasons and there is no scientific evidence to prove it, but please do not buy a manicure set for your friend's baby shower.

　　另一個有趣的例子是不能送雨傘給男女朋友，因為有分手的意思。台灣人還相信孕婦不能碰尖的東西，像針還有剪刀之類的，因為會害人流產。我知道這完全是迷信，一點科學根據都沒有，可是如果你朋友要辦孕媽媽寶寶臨盆前的派對，你千萬不要送她修指甲的剪刀組！

 ## Instructions

- 不能只是閱讀每個人物如何回答唷！這是口說測驗，所以一定要開口説。
- 現在請跟著 CD 覆誦，同步練習「説」跟「聽」，第一次請跟著 CD 以相同語速覆誦，第二次和第三次可以逐步拉長到 CD 唸完第一句、第二句後再開始覆誦，能神奇地提升你的聽力專注力喔！

1　道地高分句

2　一問三答

3　話題卡回答

4　即席應答

12 Lifestyle 生活型態

Q 01

Do you consider your lifestyle healthy?
你覺得你的生活型態健康嗎? MP3 102

I think my lifestyle is relatively healthy because I like to look after my body, eat well, and exercise regularly. I try to stay away from junk food as much as I can, like fried chicken and burgers. I always make sure I eat enough fruits and vegetables aswell. I think what I eat is not a concern, but I do have a very bad habit which is to stay up late at night.

我覺得我的生活型態還算健康啦！因為我還蠻注意飲食跟規律的運動。我是盡量不吃像炸雞或漢堡之類的垃圾食物。而且我蔬菜水果會吃足量。我覺得我最大的問題不是吃，而是我喜歡晚睡的壞習慣。

I find it very soothing to just sit there and watch TV alone at night. Sometimes I struggle to turn off the TV and go to bed. By the time I look at the clock, it would be 12:30, or 1 am even. I get tired quite easily, so I can't really say my lifestyle is 100% healthy.

我很喜歡晚上一個人坐在那裏看電視的感覺，很放鬆，放鬆到我有時候真的不想關電視去睡覺。等我抬頭看時間的時候，已經 12 點半了！有時候甚至已經 1 點了！我是蠻容易累的，所以我不能說我的生活型態百分百的健康。

 Instructions

- 不能只是閱讀每個人物如何回答唷！這是口說測驗，所以一定要開口說。
- 現在請跟著 CD 覆誦，同步練習「說」跟「聽」，第一次請跟著 CD 以相同語速覆誦，第二次和第三次可以逐步拉長到 CD 唸完第一句、第二句後再開始覆誦，能神奇地提升你的聽力專注力喔！

Q 02 What do you think is betterfor you?Home cooking or eating out?
你覺得怎樣比較健康？在家吃還是出去吃？
🔊 MP3 103

Ever since food safety became an issue in Taiwan, I am deeply convinced that homecooking is much better for you than eating out. However, I still cannot guarantee that home cooking is 100 percent safer because we still don't know whether the ingredients we bought from the shops were produced properly, such as cooking oil.

自從食安問題在台灣延燒之後，我深深地相信家裡煮的東西是比外面的東西健康，可是就算這樣説，我還是無法保證家裡的東西是安全無虞的，因為我們不知道我們買回來的原料是不是好的，例如煮飯用的油。但是比起外面的東西，至少我們還能控制我們自己煮到底加了什麼東西進去。

But I guess I have more control on what is actually in a dish if I cook at home. I know it definitely doesn't have any preservative or artificial flavouring in it. However, home cooking is still home cooking. It is not restaurant quality food. I would still eat out because the restaurant food just tastes so much better. I am willing to risk my health once in a while!

　　我可以保證絕對沒有防腐劑還有人工調味料。然而，家裡煮的東西也只是這樣而已，真的沒有外面餐廳的水準。所以我還是會出去吃因為餐廳的東西真的好吃很多，好吃到我情願拿健康來冒險！

 Instructions

- 不能只是閱讀每個人物如何回答唷！這是口說測驗，所以一定要開口説。
- 現在請跟著 CD 覆誦，同步練習「説」跟「聽」，第一次請跟著 CD 以相同語速覆誦，第二次和第三次可以逐步拉長到 CD 唸完第一句、第二句後再開始覆誦，能神奇地提升你的聽力專注力喔！

Shopping 購物

Do you prefer to shop online or visit the stores?

你喜歡上網購物還是到實體店面去? MP3 104

I actually like them both, but it depends how much time and how urgent I need the item. If I had a lot of time and just trying to pick out something I want for a long time, I will browse online and compare the price and specification. I know it will take a few days at least for it to be delivered, but I can wait because I am in no hurry.

我其實兩個都喜歡,可是要看我有多少時間或是我急不急著要那個東西。如果我有很多時間可以只是想慢慢挑一個我喜歡的東西,那我會上網逛逛比較一下價格跟規格。我知道送來要等好幾天,可是無所謂我不急。

However, if I need to pick out something at the last minute, say I just realised it is a friend's birthday, and I need a present for him today, I will definitely go to the stores. I know I might pay more in the store, but it doesn't leave me with a choice really.

　　可是如果今天是臨時需要一個東西，就好像剛發現朋友生日，需要一個禮物，那我就會去店面裡買。我知道可能會貴一點但是我也沒辦法。

 Instructions

- 不能只是閱讀每個人物如何回答唷！這是口說測驗，所以一定要開口説。
- 現在請跟著 CD 覆誦，同步練習「説」跟「聽」，第一次請跟著 CD 以相同語速覆誦，第二次和第三次可以逐步拉長到 CD 唸完第一句、第二句後再開始覆誦，能神奇地提升你的聽力專注力喔！

How do big supermarket chains affect the local traditional markets?

Q 02

大型連鎖超市對當地的傳統市場有什麼影響?

MP3 105

I believe big supermarket chains would impact the profit of the local small business vendors, such as corner grocery stores, local butchers, fish mongers which is most of the stalls you found in a traditional market. I must say most of the younger generation are drawn to chain supermarkets because it is a one-stop shop, they are very well stocked with a wide range of goods, you can even get make-up items there, and inside the store is bright and clean inside which is opposite to the traditional market.

我相信大型的連鎖超市絕對會影響傳統市場攤商的生意，尤其是像一般的雜貨店，賣肉的，賣魚的攤販。我必須要說，年輕一輩的都會被大型連鎖超市吸引，因為超市裡什麼都有賣，各式各樣的商品，就連化妝品也有，而且店裡面明亮又乾淨，跟傳統市場完全相反。

Without the younger generation's support of the local business, I think their business will really struggle especially when the younger generation start to take up the responsibility of cooking at home. The local market might not even exist by then.

如果沒有年輕一輩的來支持傳統市場，我相信攤商的生意會很難做，尤其是等到年輕的這批人開始擔起家裡煮飯的責任，傳統市場可能也不存在了。

 ## Instructions

- 不能只是閱讀每個人物如何回答唷！這是口說測驗，所以一定要開口說。

- 現在請跟著 CD 覆誦，同步練習「說」跟「聽」，第一次請跟著 CD 以相同語速覆誦，第二次和第三次可以逐步拉長到 CD 唸完第一句、第二句後再開始覆誦，能神奇地提升你的聽力專注力喔！

Q 01 **How does the Internet change the way that people have relationships with each other?**
網路對人與人的交往有著什麼樣的影響和變化? MP3 106

I don't know whether the internet has brought people closer or pushed us further apart because everything is just one click away, meeting or talking to people in person just seems like an idea of the past.

我不知道該説網路是讓人與人更靠近還是距離更遠,因為所有的事都可以上網處理。面對面的見面或聊天好像是過時的事。

I remember when I was younger I used to fight with my brother through Facetime, and mind you, he was only upstairs in his bedroom ! But by the same token, I never really felt he was far away when he moved out of home to pursue further studies. We chat all the time online. I found it very comforting to be able to see him while talking to him. I guess we are now accustomed to talking to a flat screen than a real person in front of you.

　　我記得我小時候都跟我哥用 Face-time 吵架，可是其實他就在樓上的房間裡。同樣的，當他因為讀書的原因搬出去的時候，我不覺得他離得很遠，因為我還是可以上網跟他見面聊天，讓我覺得有安心。我覺得大家應該很習慣對著平面的螢幕講話，反而不習慣跟人面對面聊天了。

 Instructions

· 不能只是閱讀每個人物如何回答唷！這是口說測驗，所以一定要開口說。

· 現在請跟著 CD 覆誦，同步練習「說」跟「聽」，第一次請跟著 CD 以相同語速覆誦，第二次和第三次可以逐步拉長到 CD 唸完第一句、第二句後再開始覆誦，能神奇地提升你的聽力專注力喔！

Q 02 Do you think meeting people online is a good thing?

你覺得上網交朋友是一件好事情嗎? MP3 107

I don't see any harm in trying and honestly I think it is worth a shot especially when there is no other way to meet new people in the day-to-day routine. I know there are lots of dating sites or chat rooms where you can find people who are more like-minded or people who share common interests. I think all friendships have to start somewhere！

基本上我不覺得嘗試下有什麼不好的，因為如果每天固定的作息都沒辦法遇到其他人的話，那我覺得為什麼不試試看？我知道有很多交友網站或是聊天室可以加入，認識一些想法類似或是有共同興趣的人，友誼就是這樣開始的！

People seem to have this negative reaction when you told them you meet someone online. But I believe not everyone you meet online is there to get you. It is no different than meeting someone in a bar. You still need to practice your common sense and be aware of the stranger danger regardless of where you meet them.

　　可是大部分的人如果聽到你説你們是在網上認識的，都會有種負面的反應，可是我相信不是每個人都是壞人。這跟在酒吧認識人沒什麼兩樣，反正不管你們是在哪裡認識的，你還是要保持理智知道面對陌生人要小心。

 Instructions

· 不能只是閱讀每個人物如何回答唷！這是口説測驗，所以一定要開口説。

· 現在請跟著 CD 覆誦，同步練習「説」跟「聽」，第一次請跟著 CD 以相同語速覆誦，第二次和第三次可以逐步拉長到 CD 唸完第一句、第二句後再開始覆誦，能神奇地提升你的聽力專注力喔！

Do you prefer domestic travel or international travel?
你喜歡國內旅遊還是出國旅遊？ MP3 108

I would prefer international travel if I can afford it, because going to a foreign country is very exciting, especially going to an exotic country like Brazil or somewhere in the Middle East. The cultural and food are so different, just imagine you are in a carnival dancing with all the beautiful Brazilian girls or surrounded by the belly dancer while you are having lamb and flat bread.

　　如果我負擔的起的話，我會比較喜歡出國旅行。到陌生的國家總是很有新鮮感尤其是那些異國風很濃的地方就像巴西或是某個中東國家。特別是文化跟當地食物會很顯著的不同，想像一下你在巴西的嘉年華會跟那些美女一起跳舞，或是一邊享用著羊肉還有中東餅，桌邊被肚皮舞孃環繞著。

It would be a once-in-a-lifetime experience！It is not something that you can experience in Taiwan. I would love to support domestic tourism more as well, but Taiwan is a small country, I think I have pretty much been to most of the tourist attractions anyway. It is just not as exciting as going overseas.

那些是一生難得的回憶，是在台灣感受不到的體驗。我也想支持國內旅遊可是台灣是個小國家，我覺得我好像大部分的觀光勝地我都去過了，真的沒什麼新鮮感了。

 Instructions

- 不能只是閱讀每個人物如何回答唷！這是口說測驗，所以一定要開口說。
- 現在請跟著 CD 覆誦，同步練習「說」跟「聽」，第一次請跟著 CD 以相同語速覆誦，第二次和第三次可以逐步拉長到 CD 唸完第一句、第二句後再開始覆誦，能神奇地提升你的聽力專注力喔！

Q 02 ◀ Do you prefer joining the pre-organised tour group or self-guided tour?
你比較喜歡跟團旅遊還是自由行？ MP3 109

I actually like the combination of both. I like to explore a new place at my own pace and interests. I will do my research prior to departure to work out a plan on what I would like to see and do once I get there. I will also research methods of transportation from point A to point B.

我其實喜歡混搭。我去旅遊的時候我喜歡照自己的意思走。我在出發之前會先做好功課，決定我到了當地之後想做什麼。我同時也會研究一下從 A 處到 B 處的交通方式。

If I get enough information and am confident about getting there on my own, I will go fully self-guided. However, in some places I will prefer to join the local tour because sometimes it works out more economically and othertimes it is just much easier in terms of transportation, especially those areas where there is no direct road to get there.

　　如果我的資訊很充足，而且沒有什麼問題的話，那我就會完全自己走。可是有些地方我是會比較想參加當地旅行團的，因為有時候其實參加旅行團比較便宜，不然就是交通上方便多了，尤其是想去那些很難自己可以去得到的地方。

 Instructions

- 不能只是閱讀每個人物如何回答唷！這是口說測驗，所以一定要開口說。
- 現在請跟著 CD 覆誦，同步練習「說」跟「聽」，第一次請跟著 CD 以相同語速覆誦，第二次和第三次可以逐步拉長到 CD 唸完第一句、第二句後再開始覆誦，能神奇地提升你的聽力專注力喔！

Q 01 **Do you think people are spending too much time looking at their phones nowadays?**
你覺得現代人是不是花太多時間在看手機?

MP3 110

It is a definite yes from me. I think I am guilty as charged. I find it hard to put my phone down, and I am constantly checking my phone to see if there is a message from someone. I must say I do get a bit sad if I don't hear from my friends for too long. It almost feels like I am addicted to my cell phone !

沒錯,我就是這樣!我有時候真的沒辦法把電話放下來不看,而且我會一直拿出來看是不是有人傳訊息給我, 我沒接到。我承認如果我朋友太久沒有傳訊息給我的話,我還會有點失落感,可以説我幾乎手機上癮了。

But the thing is, I know I am not alone, and most people are like me these days. The phone is not only a phone anymore, it is so versatile that can transform into anything. You can check your email, you can use it as a GPS, you can shop online. You name it!

可是，我絕對不是唯一一個，大部分的人都跟我一樣啊！手機已經不再只是手機了，隨時隨地都可以變成你想要的東西。你可以查你的電子郵件，你可以用它來當導航系統，還可以上網購物。你想得出來它就做得到！

 Instructions

・ 不能只是閱讀每個人物如何回答唷！這是口說測驗，所以一定要開口說。

・ 現在請跟著 CD 覆誦，同步練習「說」跟「聽」，第一次請跟著 CD 以相同語速覆誦，第二次和第三次可以逐步拉長到 CD 唸完第一句、第二句後再開始覆誦，能神奇地提升你的聽力專注力喔！

How does technology help our lives?
科技對我們的生活有什麼幫助? ⓘ MP3 111

I think technology definitely makes our lives much easier or maybe I should say it probably made us lazier because it brought a lot of convenience to our lives. We take so much for granted compared with our parents' generation. I remember my mother was telling me she had to go and collect firewood for the wood stove, so my grandmother could cook in the kitchen.

我覺得科技的進步讓我們的生活容易很多,或是我應該説科技進步讓我們變得很懶惰因為它帶來了很多的方便性。比起我父母的年代,我們真的太不知道感恩。我記得有一次我媽跟我説她小時候需要去撿柴回家在灶裡生火,這樣我外婆才可以在廚房煮飯。

I guess we are the lucky generation, we grew up with a lot of technology already in place such as telephone, TV, gas stove and microwaves. I am happy about how technology has advanced. I cannot picture myself going and finding firewood to collect！I don't think I would survive in that era.

　　所以我覺得我們真的是很幸福的一代，我們從小就對科技不陌生有電話、電視、瓦斯爐還有微波爐。我很慶幸有跟上科技進步的速度，我無法想像還要去撿柴的生活，我覺得我在那個年代應該活不下去。

 Instructions

- 不能只是閱讀每個人物如何回答唷！這是口說測驗，所以一定要開口說。

- 現在請跟著 CD 覆誦，同步練習「說」跟「聽」，第一次請跟著 CD 以相同語速覆誦，第二次和第三次可以逐步拉長到 CD 唸完第一句、第二句後再開始覆誦，能神奇地提升你的聽力專注力喔！

1 道地高分句

2 一問三答

3 話題卡回答

4 即席應答

Would you try to speak to someone when something troubles you?
如果你心裡有事的時候，你會找人談談抒發情緒嗎？ MP3 112

Well, I think mostly I will, but sometimes I just don't get a chance to. I know it is better for me if I can talk to someone and release some of the stress inside me. I don't intend to bottle up my feelings and keep things to myself, but sometimes when I need someone to talk to, my friends might be away or busy with their own life issues at that time.

嗯，我大部分時候會的，可是有時候我沒有機會。我知道找個人講一講抒發情緒對我比較好。我也沒有故意要把情緒鎖在心裡不跟人說，只是有時候想找人的時候找我的朋友們可能不在，或是在忙他們自己生活中的瑣事。

And once that moment passes, I tend to just move on and not to think about it anymore. I don't really like when people start to give me advice on how to fix things, because honestly, I really just want someone to listen to me and let me blow off some steam !

當那個情緒過了我也就不再去想了。說真的，我最不喜歡旁人開始給我意見教我怎麼做。因為只是想找個人聽我說，讓我發洩一下而已。

 Instructions

- 不能只是閱讀每個人物如何回答唷！這是口說測驗，所以一定要開口說。
- 現在請跟著 CD 覆誦，同步練習「說」跟「聽」，第一次請跟著 CD 以相同語速覆誦，第二次和第三次可以逐步拉長到 CD 唸完第一句、第二句後再開始覆誦，能神奇地提升你的聽力專注力喔！

What will you do if you see people behaving badly?

如果你看到人有不好的行為，你會有什麼反應？ MP3 113

If it is something minor, like eating in a place that you shouldn't, I would be upset, but I might just let it go and not say a thing because it is not doing anyone any harm. However, if it is a serious matter or someone's rights are being violated, such as if I caught someone shoplifting or bullying others, I will do something but discretely.

如果是小事，就像在不能吃東西的地方吃東西，我看到是會不太高興，可是我會當作沒這回事。可是如果是很重大的事，例如有人偷東西或是有人欺負別人的時候，我會有所作為，可是不會太張揚。

I find it hard to speak up in public; therefore, I don't think I will yell out at that moment, but I will definitely inform the shop owner or call the security guard.

　　我覺得我沒辦法在公開的地方大聲制止人，所以我當下不會大叫，可是我會跟店家或是保全說。

 Instructions

· 不能只是閱讀每個人物如何回答唷！這是口說測驗，所以一定要開口說。

· 現在請跟著 CD 覆誦，同步練習「說」跟「聽」，第一次請跟著 CD 以相同語速覆誦，第二次和第三次可以逐步拉長到 CD 唸完第一句、第二句後再開始覆誦，能神奇地提升你的聽力專注力喔！

Environmental issues
環保問題

Q 01

What can we do to slow down global warming?
我們可以怎樣減緩全球暖化的速度嗎?

MP3 114

People talk about reducing the carbon footprint a lot. Carbon dioxide seems to be the major contributor to global warming. I think there are a lot of things we can do as an individual, such as turning off the light when you are done with it, taking public transport or carpooling instead of driving on your own, or reducing the amount of rubbish.

　　常常聽人家說節能減碳的概念,二氧化碳應該是全球暖化最主要的原因了。我覺得我們可以盡一己之力的事很多,例如不用燈的時候就把燈關掉,搭乘大眾交通工具或是與人共乘,盡量減少自己開車,或是垃圾減量。

My favourite is tree planting. It would not only help reduce the carbon footprint, but also make the environment look nice. I know it seems very minimal, how we can help to slow down the problem, but I am fully aware if we don't start doing something about it now, global warming could get much worse very quickly.

　　我最喜歡的是植樹，因為不只可以節能減碳，還可以美化環境。我知道對於全球暖化我們能做的事很微不足道可是如果我們不從現在開始做，全球暖化會來得又快又急！

 ## Instructions

· 不能只是閱讀每個人物如何回答唷！這是口說測驗，所以一定要開口說。

· 現在請跟著 CD 覆誦，同步練習「說」跟「聽」，第一次請跟著 CD 以相同語速覆誦，第二次和第三次可以逐步拉長到 CD 唸完第一句、第二句後再開始覆誦，能神奇地提升你的聽力專注力喔！

How important is recycling?
你覺得資源回收很重要嗎? 🎧 MP3 115

I used to think recycling is just a way for some people to make a few extra bucks because it is a time-consuming and labour intensive exercise to separate the recyclables from the waste. However, ever since I realised how much rubbish we generate every day and how little room we have to accommodate it, it totally changed my attitude towards recycling.

我以前覺得回收只不過是某些人想多賺幾塊錢的方式,因為要分類回收物既費時又費力。可是,自從我知道原來我們每人每天製造的垃圾量有這麼多而且可以處理垃圾的地方這麼少,我對回收的態度就改觀了。

I must say it is a common understanding that no one wants to live next to a rubbish tip, but not a lot of people realise how recycling would help us to reduce the needs for more rubbish disposal sites. I think recycling is one of the most effective ways to reduce the amount of waste. It instantly turns the rubbish into gold!

　　老實説，每個人都不想住在垃圾場旁邊，可是很少人了解資源回收可以減少我們對垃圾處理場的需求。我覺得回收是一個對垃圾減量最有效的方式之一，立馬就把垃圾變黃金。

 Instructions

- 不能只是閱讀每個人物如何回答唷！這是口説測驗，所以一定要開口説。
- 現在請跟著 CD 覆誦，同步練習「説」跟「聽」，第一次請跟著 CD 以相同語速覆誦，第二次和第三次可以逐步拉長到 CD 唸完第一句、第二句後再開始覆誦，能神奇地提升你的聽力專注力喔！

1　道地高分句

2　一問三答

3　話題卡回答

4　即席應答

國家圖書館出版品預行編目(CIP)資料

一次就考到雅思口說6.5+ (附MP3) / 倍斯特
編輯部著. -- 初版. -- 臺北市：倍斯特,
2018.05　面；公分. --（考用英語系列；8）
ISBN 978-986-96309-0-0（平裝附光碟片）

1. 國際英語語文測試系統 2. 考試指南

805.189　　　　　　　　　107005618

考用英語系列　008

一次就考到雅思口說6.5+（附MP3）

初　　版	2018年5月	
定　　價	新台幣429元	

作　　者	倍斯特編輯部
出　　版	倍斯特出版事業有限公司
發 行 人	周瑞德
電　　話	886-2-2351-2007
傳　　真	886-2-2351-0887
地　　址	100 台北市中正區福州街1號10樓之2
E - m a i l	best.books.service@gmail.com
官　　網	www.bestbookstw.com
執行總監	齊心瑀
行銷經理	楊景輝
執行編輯	倍斯特編輯部
封面構成	高鍾琪
內頁構成	菩薩蠻數位文化有限公司
印　　製	大亞彩色印刷製版股份有限公司

港澳地區總經銷	泛華發行代理有限公司	
地　　址	香港新界將軍澳工業邨駿昌街7號2樓	
電　　話	852-2798-2323	
傳　　真	852-2796-5471	

Simply Learning, Simply Best!

Simply Learning, Simply Best!